TOYS FOR KIDS

Sarah Stacey

with lots of help from
Rona Kemp

Photographs by Christopher Ridley

ELM TREE BOOKS · LONDON

CONTENTS

All the measurements given in this book are in metric, and the ruler above may help you to convert to inches if you need to.

1 inch = approximately 2.5 cm 10 cm = approximately 4 inches
1 yard = approximately 90 cm 1 metre = 39.3 inches

I could only buy stuffing in grams; if you find it in ounces:

1 lb = 453 gms 1 oz = 28 gms
100 gms = approximately 3½ oz

The designs in this book are copyright and must not be copied, produced or sold by way of trade without the prior written consent of the author

Special thanks to Bryan Kemp for his generous help with the design

ELM TREE BOOKS

Penguin Books Ltd, 27 Wrights Lane, London W8 5TZ (Publishing & Editorial)
and Harmondsworth, Middlesex, England (Distribution & Warehouse)
Viking Penguin Inc., 40 West 23rd Street, New York, New York 10010, U.S.A.
Penguin Books Australia Ltd, Ringwood, Victoria, Australia
Penguin Books Canada Ltd, 2801 John Street, Markham, Ontario, Canada L3R 1B4
Penguin Books (N.Z.) Ltd, 182–190 Wairau Road, Auckland 10, New Zealand

First published in Great Britain 1987 by
Elm Tree Books/Hamish Hamilton Ltd

Copyright © 1987 by Sarah Stacey
Diagrams by Hilary Jarvis

British Library Cataloguing in Publication Data

Stacey, Sarah
Toys for kids.
1. Soft toy making
I. Title
745.592′4   TT174.3

ISBN 0-241-12322-4

Typeset in Great Britain by
Rowland Phototypesetting Ltd, Bury St Edmunds, Suffolk
Printed and bound in Great Britain by
William Clowes Ltd, Beccles, Suffolk

INTRODUCTION

My formative years were spent attached to a large pink bear called Lalla. We were inseparable until I was in my mid 20s when the stuffing fell out of her paws, her pink fur turned to grey and she retired to an old post office in Buckinghamshire. She sits in a rocking chair in the spare bedroom and I visit her quite often.

Over the years her place has been filled by other friends, notably a blue rabbit with loppy lugs and a small black dog with great charm but too many hard corners.

Despite my affection for these cuddly toys, I had never dreamt of making them myself. Toys were things you bought in shops and they were jolly expensive so you tried to buy them at Women's Institute stalls and village fêtes instead. The idea of designing and making a bookful of teddy bears, rag dolls, various cuddlies and even pom-pom ducklings was a million miles away.

Picture my astonishment then when Elm Tree asked me to do just that. "But I've never made a toy, I don't know what to do," I said feebly. "What about the gussets?" I had heard about them – they were a Big Problem for people like me who could only just sew an A-line skirt or make a tray cloth. These publishing people finally persuaded me that they meant business, however, and I set off to find someone who could help.

Without Rona Kemp, this book could not have been written. She is an expert seamstress and pattern cutter whose talents solved the gusset problem and many others. She helped to design the toys and gave endless practical and moral support. By the time I had finished the book, I could even cut a tolerable pattern myself and you will probably be able to do the same.

All the toys are easy to make but some are more fiddly and time-consuming than others. It helps to start with one of the quickest, the seal or a teddy bear perhaps, or even the Mother Duck and her demented ducklings. As each toy was finished, it came out visiting to play with small children. I wanted to make sure that each design was able to stand up to a reasonable amount of strain and, even more important, was appealing to children. So the contents of this book really have been consumer-tested.

I loved making these toys and dreaming up new ones and I had a lot of help from my friends. My opposite neighbour, Rebecca Lawrence, aged 16, used to dash in for tea and an update after school every day and she gave me lots of ideas, advice and enthusiastic support. Val Mangold and Annie Lickett provided ideas and inspiration for Christmas Tree decorations. Susannah Webster advised me about the safety side and Clive Syddall made endless comforting cups of hot chocolate.

Very special thanks must go to the photographer, Christopher Ridley, who gave unstintingly of his time and talent, and to Kyle Cathie, who thought of the original idea.

And finally thank you to all the children who appear in the photographs: Abigail and Jessica Mangold playing the Swimming Pool Game; Jonathan Taggart with the Crocodile Oven Glove; David Hearn feeding cornflakes to the Elephant; Poppy Ridley disporting herself with the Blue Bear; Kate Pakenham strapping on the Bear Bag watched by Gary Allen; small Emily Wallace who was snatched from her fishfinger lunch to appear in the Packing Doll picture; and Max Webster who said we could take a hundred photos of him if we really wanted, perched precariously on a wall with the American Footballer.

I hope these toys give you as much pleasure as they have given to all of us.

GENERAL GUIDELINES

EQUIPMENT

FOR PREPARING PATTERNS

Tracing paper (available from stationery stores) or greaseproof paper, pencils, quartz rubber

NEEDLES

The size of needle you use is unexpectedly important. The best thing is to buy those packs of assorted needles and be prepared to swop in mid-seam if necessary. For fine work, you need a small thin needle, but to sew most of the toys it is easiest to use a medium to long needle which is quite strong, so that you can push easily through thick materials like double fur fabric seams. You will also need a large needle with a wool eye (like a darning needle) for sewing nose and mouth on bears and such like.

SCISSORS

Although it is not strictly necessary, it is worth having three pairs of scissors:
- One large pair of sharp cutting-out scissors to cut materials
- One small pair to snip threads, cut small bits of felt etc.
- One medium sized pair solely for paper cutting. N.B. Don't use the cutting out or snipping scissors for paper cutting, it blunts them instantly.

THIMBLE

You will definitely need one of these.

QUIK UNPIK

This is a useful tool for unpicking misplaced stitching.

STUFFING STICKS

For pushing stuffing into bodies and particularly into corners, there are several useful tools: chopsticks, thick gauge knitting needles, the handles of wooden spoons, lengths of dowelling or cane with a V-shaped notch cut in the end so that the stuffing is gripped in the pusher — make sure that the notch is smooth or you will find the filling doesn't leave the stick.

GLUE

I found Copydex the most useful all-purpose glue; other people swear by UHU.

FRENCH CHALK/MARKER PENS

To mark seam allowances, stuffing spaces, etc.

MATERIALS

FUR FABRIC

I bought almost all the fur fabric used in this book from John Lewis, who have a far better range of toymaking materials than any other store. The range of colours is glorious, although sadly, with a couple of exceptions, they are all shaggy rather than close pile fabrics. I have looked all over the place for that velvety synthetic fur which is short and springy, but have never found it — perhaps you will have more luck.

Fur fabric is not vastly expensive and it is worth buying 0.5 metre at a time, although some of the toys in this book will need rather less; any left-overs from the larger quantity always come in useful later. (It's also excellent playstuff for rainy days – Max Webster made an owl from leopard remnants and computer paper.)

All synthetic fur fabric is washable, can be combed out and is kind to the less expert seamstress – the fluffy fur hides a multitude of odd stitching.

The following tips are essential knowledge when you are using fur fabric:

☐ When positioning the pattern on the wrong side of fabric, always check that the fur is running the right way before cutting.

☐ Cut fur fabric through cloth not fluff (i.e. wrong side up).

☐ When you pin the seams with right sides together, tuck the fluff on the raw edges *inside* the two pieces of fabric: it is easier to sew and the fur will be more plentiful on the seam line, which makes it look better.

☐ When you have finished the toy, tease captive fur out from seams with a darning needle or wire comb.

☐ Seam allowance: 7 mm to 1 cm.

TOWELLING

Towelling is a wonderful fabric for soft toys, both cuddly and washable. If you want to make a bath toy, use towelling for the shape and foam chips for the stuffing. The disadvantage is that it frays, so you must be sure to leave a generous seam allowance – 7 mm to 1 cm. It is worth oversewing the raw edges, either by hand with blanket stitch if you have the patience, or machine edges in blanket stitch or zigzag. Towelling is slightly more expensive than fur fabric, but you could recycle old towels – which usually wear out in patches, rather than overall – as cuddly toys.

FLEECE

With the difficulty of finding shortpile fur fabric, I turned to fleece. This is a soft cuddly fabric often used for dressing gowns, so your ancient housecoat might turn into Mrs Paddlequack (see page 53).

It is totally synthetic and thus washable, easy to work with and about the same price as towelling.

Allow about 7 mm seam allowance.

COTTONS

Cotton is an easy and relatively inexpensive material to use. Amongst the most useful cottons I have found are ginghams, lining materials and T-shirt or sweatshirt material.

Because I am in the middle of making curtains for a new house, I have scraps of curtain lining all over the place. It proved to be an admirable fabric for rag doll bodies.

Most T-shirts and sweatshirts are pure cotton. The material is easy to work in but it is usually stretchy, so make sure you allow for this when cutting out the pattern pieces – you should see which way the fabric stretches and skip the seam allowance in that direction; this doesn't apply to basic patterns like dolls' bodies, but for any tight-fitting clothes, such as socks or tights.

Cotton doesn't fray significantly so you need only allow 5 mm for the seam allowance. It is washable but beware when you wash lining or any other glazed cotton – the surface glaze disappears with washing so the fabric becomes matt after a time.

FELT

Use a good quality felt for toymaking; the poorer ones are thin in patches, leading to leaking stuffing. Because felt doesn't fray at all, it is wonderful for small toys which are much better sewn together on the outside. The disadvantage with felt is that you cannot wash it – I imagine you can dry clean it although I have not experimented with this.

Choose the brightest coloured felts you can find; the dark ones tend to be lifeless and need a lot of surface decoration to overcome this.

OTHER MATERIALS

Very soft *leather* (suede, chamois, kid, etc.) can be used for toys; leather scraps are useful for accessories, shoes, facial details, harness etc.

Velvet, velveteen and velours are difficult to work with and I have not attempted it.

STUFFING

Modern polyester stuffing, which is advertised as clean, hygienic and safe, is much easier than the old-fashioned kapok. Polyester filling doesn't fly around the room, doesn't have twigs in it and doesn't get up your nose. It is available in large bags containing approximately 400 gm and one bag should fill four medium-sized toys.

Use foam chips to stuff a towelling toy if you foresee it ending up in the bath.

COTTONS, THREADS, ETC.

My sewing machine objected to thick pure cotton thread so I used Gütermann or Drima polyester thread for everything.

Use contrasting coloured thread for tacking – it's easier to see.

Darning wools are useful for animal noses and stranded embroidery silks are the most suitable for embroidering dolls' features. The silks come in six-strand skeins but you need only thread your needle with two or three strands at a time.

THINGS TO HOARD

Bits and pieces which you might throw away without a backward glance come into their own when you are making dolls' clothes and accessories. A friend of mine, Sevilla Hercolani, is a dress designer and showered me with wonderful 'rag bags' which were like an Aladdin's cave of scraps.

Here are some of the items I have found useful:
☐ scraps of material of all kinds
☐ old T-shirts and sweatshirts
☐ worn gloves, or other items, made from supple leather
☐ lengths of used but intact elastic
☐ buttons of all sorts, sizes and shapes
☐ zips from old clothes and cushions
☐ trimmings – e.g. cushion or curtain braid, lace, broderie anglaise, ribbon, fake flowers, sequins, feathers, net
☐ pipe cleaners

SAFETY

The British Standards Institution guidelines on 'Safety of Toys' are concerned with the safety of children under 36 months. The most relevant section of their latest edition is the following, which applies to the eyes for teddy bears and other cuddlies:

'3.2.2.2
Non-detachable components. In the case of toys for children under 36 months to which components made from glass, metal, wood or other non-pliable material are attached, these components shall either: be so embedded that the child cannot pull them out with his teeth or fingers; or be so fixed to the toy that they cannot become detached or loosened when they are submitted to . . . a force of 90 N when the largest accessible dimension is greater than 6 mm.'

The old-fashioned hook-in or button eyes are obvious dangers. Lock-in safety eyes are now available at most haberdashery shops and in department stores which have a toymaking section. They are fixed like this:

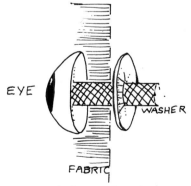

Always insert eyes before stuffing the toy. Make a small hole in the fabric with the Quik Unpik to put through the stalk of the eye. Snap washer and eye firmly together to lock, one hand on the washer, the other on the eye.

Other possible risks are bells and similar small hard objects which could cause a child to choke, also sharp items such as fish gut, pipe cleaners etc. I have used these in the book but if you intend to give the toys to a child under three years old, it would be wise to omit them.

Felt toys are not actually dangerous to babies or toddlers if eaten but it seems generally undesirable. To reduce the risk, firmly *sew*, rather than glue, any features made of felt, e.g. the cat's tongue (see page 71).

One mother I know suggests keeping an eye on shaggy cuddlies; bald patches may indicate that a child is sucking the fur which can be harmful to the lungs.

PREPARING PAPER PATTERNS

Read instructions carefully before starting. Trace patterns on to good quality tracing paper or greaseproof paper. If you want to make your patterns more permanent, transfer the designs to cardboard: cereal packets are ideal. To do this, trace the design on to paper, turn the paper over and scribble all over every line in pencil. Turn the paper right side up again and put it on top of the cardboard. With a sharp pencil, retrace the lines, thus pushing the carboned design on to the cardboard – just like copying maps at school.

Copy all sewing instructions and letters on to paper pattern pieces.

A simpler but more expensive option is to photocopy the relevant pages, cut out the pattern pieces and glue on to cardboard, then trim cardboard to size.

Unless you are using double-sided fabric (the same on both sides), remember to reverse the paper pattern on the fabric when you cut the second piece of a pair (e.g. side of elephant, ear, etc.).

Before you lay the pattern pieces on the fabric, check that the fabric is smooth and flat. If not, take five minutes to press it.

SEAM ALLOWANCES

Because of the difficulties involved in fitting large stencils on to a double page, only a few patterns have seam allowances included, most do not. Please note whether you have to add on a seam allowance. If you do, you can *either*:

☐ cut out the pattern pieces *without* the seam allowance. Pin the pattern pieces to the fabric leaving room between the pieces to add the seam allowance. Mark round the pattern (i.e. the seam lines) with chalk or marking pen. Cut the fabric 1 cm (or less depending on fabric used – see below) outside the seam line. The advantage of this method is that you have a marked seam line to sew on. *Or*

☐ when you trace the pattern, leave room round the pieces to draw in the seam allowance at this stage: this means that your paper pattern pieces will be marked with a seam line and a seam allowance 1 cm (or less) outside the seam line. I found it easier to add in the seam allowance in this way, where necessary, because then I couldn't forget the seam allowance when it came to cutting the fabric; the disadvantage is that you do not have a seam line to sew on. Seam allowances vary from fabric to fabric. As a rough guide, allow:

☐ 3 to 4 mm for felt
☐ 5 to 7 mm for fine, non-fraying cottons
☐ 7 mm to 1 cm for fur fabrics
See page 8 for more details.

Rule of thumb: It is better to allow too much seam allowance than too little – you can always cut off the surplus.

BASIC SEWING TECHNIQUES

Pin, tack and then machine, or handsew, all pattern pieces.

I used a combination of my sewing machine and hand sewing to make most of the toys in this book. The exceptions are the felt toys – the little felt horse on page 104, the felt Christmas Tree decorations (page 102) and the goldfish and dolphins (page 108) – which are all hand sewn in blanket stitch.

MACHINING

(This note is for beginners, not experienced seamstresses).

It helps immeasurably to read the instruction book that accompanies your machine. I used to finish off every seam by hand until I discovered the reverse button, which – at the flick of a switch – sews backwards, firmly securing every seam in sight. The manual should also give you useful information about stitch lengths and sewing cotton. Medium and small stitches were used for all the toys in this book: medium for straight seams, small for corners and short curves so that you keep the detail.

HAND SEWING

You can sew any or all of the toys by hand if you prefer. If you choose to hand sew seams, the best stitch is back stitch: other useful stitches include blanket, running (gathering), satin, feather, chain and ladder.

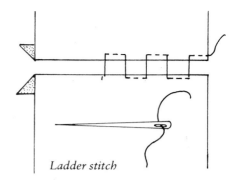

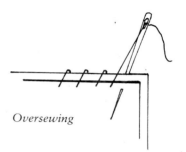

Ladder stitch

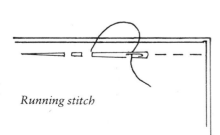

Slip stitch

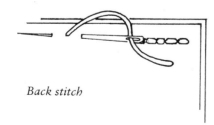

Back stitch

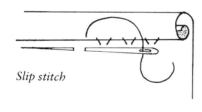

Running stitch

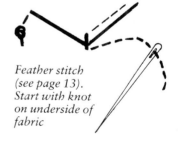

Oversewing

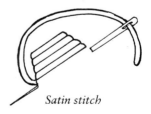

Feather stitch (see page 13). Start with knot on underside of fabric

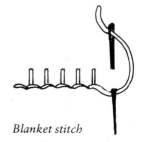

Satin stitch

Blanket stitch

When you turn a toy with curved seams to the right side, you must cut into the curved seams so that the seam will lie flat. Depending on the way the seam curves, you make a V-shaped notch or a little nick. If the finished seam curves in, e.g. the doll's heel, you make little Vs into the seam allowance to take out some of the excess material on the inside.

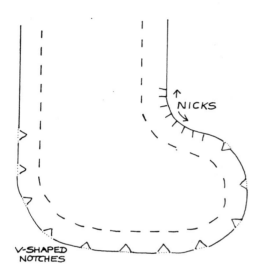

If the finished seam curves out, e.g. the front of the doll's ankle, you make a nick to allow the seam allowance to spread out.

In the same way, you will need to clip into corners so that you can satisfactorily turn the corner right side out.

I went to work on this with great enthusiasm and cut too deeply so that my notches and clips went into the seam and made a hole – this is not a good thing.

ENLARGING THE STENCIL

The toys photographed in this book were all made from the stencils given with the instructions and they are a good size for children to play with (grown-ups too). However you may wish to make a bigger toy (like the big bear on page 18). I have not experimented with every single toy but there

seems to be no reason why other patterns should not work just as well as the bear pattern when enlarged.

There are two ways of enlarging the basic patterns:
- ☐ Take it to an office equipment shop or large public library with a photocopier which enlarges – this will probably cost you between £1 and £2. If you know a helpful office manager, you may only have to pay the price of the photocopy – 10 to 20p. *Or*
- ☐ Use Rona's method:

Draw a rectangular (or square) frame round your pattern. Draw a diagonal line from bottom left to top right of the frame. By extending this diagonal upwards and the bottom horizontal to the right, you will be able to make a larger frame in exactly the same proportion as the original.

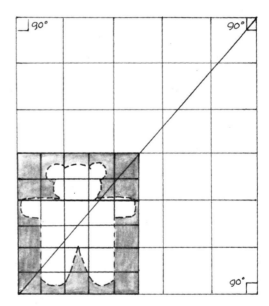

Repeat squares in larger frame

Divide the small frame into even sized rectangles or squares and then repeat the number on the larger frame. Fill in the larger rectangles or squares with exactly the same pattern lines as the smaller, until you have recreated the whole pattern.

FACES

A stitch up or down, the colour and size of a pair of safety eyes, can make all the difference to a toy's face. Some of the faces on old teddy bears and dolls were at worst grim, at best charmless.

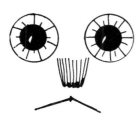

Cross face

Here are a few ideas to make your toy's face lovable.

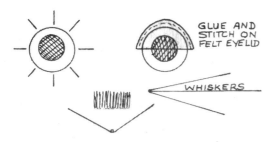

Happy, interesting face

☐ eyes are better set too wide apart than too close together.
☐ every toy benefits from a wide, upturned mouth made from a big stitch caught in the middle to make the curve (i.e. a feather stitch: see page 11).
☐ a small colourful detail, such as the cat's red and pink tongue (see page 71), can bring instant life to a dull face.
☐ sew on eyelashes or whiskers – or both.
☐ to make soft, melting orbs – or to make too-small eyes bigger – cut a small circle of dark felt or suede, 1 to 2 mm larger than the eye, and insert at the back of the eye. (See Seal, page 79.)
☐ if you can't find readymade eyes, see page 71 for details of how to make felt eyes.
☐ make felt eyelids for glass eyes to alter the shape; this is particularly appropriate for cats.

STUFFING

More is not necessarily better when stuffing these toys. Cuddly toys must not be hard and unyielding. The rag dolls need nice, bendy limbs so that they are easy to dress and undress. The little felt toys may split at seam junctions if great wads of stuffing are forced in.

Stuff toys with small amounts at a time so that you can see exactly what is happening and also avoid lumps forming. Having said all that, stuffing tends to go down after a little while, so don't skimp – firm but squashy is the ideal.

Whilst you stuff the toy, you also need to mould it into the right shape. If there seems to be a vast gulf between your toy and the one in the photo, it may well be that you simply need to mould and push your toy into shape. The only way to become expert at this is to practise, but it is not at all difficult. Stuffing always takes longer than you imagine, so leave plenty of time.

TEDDY BEARS

This bear pattern is very easy. It is also versatile:
you can make a glove puppet from the same basic pattern as the
honey bear, a much bigger bear like the blue bear or a bear bag. You
could use different colours of fur fabric to make a whole family of bears.
It's a curious thing about bears – they are meant for children but grown-ups
never lose their attachment to teddies. Tired friends in need of comfort sit on my
sofa cuddling the bears I made for this book; the honey bear is a particular
favourite. These bears cost well under £5 each to make, even if you
have to buy everything new, such as a full bag of stuffing. (Like all
the toys in this book, the cost is less as you gather more
materials around you. The glove puppet was made of
scraps left over from bigger toys.)

HONEY BEAR

YOU WILL NEED

- ☐ 50 cm fur fabric
- ☐ 150 gm stuffing
- ☐ 1 pair 15 mm safety eyes
- ☐ Darning or double knitting wool for nose
- ☐ At least 60 cm ribbon for bow
- ☐ Sewing thread – same colour as fur fabric
- ☐ Tacking cotton

PREPARATION

Trace pattern pieces, leaving room to add the 7 mm to 1 cm seam allowance on to each · pattern piece (see page 10).

Write the cutting and sewing instructions and letters – e.g. A, B – on each piece.

Pin pattern to wrong side of fabric with fur lying in direction of arrows.

With the ear and cheek patterns, cut the first one, then *reverse* the paper pieces and cut the pair, making certain the fur will lie in the corresponding way to the first piece.

Cut out each piece. *Make sure not to cut* between the legs of the main body pieces until after stitching. If you want longer paws or floppier ears, cut them a bit larger.

MAKING UP

Remember that all pieces should be joined with right sides together. It really is worthwhile pinning and then tacking the pieces before you machine or firmly hand stitch together. Start off by joining cheek pieces together from A to B. Finish stitching on point B.

Join centre head section to cheek pieces from C to C through B. It is easiest to do it in two stages: sew from C to B on one side, finish off, then sew the second C to B. Make certain that all the seams lie flat.

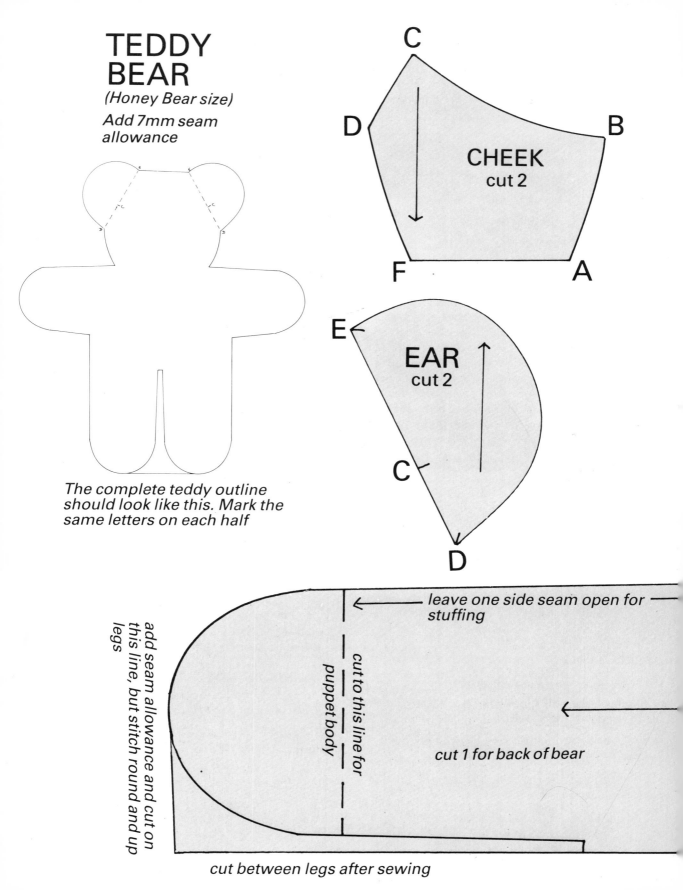

TEDDY BEAR

(Honey Bear size)

Add 7mm seam
allowance

The complete teddy outline
should look like this. Mark the
same letters on each half

CHEEK
cut 2

C
D
B
F
A

EAR
cut 2

E
C
D

leave one side seam open for
stuffing

cut to this line for
puppet body

cut 1 for back of bear

add seam allowance and cut on
this line, but stitch round and up
legs

cut between legs after sewing

Arrows indicate direction of fur

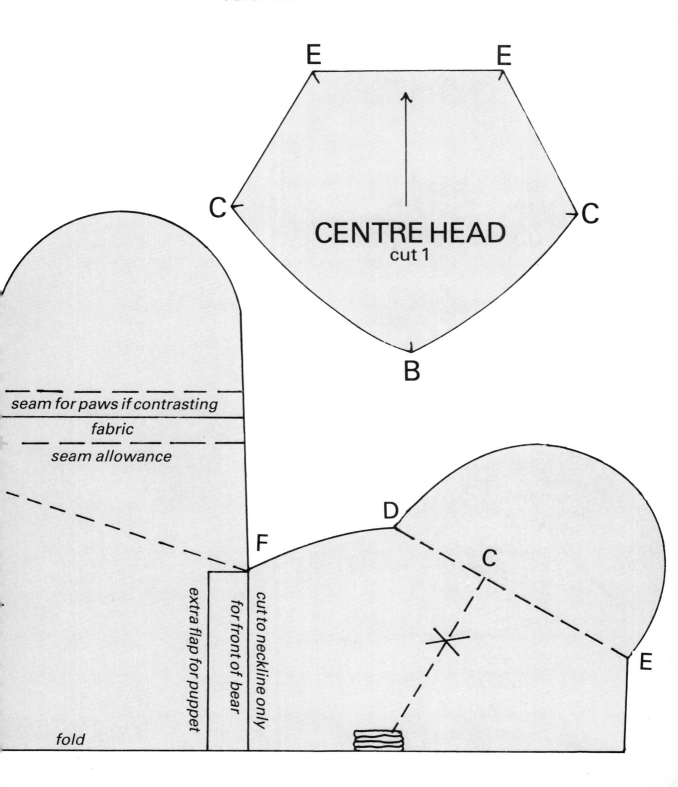

E   E

C   C

CENTRE HEAD
cut 1

B

seam for paws if contrasting

fabric

seam allowance

D

C

F

E

extra flap for puppet

for front of bear

cut to neckline only

fold

Join ear sections to front head shape from D to E through C.

Join front head to front body from F to F and finish off stitching firmly at each point.

Make the nose by sewing several satin stitches (see page 11) in the position shown. Sew mouth with double feather stitch (see page 11), caught in the middle to make him smile or look serious.

It is easiest to fix the safety eyes into position at this stage.

Decide where on the seam they will look best, undo a stitch with the Quik Unpik, push the stem of the eyes through, then lock them in place with the metal disc on the wrong side of the fabric.

Join back bear to front bear all round outer edge *except the opening for the stuffing*. Finish off stitching at both points F, that is where head meets body on either side, and then start stitching again. This will help enormously when you clip the seam allowance and turn the bear right side out.

Make a single cut between the legs to separate; trim seams and clip into corners at neck, ears, underarm and between legs and clip curves (see page 12). Be careful not to cut through to machining.

Turn through to right side and pull into shape.

On the outside, machine or hand stitch back and front of bear together across each ear from D to E along seam line, so that the ears are separate from the face and don't get stuffed.

Stuff each arm lightly and then machine or hand stitch back and front together between F and the underarm.

Stuff the rest of the bear, pushing the stuffing well into corners. Sew up the opening by hand in ladder stitch when stuffing is completed.

Ease out fur caught in seams, with a wire comb or darning needle. Tie bow round neck to finish.

BIG BEAR

See page 6 for photo

I took the Teddy Bear pattern to a copy centre and asked them to enlarge it by 50%. I made the bear in exactly the same way with one addition — I seamed the legs in the same way as the arms are seamed on the Honey Bear; this means that the big bear will sit happily in a chair. He is very impressive and despite the extra cost of the photocopy, he is still extremely good value. If you are far from a photocopier, you could enlarge the pattern yourself (see page 12). You will need 50 cm fur fabric; one pair 17 mm safety eyes and about 300 gm stuffing.

BEAR BAG

I don't know exactly when the vogue for animal bags hit the population but they are incredibly popular. I made this one using the basic bear pattern which I had enlarged to make the big bear. The zip lies across the back of his neck and the only difference to the pattern is that the back of the bear becomes two pieces instead of one.

You can either wear the bear round your waist on a stretchy belt, or sling it over your shoulder on a longer, buckled belt. The belt should be made of some fabric light enough to be sewn into the bear's paws — leather, unless it is very soft, would be too heavy.

YOU WILL NEED

- ☐ 50 cm fur fabric
- ☐ 2 rectangles of tough cotton (such as lining cotton) measuring 13 cm by 18 cm and 13 cm by 16.5 cm
- ☐ 10 cm zip preferably with closed end

- Pair of safety eyes 17 mm in diameter
- About 100 gm stuffing
- Matching cotton and tacking cotton
- Stretchy webbing belt with clasp or buckled belt, long enough to make a shoulder strap for your child.

PREPARATION AND MAKING UP

Trace the pattern for the Teddy Bear (pages 17–18) and enlarge it; or use the pattern for the big bear if you already have it. Cut the front as detailed in the pattern for the Honey Bear, two ears, two cheeks, one centre head, and one body. Sew these together as in the basic pattern, with all the features in place.

Cut the whole pattern in two at the neck to make the back, or trace it in two pieces – the body and the head. Cut out the back in fur fabric, adding on 1 cm seam allowance to each piece at the neck.

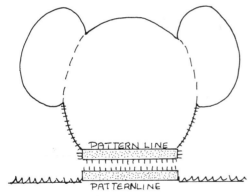

Allow extra seam allowance at top of body and bottom of head

Lay the two pieces on your work top, wrong side up. Turn the seam allowance back and tack it down. Lay the lining fabric rectangles on top of the fur fabric with the short edges along the neck line. Use the longer rectangle for the head piece. Turn the seam allowance under so that the raw edges are turned in to meet the raw edges of the fur fabric. Make certain that the lining comes right up to the neckline of the fur fabric on both pieces. If you don't, you will find the fur keeps getting caught in the zip.

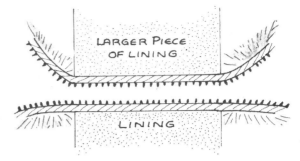

Shaded areas to each side are the wrong side of fur fabric

Tack the lining pieces down on to the fur fabric along the neck line each side.

Lay the head and body edge to edge so that it looks like a whole bear with a gap of about 5 mm between the two pieces. Put the zip in so that the teeth are exposed along this line. The handle for the zip will be face down, because you are working inside out. Pin, tack and machine the zip in. Finish off with a row of machining about 2.5 cm long at each end of the zip, through all thicknesses.

Lay the bear bag flat and pull the top longer rectangle of lining down to lie on top of the other – they should now match in size. Machine the lining round the open sides so that you make the bag; you may need to fiddle a little at the top where it meets the zip, possibly hand sewing through all the thicknesses to make sure it is secure.

Cut the belt in two pieces and put one end of each in a paw seam – tuck the rest of each belt piece inside the bear's body, so that they will appear on the outside of the bear bag. If you are making a belt bear bag, insert the pieces into the ends of the bear's paw, if you are making a shoulder bag, put them in over his wrists:

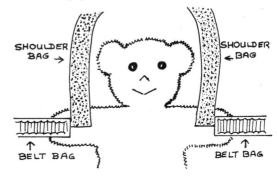

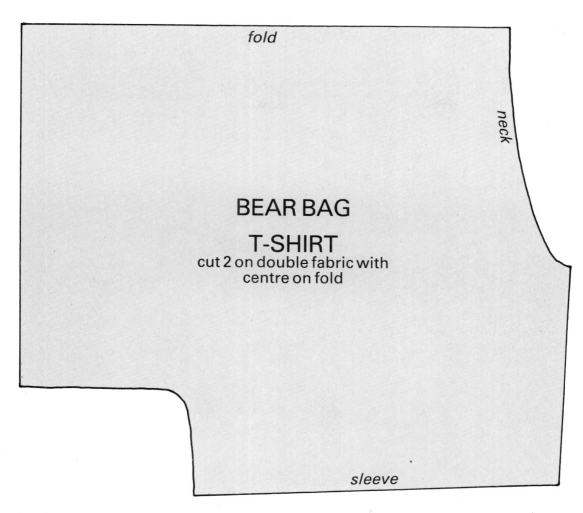

fold

neck

BEAR BAG

T-SHIRT
cut 2 on double fabric with
centre on fold

sleeve

Right sides together, sew the back head to the front as for the basic Honey Bear pattern and sew round the rest of the bear, leaving a space up the side of one leg open for stuffing. Cut and clip the seams into the corners and round the curves.

Turn the bear right side out and stuff him lightly but firmly.

If you wish to joint his arms and legs, oversew them by machine or hand through all thicknesses.

Fill the zippered bag with all sorts of delightful and interesting items. If the fur gets caught in the zip, just snip it back with a small pair of scissors.

I thought this bear looked rather a bohemian,

South of France sort of bear, who might wear a faded blue T-shirt to match his eyes, so I made him one. The pattern is simply the pattern of the bear's body without seam allowances, cut out with pinking shears from an old T-shirt and machined on the outside up the side seams and across the shoulders. I added the red tennis racquet motif because it looked good.

GLOVE PUPPET
Sam Talhi's mother Rosamund put in a special request for a glove puppet pattern. Sam had come back from school one day asking her to make one with such fervour that she went to look for a book with simple instructions. She couldn't find one and asked me if I could help. This enormously engaging bear with his Robin Day bow and leather satchel is the result.

YOU WILL NEED

- ☐ 25 cm fur fabric, scraps of contrasting fabric for paws and face if wanted
- ☐ A pair of 15 mm safety eyes
- ☐ Double knitting or darning wool for nose and mouth
- ☐ About 25 gm of stuffing
- ☐ Spotted cotton for bow tie – 25 by 15 cm for bow, 30 by 4 cm for strap
- ☐ Matching cotton for sewing, contrasting cotton for tacking
- ☐ Scraps of leather or felt and a popper for satchel, or bought plastic purse
- ☐ Cord for strap

PREPARATION

Use teddy bear pattern, but instead of cutting round legs, just cut a straight line across the bottom where it is marked on the pattern.

If you want to give the bear different coloured paws, cut across the line marked on the pattern, remembering to leave a seam allowance for each paw and the arms of the main body of the bear.

Also cut one piece of strong cotton (I used lining material) to the pattern of the back of the bear's head – again remembering to leave a 1 cm seam allowance. This is so that you can stuff the bear's face but still leave a gap at the back of his head for fingers. The dotted line just below his neck on the pattern is the line you must cut on so that you have enough material to turn up.

MAKING UP

Make up the bear's face – two ears, one centre head, two cheeks – as in instructions for the Honey Bear. Put in eyes, embroider nose and mouth.

Now pin and tack piece of lining to back of face. Because the lining is smaller than the face, pin edge to edge and don't fuss about the face creasing in the middle. *Do not pin, tack or sew down lining on neck line.* Machine tacking.

Now make up bear as for main pattern. Pin, tack and machine (or hand stitch) paws together if using contrasting material then pin,

tack and machine (or hand stitch) back bear to front bear. Turn hem in about 1 cm and machine or hand stitch.

Turn bear head right side out. Leave paws and body pulled up wrong side out around neck.

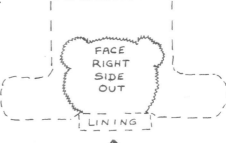

Pull the paws and body wrong side out over the puppet's head. Insert stuffing into face as shown by the arrow

Stuff face firmly. Pin and slip stitch lining to neck front so that stuffing is firmly wedged in. This is easy to do if you have left the paws and body of the puppet over his head; it doesn't matter if you cobble the seam together as long as it is secure.

Pull the paws and glove down when you have sewn the stuffing in, turn the teddy bear puppet the right side out, and attach bow tie, badge etc.

Satchel Use a rectangle of soft leather or felt about 22 cm by 8 cm, or buy a tiny flap-over purse and stitch shoulder strap firmly on.

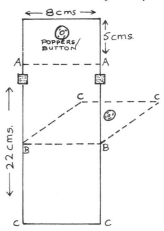

Stitch/oversew side AB to side CB on the outside of both sides of the bag. Sew on shoulder straps at A; sew on popper

23

RAG DOLLS

Using this one basic pattern, you can make lots
of different dolls, from American footballers to more traditional dolls.
Rag dolls were originally just that
— made out of old rags and scraps of left-over material; even the stuffing
was shredded rags. Today there is still no need to buy very much to make
your rag doll: I refused to go on shopping expeditions especially for one doll so,
apart from the synthetic stuffing, the dolls and all their clothes are made of things
I had round the house. The first time I made the actual doll, it took me
about three hours — because I didn't read the pattern properly
— now it takes less than two hours.

BASIC RAG DOLL PATTERN

YOU WILL NEED

- ☐ 50 cm skin-coloured cotton fabric, 115 cm wide
- ☐ 250 gm stuffing
- ☐ Scraps of felt for eyes
- ☐ Pink embroidery silk for nose and mouth
- ☐ Matching cotton for sewing, contrasting cotton for tacking
- ☐ 50 gm chunky knit wool for hair (skein of tapestry wool is ideal)
- ☐ Glue

PREPARATION

Trace off the doll pattern pieces (pages 28–30) separately and draw in all the necessary markings. 5 mm seams are allowed on all pieces. Join fabric with right sides facing. Cut all pieces with the straight grain of the fabric in the direction shown on the patterns. (Note that the doll's body is cut on the bias.)

MAKING UP

Legs Join leg shapes in pairs round the edges leaving the top edge open, clip seams on curves. Turn right side out and stuff firmly up to 2.5 cm from top edge; don't be tempted to fill further, you need the slack. Pin the top edges of each leg together so that the two seams lie in the centre of each leg at back and front. Make a small inverted pleat at each side and tack the top edges together.

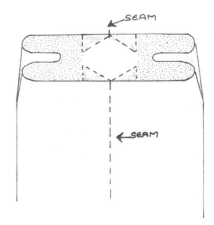

Face and body Mark in with tiny chalk marks or tailor tack the facial features on the right side of one piece. Mark the neck darts on the wrong side of each piece and then fold the fabric from corner to corner of the dart and stitch on the curved line.

Join the body round the edges leaving the top and lower edges open. Turn right side out, turn in lower edges of body 1 cm and tack. Insert about 1 cm of the top of each leg between the body pieces and machine or hand stitch into

24

place through all thicknesses. Stuff body and then head firmly, pushing the stuffing into the corners with a chopstick or something similar (see page 13). Turn raw edges in 1 cm on top of head and tack. Run a strong double gathering thread round and then pull it up to draw edges together as tightly as possible. Fasten off.

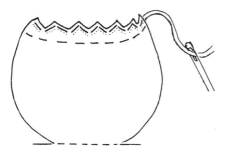

Use running stitch in double cotton to gather top of head

Arms Join arm shapes in pairs round the edges leaving the top edge open. Clip round curves, especially into the corner between thumb and hand. Turn right side out and stuff firmly to within 2.5 cm of top edge. Turn in top raw edges 1 cm and bring seams together in the middle and make a small inverted pleat each side (like the legs).

Oversew top edges of each arm together, catching pleats into place at the top and then sew arms securely to shoulders at position shown on pattern. It is neatest to sew the arms from underneath; this also gives her a little bit of a shoulder.

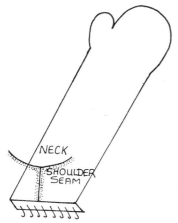

Oversew arm from underneath

Hair For the fringe: cut 14 strands of wool 20 cm long, fold in half and lay with the cut edges to the back of the head, the folds falling down to her face. The fold should be on the fringe line. Catch each fold down on to the forehead with a small stitch in matching cotton.

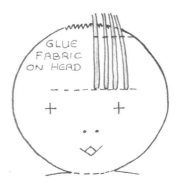

Secure the ends at the back with a row of stitching and glue if necessary. For the remaining hair – cut the rest of the wool into equal lengths of about 38 cm. (I bought tapestry wool in 50 gm skeins: this was very easy because all I had to do for the remaining hair was slit the skein at either end.) Spread glue on the doll's head from the top of the fringe backwards, down the sides and back; don't spread it too far down the sides and back because you may not want the hair to stick that far down. Place the skein on the doll's head, hanging down evenly on either side. Make sure that it is lying across the back of the head as well (see the picture of the Fergie doll). Using a large needle threaded with double cotton the colour of the hair, stitch it firmly into place using backstitch. Tie loose ends into bunches with ribbon. Trim the ends if you wish.

Neck To hold the head firmly and stop the neck from stretching, thread a medium to large needle with a long piece of flesh coloured cotton and double it. Push the needle in at one side of the neck, and make two small back stitches. Wind the cotton round the neck at least twice, ending up by the seam on the other side of the neck. Finish off with small back stitches.

Eyes Cut two circles of felt 1 cm in diameter and glue in position shown. Stitch securely if this doll is for a small child.

Mouth Use two strands of stranded pink embroidery thread to work this. Consult the stitch diagrams on page 00. The mouth is two large feather stitches – fasten the threads on and off under the hair line so that there are no loose ends showing.

Cheeks To colour the cheeks put a little lipstick on to the tip of your finger and lightly rub in the position marked on the pattern. Or dot the lipstick straight on to the face. It dries firmly after a while. (Practise on a spare piece of fabric first.)

Nose The easiest way to make her nose is to apply two small dots of pink lipstick; alternatively you can sew it on in pink embroidery silk using two French knots or tiny cross stitches.

FERGIE DOLL

This charming doll with her mane of red hair and blue eyes was inspired by the Duchess of York and is affectionately known as the Fergie Doll. Strangely enough, she is the great pin-up of an extremely macho small boy, Rory Edgerton, aged 5, who roars around the New Forest. Given a choice of any of the toys in this book for his birthday present, Rory demanded the 'beautiful girl'.

I gave her different shoes so that you can see how easy it is to ring the changes from the one basic shoe pattern.

FERGIE'S DRESS

This enchanting dress takes time and you may gnash your teeth and roar with exasperation if you try to make it in a hurry. It is worth the time and trouble because it looks so wonderful but I think you should allow a long afternoon to make it.

I used some Viyella material left over from a grown-up dress and the braid from some cushions to trim it. The buttons down the back come from an old woolly; I used them because I couldn't find any poppers in the house and I was determined not to make a shopping trip especially for this dress.

YOU WILL NEED

- ☐ 50 cm fabric, 90 cm wide
- ☐ Shirring elastic
- ☐ 3 buttons, poppers or press studs
- ☐ Cottons for sewing, contrasting cotton for tacking
- ☐ Braid, etc. for trimming

MAKING UP

Trace pattern (page 31–32) on to tracing paper and note sewing instructions.

Join front and back bodice together at the shoulder. Use the other two pieces to make another bodice exactly the same for the lining, but machine side seams together.

Gather top edge of each sleeve where indicated on pattern and tack, pulling up gathers to fit.

Insert sleeves into bodice. This is a real fiddle because the dress is so small; I found the easiest way was to start pinning at the centre. That gives you something to work from. Tack both sleeves in and then machine or hand stitch. Neaten raw edges by oversewing if you wish. Clip the corners between the sleeves and the side seams.

Make a small hem on the lower edge of each sleeve and gather either by using shirring elastic or by making a deeper seam and inserting narrow elastic.

Join lining to main bodice right sides together along back centre edges and neckline. Clip seams and turn through to right side. Press. Turn under raw edges of lining at armhole to neaten and slip stitch into place.

Sew back seam on skirt to within 6 cm of upper edge. Gather top edge to fit bodice and sew to outer edge of bodice only. Turn in raw edges on back seam to neaten.

Turn under bodice lining along lower edge and hem into place over gathered edge of skirt.

Trim and hem the lower edge of her skirt.

Sew buttons or press studs down back to finish.

Her sash is a strip of fabric about 5 cm wide and as long as you have fabric – mine was about

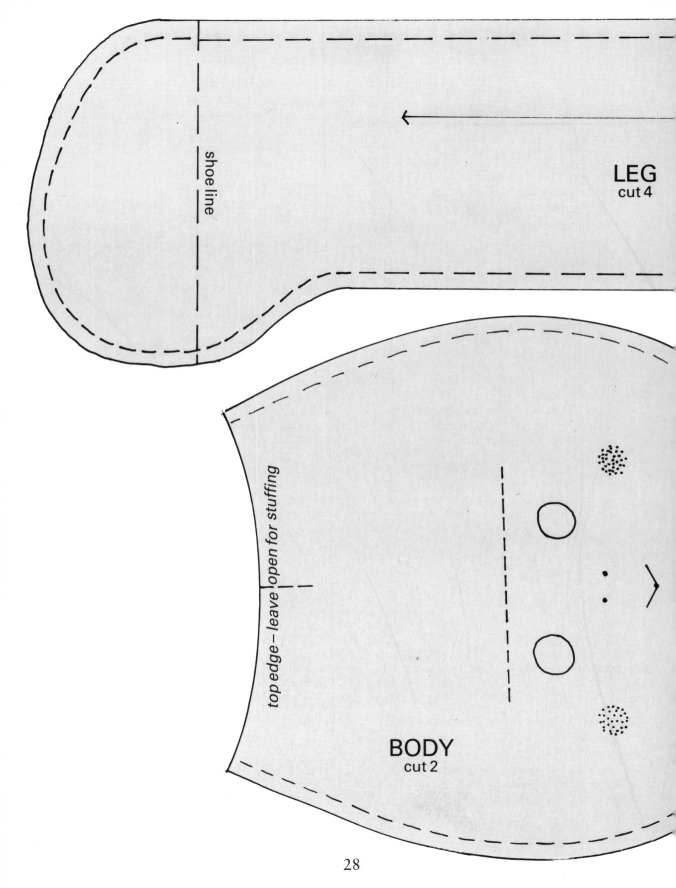

shoe line

LEG
cut 4

top edge – leave open for stuffing

BODY
cut 2

28

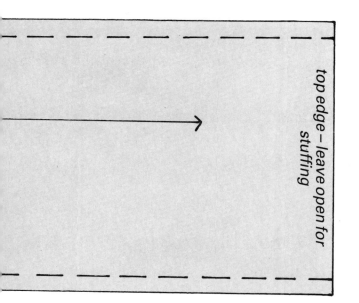

RAG DOLL
Arm pattern on page 30
5 mm seams included

top edge – leave open for stuffing

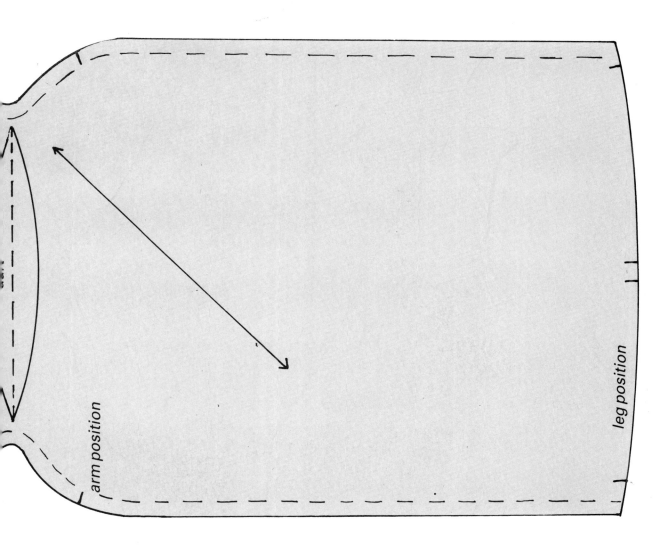

arm position

leg position

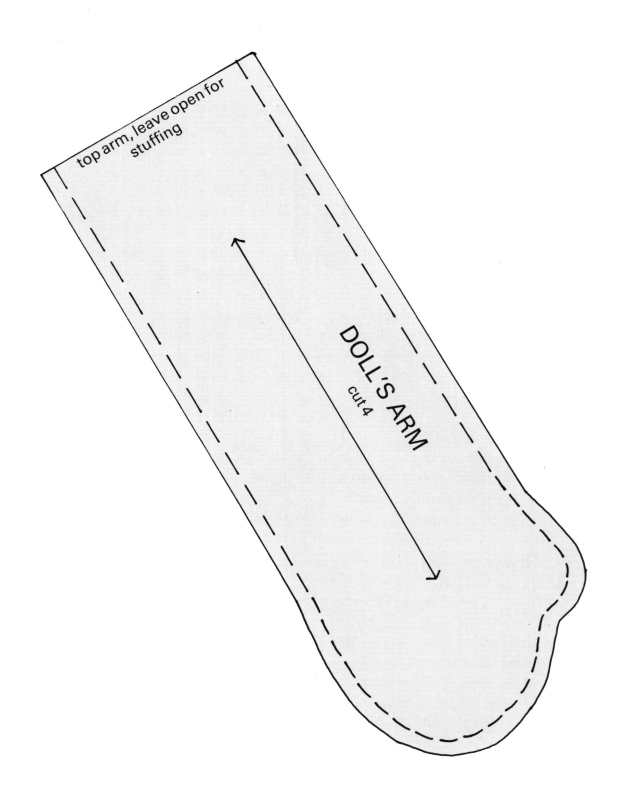

top arm, leave open for stuffing

DOLL'S ARM
cut 4

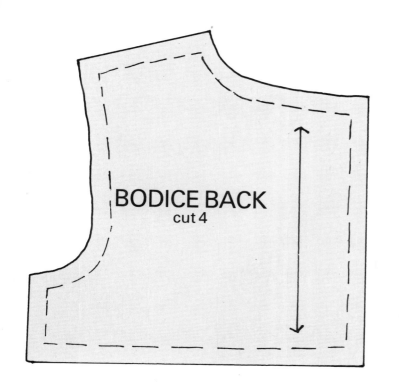

FERGIE'S DRESS
5mm seams included
Sleeve on page 32

BODICE BACK
cut 4

SKIRT
cut a rectangle 25cm by 90cm

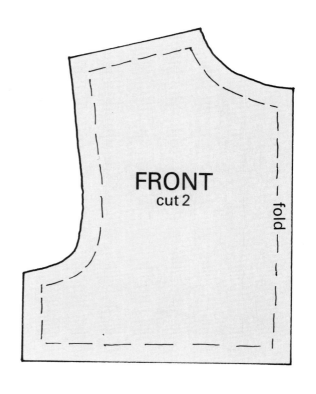

FRONT
cut 2

fold

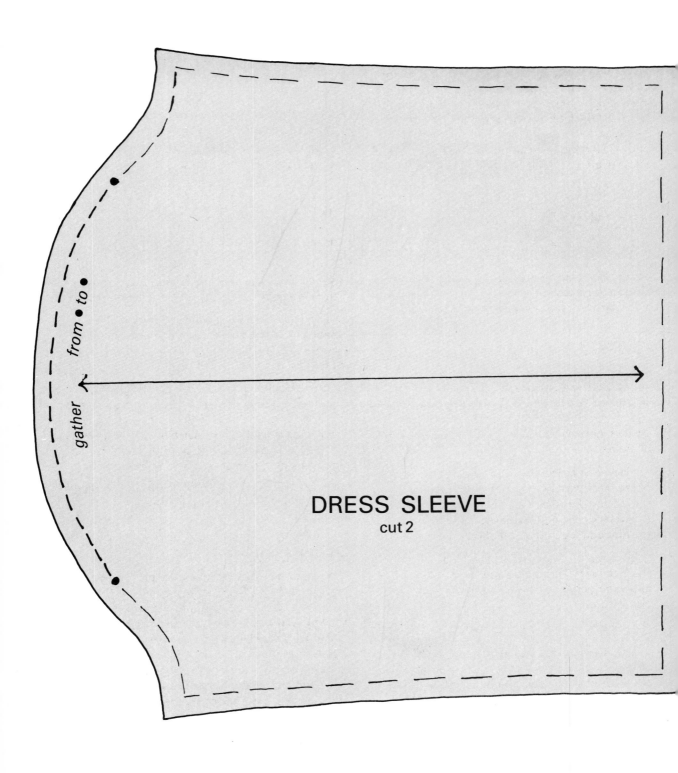

gather *from • to •*

DRESS SLEEVE
cut 2

50 cm – seamed, turned inside out and trimmed with braid. I stitched it down at either side so that it would not immediately be lost.

If you want to sew on a ruff collar as I have done, take a strip of material 5 cm wide and three times the neck measurement of the dress. With right sides together, machine up one end and the length of the fabric, then turn right side out. Press. Pin to neck in pleats. Finish band by turning in end. Tack band in position, and machine or hand stitch firmly.

SOCKS

YOU WILL NEED

- Scraps of white (or coloured) T-shirt material
- Cotton to match
- Very narrow, or shirring, elastic

MAKING UP

Use the doll leg pattern. You can make ankle socks, knee socks or stockings depending on where you cut the top of the fabric. Allow an extra 1 cm because each sock or stocking is held up with narrow elastic inserted in the turnover at the top.

Place the pattern on the fabric with the weave of the fabric running up and down so that the stretch runs from side to side. Cut the fabric on the scant side – the sock has to be stretched over the foot and leg so that it fits well.

With right sides together, machine or hand stitch the seam leaving a good 5 mm seam allowance, either with small straight stitch or zigzag stitch.

Nick curves and then turn right side out.

Turn over the top and use running stitch to make a channel for narrow elastic. Thread elastic through using small safety pin.

Tack the ends of the elastic together, try socks for size and then stitch firmly.

See also instructions for knitted socks on page 41.

SLIPPER SHOES

YOU WILL NEED

- Scraps of felt or stretchy towelling material
- Matching cotton and ribbon or more scraps for decoration.

MAKING UP

Use leg pattern of rag doll and cut four pieces along the line marked 'shoe line'. Join in pairs to make up shoes. If you are using felt, machine or hand stitch round the outside on the right side of the material; if you are using towelling or similar material, sew on the wrong side of the material and then turn right side out.

Stay stitch along the top edge to neaten, either by machine or hand – you can use a decorative stitch in a contrasting colour if you feel energetic.

If you use towelling, which stretches to the shape of the foot and so keeps the shoe on, hand sew the seams, make a tiny bow for decoration and sew it firmly on to her toes.

If you use felt (as I have in the photograph), make a bar out of doubled up felt, about 7.5 cm long by 2 cm wide, fold in half lengthways and stick together with glue. When it has dried, put the shoe on the doll's foot and position the bar so it looks realistic, then sew firmly in place.

Decorate with a ribbon bow, felt flower, small button or whatever takes your fancy.

NECKLACE

This pearl necklace is made from pearl beads bought in the local haberdashery store. They come in packets costing about 55p and seem to be widely available. My neighbour Rebecca Lawrence, aged 16 and an authority on dolls' accessories, threaded them on shirring elastic which is stretchy enough to pull over the doll's head so that you don't need a clasp. The only difficulty was persuading the elastic through the eye of a needle small enough to fit through the hole in the beads; it is a good idea to try out the needle for size before you start pushing the needle through the beads.

SUNSHINE SUSIE

Susie is Jessica Cran's favourite doll. Jessica is 3 and she made straight for Susie in a room crowded with toys and played with her all morning while her mother and I played with the word processor.

The pattern is the basic Rag Doll pattern, but she has melting brown eyes made of tiny scraps of suede and her hair is braided and beaded and ribboned into eight plaits which stick out from her head. The sundress is just one length of material, with elastic at the top and waist.

SUNDRESS

YOU WILL NEED

- ☐ 35 × 55 cm rectangle cotton material
- ☐ 50 cm narrow elastic
- ☐ Coloured cotton; contrasting cotton for tacking

The 35 cm measurement is the length from top to bottom.

MAKING UP

Turn the top over 2 cm on the wrong side. Machine stitch in zigzag or back stitch by hand.

Leaving a band of about 1 cm at the top which forms a frill, run another line of sewing, straight stitch this time, above the lower line, to form a channel for the elastic.

Lay the material flat again and measure 3 cm below the second line of sewing. Mark this line (the third one). Measure another line, that is the fourth, 3 cm below that. Leaving this band on top, tuck up exactly the same amount of material (3 cm) underneath to meet the third line. You should have a pocket or fold of material running along the width of the fabric, which is 3 cm deep.

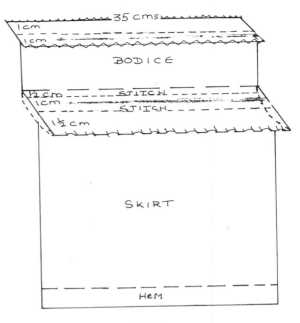

Insert elastic in the two shaded areas

Stitch along the top line of this pocket (the third line), then stitch again 1 cm down to form a channel for the elasticated waist. The rest of the pocket forms the frill at the waist, running underneath the elastic. Seam straight down the side *but do not seam over the channels where you will put elastic at top and waist.*

Run narrow elastic through those channels using a safety pin to pull the elastic through; tack the ends together, fit on the doll, then firmly sew the ends and trim.

Finish the sundress by machining or hand stitching the hem where you wish.

NECKLACE, BRACELET AND BEADS

I used an old necklace of mine and a few extra beads from the Hobby Horse to make her necklace and bracelet and for her hair. The necklace and bracelet are threaded on shirring elastic with the ends knotted loosely enough to pull over her head and wrist so that you do not need a clasp. Her earrings are two small brass curtain rings sewn tightly under her hair.

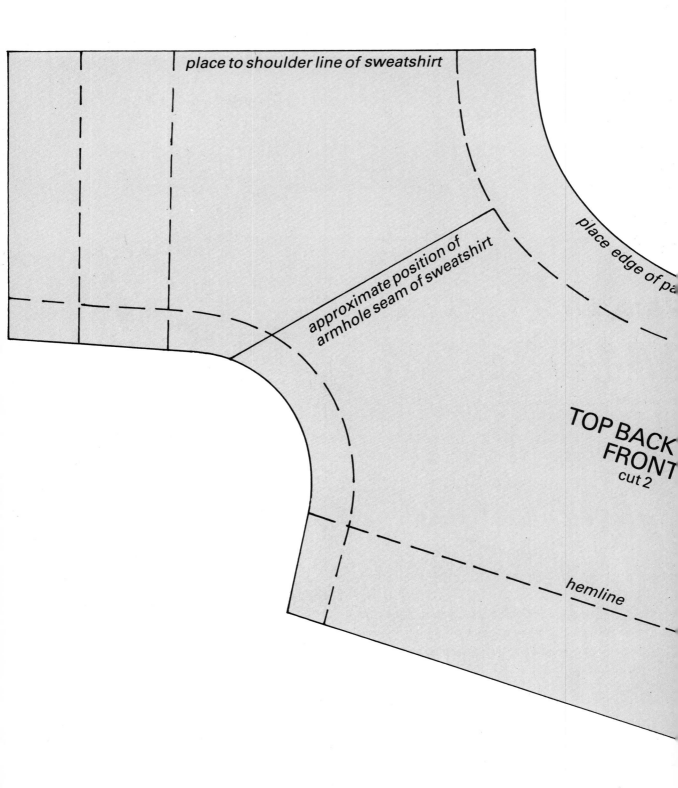

place to shoulder line of sweatshirt

approximate position of
armhole seam of sweatshirt

place edge of pa

TOP BACK
FRONT
cut 2

hemline

Yokes on page 40, trousers on page 49

JOGGING DOLL
TRACKSUIT
1 cm seams included

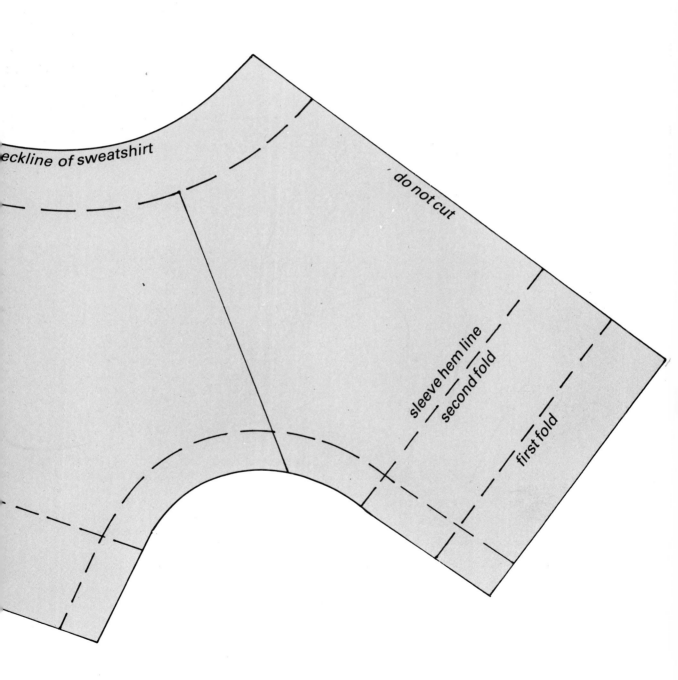

neckline of sweatshirt

do not cut

sleeve hem line

second fold

first fold

JOGGING DOLL

A friend of mine looking at this doll said that she had the sort of colouring that we would all give our eye-teeth for – flaxen blonde hair, green eyes and peachy complexion. This was coincidental because, like the rest of the rag dolls, she is entirely made of recycled bits and pieces.

Her hair is quilting wool, which was all I had in the house at the time. The peach-like bloom comes from remnants of my curtain lining, and I cut up an old paint-stained sweatshirt for her tracksuit.

She was the first rag doll I made and I am very fond of her, not least because there are lots of different bits of clothing to take on and off, and her accessories can go on for ever. I plan to make her a sleeping bag and a futon next.

TRACK SUIT

This track suit is made from a recycled crew-necked sweatshirt, preferably one with long, raglan sleeves. It is a bit fiddly so allow at least two hours to make the set and please read the pattern very carefully before you start.

YOU WILL NEED

- ☐ One old crew-necked sweatshirt
- ☐ Approximately 28 cm of 5 mm wide elastic
- ☐ 60 cm of white piping cord
- ☐ 2 non-sew poppers or press studs
- ☐ Badges or sew-on motifs
- ☐ Matching cotton for sewing; contrasting cotton for tacking

When you fit the tracksuit on the doll, remember it needs to fit loosely so that children can drag it on and off without anything splitting.

PREPARATION

Cut out all the pieces at the beginning.

Trace the pattern pieces and make careful note of the positioning of the pieces on the sweatshirt. Adjustments have to be made according to the size and style of sweatshirt used, so don't worry if the pattern doesn't seem to fit exactly.

Place the pattern piece for the tracksuit top on the neckline of the sweatshirt. I found that the sleeves of my old sweatshirt went out at a different angle from the sleeves on the pattern. If this happens to you, don't cut through the shoulders (as I did), cut the arms along the shoulder seams of the sweatshirt to the same size as the pattern, as if the pattern and the sweatshirt were an exact match.

Cut round the pattern, across the ends of the sleeves, underarm seams and hemline. Do not cut through shoulder seams.

Cut the yoke from any part of the sweatshirt.

The trousers of the tracksuit are made from the sleeves and cuffs of the sweatshirt. Cut one trouser pattern from each sleeve, placing the hem line of the pattern to the hem of the cuff.

From the welt, cut a strip approximately 20 cm by 3 cm to bind the neck.

Cut another piece from the welt about 15 cm by 5 cm to make a headband.

MAKING UP

Pin, tack and machine the underarm seams with right sides together, clipping the seam allowance on the curved edges.

Pin, tack and machine the back and front yoke together along the shoulder line. Turn back the facings on the fold lines and fix non-sew poppers or press studs in position shown.

Join the yoke to the main body by overlapping curved lower edge of the yoke with the main body piece about 2 cm all round and sewing it into place by hand. Back stitch bottom of sweatshirt neck band to yoke to keep it firm and slip stitch along top.

Bind the neck edge using the strip cut from the welt.

Turn up the hem to hip level and machine 1 cm from bottom.

In the front middle, make a slit big enough to take the cord, and button hole stitch the slit. Thread the cord through, knotting it at each end.

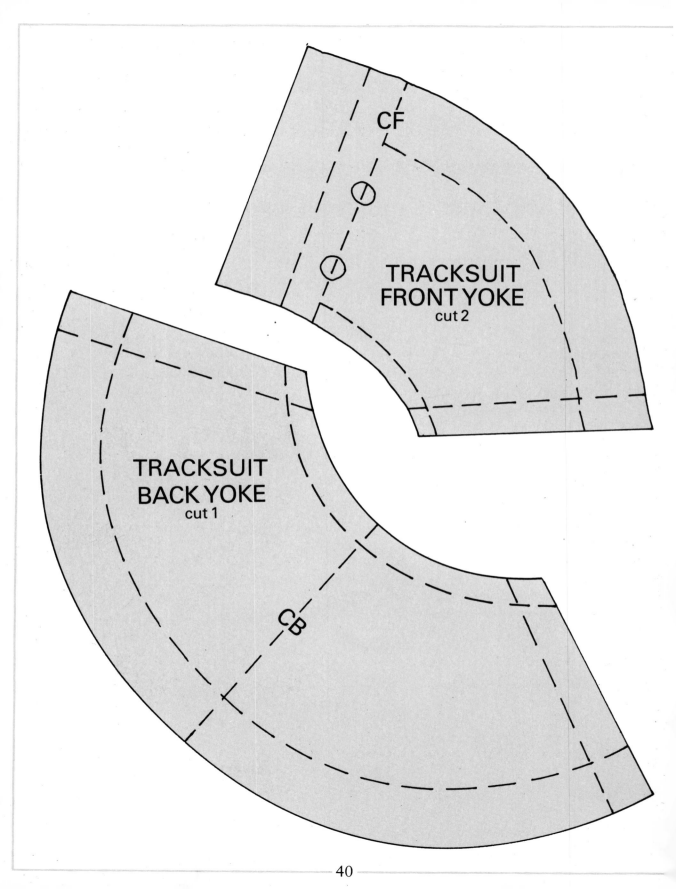

TRACKSUIT
FRONT YOKE
cut 2

CF

TRACKSUIT
BACK YOKE
cut 1

CB

Machine or hand stitch the raw edges and roll the sleeves over a couple of times.

HEADBAND

Fold strip in half, right sides together, and machine along bottom and sides, leaving top open. Turn right side out and stitch top edges in. Sew the ends together firmly to make a band.

TROUSERS

Pin, tack and machine the inner leg seams of each trouser piece with right sides together, adjusting the tightness at the hem to fit the doll's leg.

Stitch the two pieces together round the crutch seam.

Turn over the top edge on the dotted line (2 cm) and machine (zigzag if possible) close to the raw edge, leaving a gap on one of the seams to draw through the elastic.

Overlap the ends of the elastic and sew together after checking that the trousers fit. Finish off the opening by sewing down by hand. I neatened all the raw edges by machining with zigzag stitch; this isn't strictly necessary but it gives the tracksuit a longer life.

LEG WARMERS/THICK SOCKS

YOU WILL NEED

☐ Oddments of double knitting wool
☐ 1 pair each size 8 and 10 (4 mm and 3¼ mm) knitting needles

MAKING UP

Using size 10 needles cast on 31 sts and work 2.5 cm in knit 1 purl 1 rib.

Change to stocking stitch – purl 1 row, knit 1 row – for 7 cm and work in a pattern – you could make up alternate centimetre bands in contrasting colours.

Change to size 8 needles and original colour and work 3 cm in knit 1 purl 1 rib. Cast off loosely in rib.

Make a second leg warmer to match.

Sew each one into a tube along the long edge with right sides together, matching stripes carefully, then turn right sides out and press.

If you want to make thick socks, use this pattern and stitch up the ends with the shorter rib to form a sock.

TRAINERS FOR JOGGER

Use pattern for American footballer sports shoes on page 47.

SPORTS BAG

YOU WILL NEED

☐ Scraps of fabric (I used taffeta) cut into two rectangles 18 cm by 12 cm and two circles 9 cm in diameter.
☐ 15 cm zip in contrasting colour
☐ 70 cm of 1.5 cm wide petersham ribbon (same colour as zip)
☐ Matching cotton for sewing; contrasting cotton for tacking

There is a 1 cm seam allowance throughout.

MAKING UP

Turn in one of the long edges on each rectangle and lay along each side of the zip so that the teeth are exposed. Machine into place.

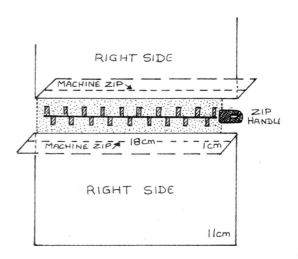

Now make the handles. Cut the ribbon into two equal lengths. Fold each length in a U-shape. With the zipped up main part of the bag flat on your work top, place the cut edges of the ribbons to the raw outer edges of the bag, about 6 cm apart.

Make sure the ribbons are not twisted; pin and tack into place.

The ribbons should be sewn down for about 9 cm from the outer edges. Machine or back stitch into place (see drawing).

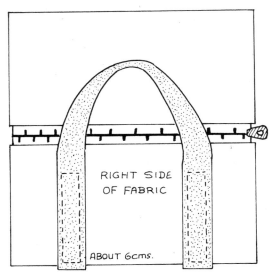

Repeat handle on other side

Now turn the bag inside out and join along the base to form a cylinder.

Undo the zip and keeping the bag inside out, insert the two circles at each end. Pin, tack and machine or hand stitch into place. I found it easier to sew by hand in back stitch.

Turn right side out and press.

She is carrying a towel in her sports bag (a spare face flannel) but there are lots of different things she might want to pack.

PACKING DOLL

This doll was finally christened Candy and she is a very leggy lady – I think I must have cut the legs on the long side – but she will show you what an undressed doll looks like.

Her blue-spotted bikini top and pants – scraps from Sunshine Susie's sundress – and all her underclothes are made to the same basic pattern, which is incredibly easy. The orange silk petticoat is a simple rectangle of material seamed down one side and elasticated.

The basket suitcase came from my local flowershop and used to hold two potted hyacinths. I washed the earthy polythene lining and lined it with pretty fabric to turn it into a splendid travelling trunk.

Her mattress, eiderdown and lacy pillow are all recycled materials, most of them rather tatty but easily refurbished and made into marvellous playthings.

BASIC UNDERCLOTHES/ BIKINI PATTERN

FOR THE HALTER OR STRAPPED TOP, YOU WILL NEED

☐ Rectangle of fabric 7.5 cm deep by 30 cm long
☐ 2 strips of matching fabric, 15 cm by 2.5 cm, *or* two 15 cm lengths of matching ribbon 1 cm wide

Fold the rectangle in half, right sides together, and seam up the side. Turn right side out and press the band so that the seam lies in the middle. Tuck in the ends and stitch down.

Run a double thread through the middle and gather.

Make narrow halter straps out of strips of material 15 cm long and 2.5 cm wide. Or if you are using ribbon, swallowtail or hem one end of each length.

Then go ahead as follows.

Put the bandeau top in position and mark where the straps should be. Fold them round the bandeau, gathering it slightly, and sew firmly in place across the tops.

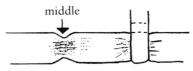

Fold shoulder strap round band, gathering slightly, and stitch on dotted lines

Fit the garment again and then sew on poppers or hooks and eyes at the back. Tie straps in place.

FOR THE KNICKERS OR SHORTS, YOU WILL NEED

- ☐ Scraps of fabric, not less than 2 rectangles measuring 15 cm by 30 cm
- ☐ 30 cm very narrow elastic

These are made from the basic tracksuit trouser pattern (page 49).

For bloomer knickers, cut to a line about 3 cm below the crotch. Hem the top and bottoms, and thread through the top hem with narrow elastic.

For Bermuda shorts, cut to a line about 7 cm below the crotch. Hem the top only and thread with elastic.

PETTICOAT

You will need a rectangle of fabric about 38 cm by 15 cm and 15 cm of narrow elastic. Seam the short sides, right sides together. Turn over the top 1 cm and stitch down, turning in raw edge as you sew. Push narrow elastic through with a safety pin. Turn up hem and decorate with lace or other trimming.

AMERICAN FOOTBALLER

Small boys like playing with dolls too and they were unanimous about the doll they wanted – an American Footballer.

The clothes are as near as possible to the real thing – apparently the 'padding bodice' really is separate from the T-shirt and is laced up at the back just like this one. This bodice is constructed from a sponge washing up cloth from a big supermarket chain – which adds a different dimension to your usual household shopping list. None of it is difficult, but the whole costume – helmet and visor, T-shirt and padded bodice, trousers, socks and shoes – will take about two evenings to make, unless you are incredibly quick. The results are worth it however: the whole effect is sensational.

I made the doll in dark brown cotton with brown suede eyes. His hair is an 18 cm circle of black fur fabric. Run a line of stitching round the edge. Do not finish off. Glue fur on head like a cap, then pull thread until it fits snugly. Finish off securely.

PADDED T-SHIRT

YOU WILL NEED

- ☐ Scarlet, or bright coloured, old T-shirt or sweatshirt
- ☐ 1 metre of 1 cm wide white tape for numbers (not bias binding)
- ☐ Cotton to match T-shirt and white cotton
- ☐ Contrasting cotton for tacking
- ☐ 5 poppers to fasten back
- ☐ 1 washing up sponge cloth 20 cm square for bodice
- ☐ 1 white bootlace (or more tape) to lace bodice

PREPARATION

There are no seam allowances so you should add 5 to 7 mm on the outside of each pattern piece for the T-shirt. Trace the pattern for front and back and cut out like this:

Front: 1 piece. Cut from doubled fabric with the centre line on a fold. Add seam allowances to every outside edge (not to fold).

Back: 2 pieces. Cut from single fabric. Add seam allowances to outside edges; increase allowances at centre back to 4 cm because of the fastenings.

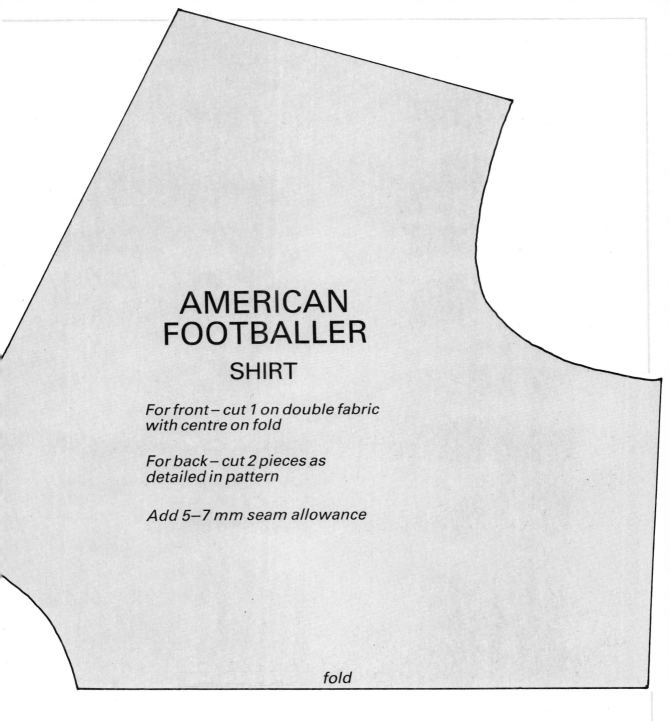

AMERICAN
FOOTBALLER
SHIRT

*For front – cut 1 on double fabric
with centre on fold*

*For back – cut 2 pieces as
detailed in pattern*

Add 5–7 mm seam allowance

fold

MAKING UP

With right sides together, machine or hand
stitch shoulder seams. Sew white tape on for
armband, 2 cm above raw edge. Then sew up
side seams. Turn in the seam allowance on raw
edges – neck, arms and hem. Either slip stitch

by hand or machine the edges under on the neck
and arms. You can get away with pinking the
hem edge or zigzag machining it.

Attach the fastenings at the back: turn the left
centre edge in 2 cm – the edge should overlap
the centre of the back towards the right side by

2 cm; pin with the raw edge just turned under again to keep it neat.

Repeat with the right side back, so that it overlaps the left and then machine, or firmly hand sew, each side with a double row of stitching 1 cm apart so that the poppers can be sewn in between the two rows of stitching.

Sew on the five pairs of poppers.

Pin the tape on to front and back to make the numbers you choose, tack and then machine or slip stitch to the T-shirt with white cotton.

Padding Fold the sponge cloth in quarters and cut a 3 cm line across the centre. This will give a diamond shaped hole in the middle of the unfolded cloth.

Cut from the back V to the centre of the outer edge. Punch three holes either side of this opening to take the bootlace. Round off the corners at the front as shown in the drawing.

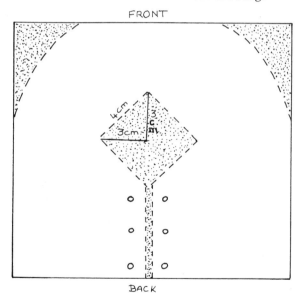

FRONT

BACK

TROUSERS

These are the Jogging Doll's tracksuit trousers (see page 41), made in white fleece left over from the duck (see page 53), used wrong side out. You could equally well use any other thickish white material, old T-shirts or towelling. I thought the footballer needed a leaner outline so the seam allowance is omitted at the sides and top. The ankles just need to be hemmed, by hand or machine, because the fleece is quite thick; if you use a lighter weight fabric, you may want to insert narrow elastic. The red bands on the trouser legs are red ribbon hand stitched down the sides after the trousers were made. On reflection, it would have been easier to sew them by machine or hand before making up the trousers.

SOCKS

These are really white legwarmers with a red stripe, made to the pattern on page 41. Follow this exactly but sew up one end of each woolly tube to make socks.

SPORTS SHOES/FOOTBALL BOOTS

YOU WILL NEED

- ☐ 20 cm square of red felt
- ☐ 0.5 metre narrow white tape
- ☐ Red cotton

MAKING UP

Use the foot part of the basic Rag Doll pattern (see page 28). Cut four foot pieces to dotted line on pattern. Trim the top edges with pinking shears if you like. Machine or blanket stitch the pieces together in pairs to within 1.25 cm of the top.

Turn the top of each piece over and stitch down near the raw edge. Run the narrow tape through with a small safety pin.

HELMET AND VISOR

YOU WILL NEED

- ☐ 20 cm square of red felt
- ☐ Red cotton for sewing
- ☐ 20 cm square of thick cotton such as T-shirt material, quilting or fleece
- ☐ Red, white or black bias binding and matching cotton for sewing
- ☐ Contrasting cotton for tacking
- ☐ 9 white pipe cleaners

It took me ages to think up the pattern for this but it is quickly made.

MAKING UP

I have only allowed 2mm seam allowance for the felt, add more if you wish. The lining needs to be slightly smaller than the outer layer, so allow 3 mm seam allowance. Cut out three full size pieces from each material to make the back of the helmet; cut out two to dotted base line from each material for the front.

Sew the felt pieces together, seaming down each side by machine or back stitch. Finish off each seam firmly. Press with a steam iron or damp cloth and ordinary iron.

Repeat with the lining material. Press. Put the lining and felt helmet shapes together, check that they fit properly, trim if necessary and pin.

Tack up helmet edges. Finish edges in one of the following ways – depending on how much time you have and what is handy:
- ☐ machine edges in straight stitch or satin stitch, in red or black cotton; *or*
- ☐ oversew all edges neatly by hand with red cotton or black embroidery silk; *or*
- ☐ bind all edges with white or black bias binding.

Make the visor with the nine pipe cleaners assembled like this:

Oversew all joints with double white cotton to secure. Fit on doll with helmet in position and adjust if necessary. Sew centre, top and side pipe cleaners into helmet very firmly with red or other matching coloured cotton. Bend visor to a satisfactory shape.

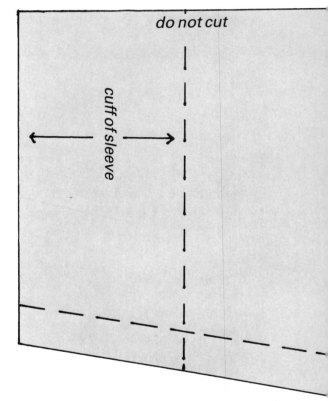

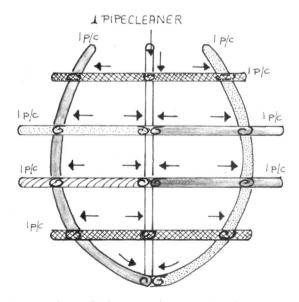

Arrows show which way to wrap one pipe cleaner round another at corners

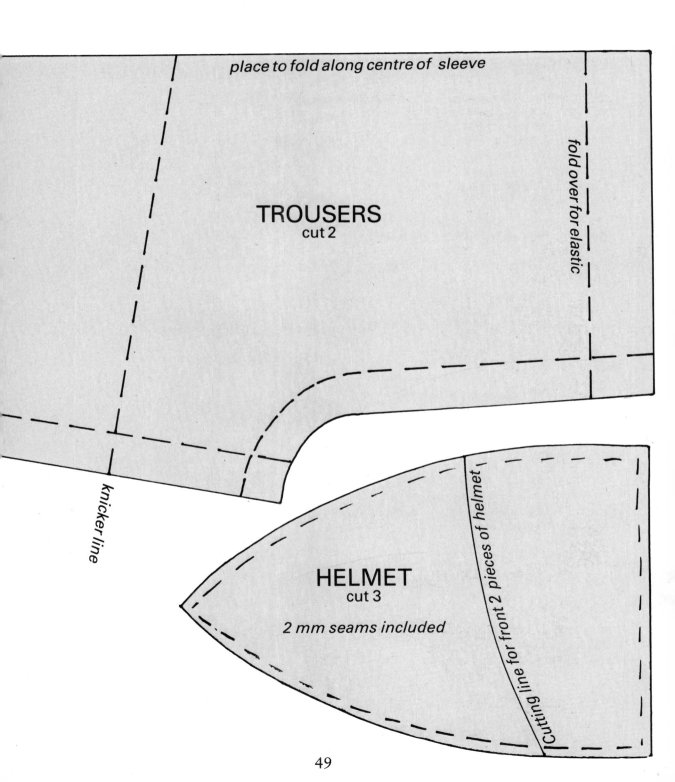

place to fold along centre of sleeve

fold over for elastic

TROUSERS
cut 2

knicker line

HELMET
cut 3

2 mm seams included

Cutting line for front 2 pieces of helmet

MR BO JANGLES

This towelling rag doll – if you can call a chap a doll – evolved from the vaguest idea. Max Webster had said he wanted a clown but various mothers had warned me that their children were terrified of the traditional clown, so I was trying to dream up a character who would have the essential qualities of a clown – a funny face, a floppy body, oddly fitting clothes – but would be very obviously warm and endearing for children to play with. Two things came out of my dreaming. The first was that towelling makes an ideal material for rag dolls, soft, comforting and washable; the second was the emergence of an amiable punk, a clown with a 1980s hairdo. This perm is knotted firmly into his scalp but even so, it is probably not suitable for younger children who might manage to eat the metallic ribbon. You could substitute short lengths of ribbon, securely sewn in, or a piece of fur fabric glued to the towelling and finished off with stitching round the edge, like the American Footballer (page 44).

The bells on his knees and a distant memory of a musical number about the original Mr Bo Jangles, who sported oversized, patched trousers with braces, gave the doll his name.

As an alternative, you could make a pierrot clown's costume on the lines of the little clown on page 117. Use exactly the same design enlarged to fit the rag doll – remember that, to be satisfactorily baggy, the costume has to be bigger than the doll. Elasticate at waist, wrists and ankles.

YOU WILL NEED

- ☐ 1 rag doll, made up in whatever fabric you prefer – pink towelling is ideal
- ☐ Oddments of present-wrapping, curly, paper ribbon, metallic or not
- ☐ Oddments of cloth ribbon
- ☐ Pink and blue embroidery thread
- ☐ Scraps of old T-shirt and contrasting cotton
- ☐ 25 cm outrageous material for trousers
- ☐ Scraps of interesting material for patches
- ☐ 20 cm narrow (5 mm) elastic
- ☐ 40 cm narrow (1.25 cm) petersham ribbon
- ☐ 2 bells
- ☐ Optional: fake flowers, scraps of towelling for boots, balloon, scoop from dishwasher powder

MAKING UP

Hairdo With a large-eyed needle, thread ribbon through the towelling. Leave about 3.5 cm of ribbon for each curl before bringing out the needle, overstitching once and knotting the ribbon. Then cut off, leaving another 3.5 cm. Repeat this with different sorts of ribbon – everything you have round the house – until you have covered his head.

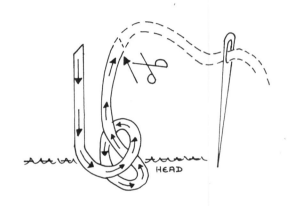

T-shirt Use the tracksuit top pattern (page 36) as a basic and draw the neckline up as illustrated. Cut out the basic pattern twice. Make a little cut in the neckline of one piece.

Cut along solid lines. Dotted line is tracksuit pattern neckline

Machine with zigzag or hand stitch with blanket stitch round all seams: down neck shoulders and outer arms, up sides and underarms, round cut in neckline. Roll up sleeves.

Trousers Use the tracksuit trousers pattern (page 49) as a basic. Add on 2.5 cm to the width on the foldline to make the trousers 10 cm baggier in all; cut straight on down the sides to the hemline, disregarding the instruction to use the cuff of the sweatshirt.

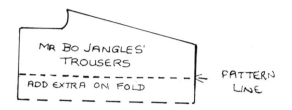

Sew up the inner legs and then from front to back across the crutch. Turn over top leaving a channel for the elastic to run through. Leave a gap at centre front to insert the elastic.

Before you put in the elastic, sew on the patches. Use contrasting thread and whatever decorative stitches you prefer. Then sew on the bells.

Push the elastic through using a safety pin and then try on the trousers over the T-shirt, adjust the elastic and stitch firmly. Turn up the hem by machining or hand stitching it in place.

Braces These are lengths of petersham ribbon, sewn on to the trousers at the back, crisscrossed and buttoned at the front. Sew the ribbons at the back. Fix the buttons on either side at the front. Pull the ribbons from back to front, cross over, and snip buttonholes in the appropriate place. Blanket stitch the buttonholes and hem the raw edges of the ribbon to finish off.

The dishwasher powder scoop is an optional extra, which seemed to suit him. It's firmly sewn to his wrist.

MRS PADDLEQUACK

Anna-Louise Lawrence, now
aged 21, tells me that her favourite game was to take
Mother Duck and her ducklings down to the pond – which is
made out of silver foil. Apparently this game went on endlessly to
the great satisfaction of Anna-Louise, her mother and doubtless the ducks.
I saw a duck in a toy store in Los Angeles who was actually called Jemima
Puddleduck; she had the story on a label round her neck to prove her identity. She
came complete with bonnet and shawl, and you could easily sew these if you wanted
to make a similar Beatrix Potter character.
You can alter the appearance of Mrs Paddlequack to some extent by
changing the position of her wings and feet. I suggest you experiment
before sewing them finally in place.
Despite my notes on stuffing (page 13), this is one toy which
should be firmly and fully stuffed. She is very very simple
to make and should not take more than two hours.

YOU WILL NEED

☐ 50 cm white fleece
☐ Scraps of yellow towelling (a face flannel would do)
☐ About 200 gm washable stuffing
☐ Two 1 cm circles of black felt and black embroidery silk for eyes
☐ White cotton for sewing; contrasting cotton for tacking

PREPARATION

Trace the pattern pieces (pages 56–59) and add a good 5 mm (or more) seam allowance (see page 8).

Lay the pattern pieces on the fabric and cut out, remembering to reverse the pattern for the second side and two of the four wings. If you use double-sided towelling (which is the norm) you need not reverse the pattern for the feet or beak.

MAKING UP

Join beak sections to head from A to B. Use a small stitch to avoid the towelling fraying.

Now join the two side pieces together from C to D across the duck's back, round her head and beak and a little way down her chest.

Join the underbody to each side along the raw edges, starting from C, her tail, each time. Leave an opening where shown on one side only.

Clip the seams carefully and turn through to the right side. Stuff Mrs Paddlequack carefully but firmly starting with her beak. Mould her head with full cheeks.

When she is full and fat, sew up the gap neatly by hand (see page 11). You may still need to push her into shape – I had to squash her down with a firm hand, so that she sat nicely.

Join the wings together in pairs, leaving the straight side open. Turn through to right side and slip stitch across the opening. Sew the wings on to the duck where you wish; the easiest way is to slip stitch the wing on to the side, making sure you stitch right through each layer of fleece.

Join the feet together in pairs, leaving a gap open at the back of each, where shown on the pattern.

Turn each foot right side out and stuff lightly. Sew up opening by hand or machine.

Stitch lines by hand or machine where shown on the foot pattern, to look like webbed feet.

Oversew the feet on to her tummy where you choose.

Cut out 1 cm circles of black felt and glue them in place as eyes. Embroider over these with black embroidery silks so that no white fleece shows through. Use a long needle and start by drawing a thread from one side of her face to the other, securing it on either side. This gives a really bird-like look to the duck. Then make some ducklings.

THE DUCKLINGS (OR HOW TO MAKE POM-POMS)

It is such a very long time since I made pom-poms that I got myself into a cat's cradle with the wool and had to be rescued by Rebecca. 'Every child,' said Becca severely, 'finds it very easy.' Here, for grown-ups, is the way to make pom-poms.

YOU WILL NEED

- ☐ Scraps of white or yellow wool
- ☐ 2 circles of card, about 7.5 cm diameter with a hole about 3 cm in the middle
- ☐ Wool needle
- ☐ Scraps of yellow or orange felt

MAKING UP

It is easiest to wind the scraps of wool into little balls which will go through the ever-decreasing hole in the middle of the card.

Start off by tying the end of the wool in a loop round the card.

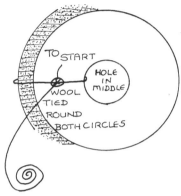

The principle of pom-poms is that you wind the wool round and round two circles of card, through the hole in the middle, until it is impossible to push through another strand; when the hole gets very small, use a needle to thread the wool through.

Then cut round the outside of the fat circle through all the wool until you reach the pieces of card. Tie a piece of wool round and round between the two pieces of card. You should then have a wild woolly ball, securely tied in the middle. Cut out the two pieces of card.

Take some small sharp scissors and trim the pom-pom into a duckling sort of shape, something like this:

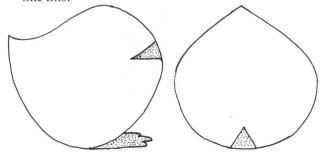

Duckling shape in profile and from above

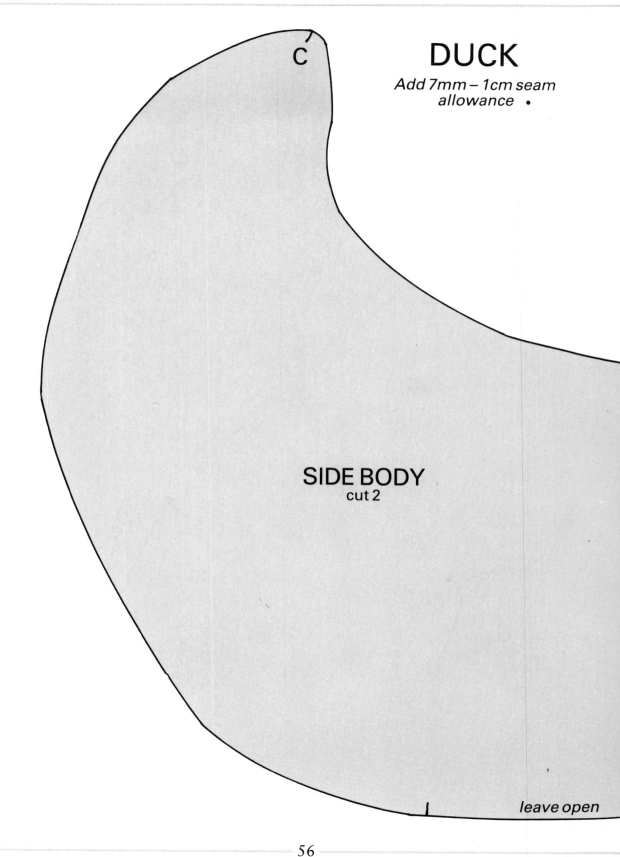

DUCK

Add 7mm – 1cm seam allowance •

C

SIDE BODY
cut 2

leave open

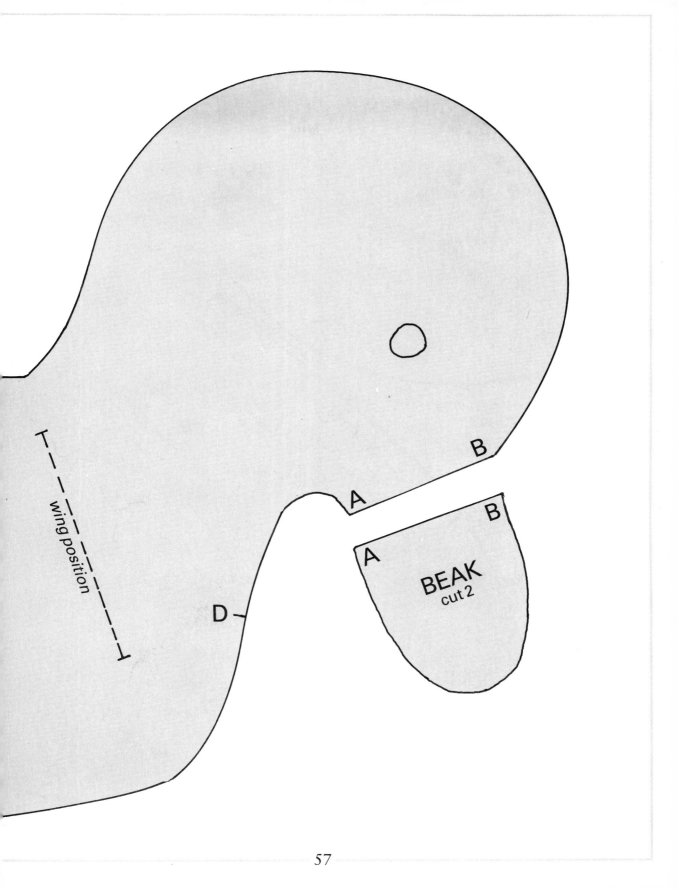

wing position

B

A

D

A

B

BEAK
cut 2

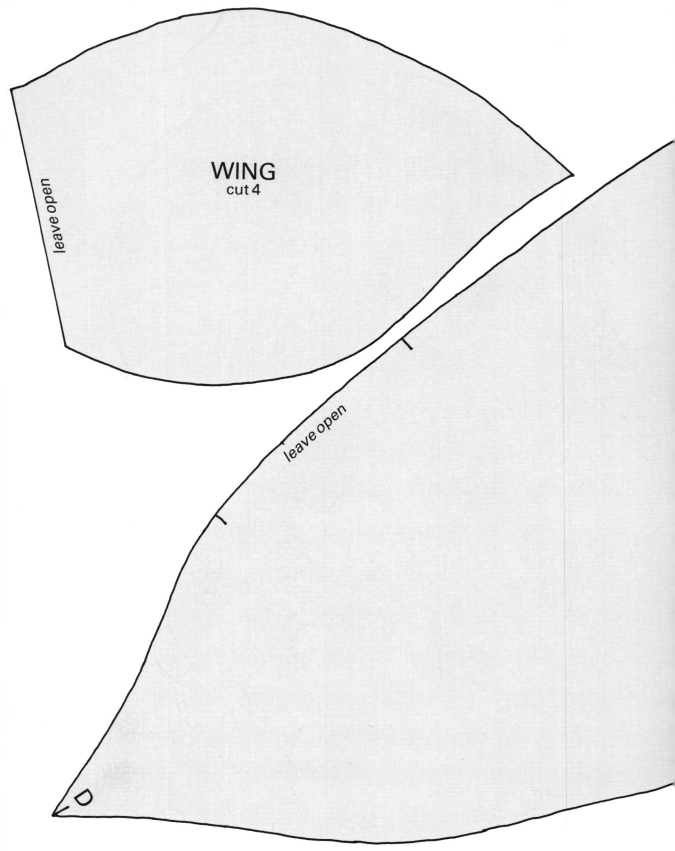

WING
cut 4

leave open

leave open

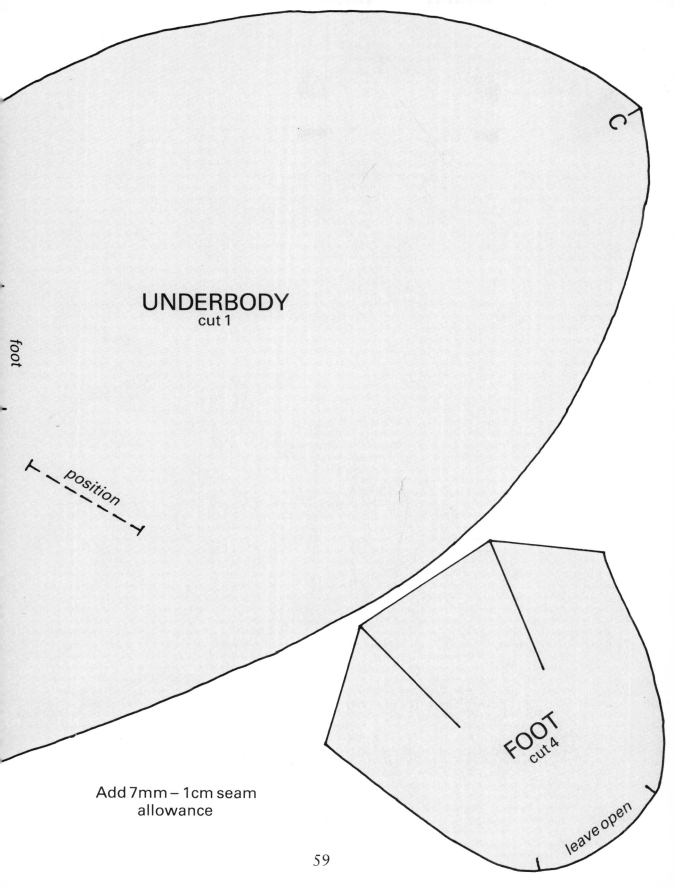

UNDERBODY
cut 1

foot

position

FOOT
cut 4

leave open

Add 7mm – 1cm seam
allowance

C

59

Cut a long, diamond-shaped piece of yellow felt
and glue it into the head end as a beak; cut out two
feet shapes and glue them on.

Sew the felt on using yellow cotton and a long
needle so that you can secure the stitches at the
centre of the duckling.

These are very good rainy day toys for children
– and grown-ups. You can make all sorts of
different baby birds, or indeed anything which
takes your fancy.

PARROT

This parrot is completely over the top. He is called Floyd
(as in Pink Floyd), because he is psychedelic and I
am a product of the Sixties. You could just as easily make
him a tasteful pink and grey and call him something serious like
Solomon. Rona called our prototype Fred – there's nothing wrong
with Fred, it's my father's name – but it never really caught the essence
of this bird; Rona just couldn't shake off the memory of the Monty Python
parrot (which was dead, unlike this one which is most aggressively alive). This
parrot is very easy and enormously cheering to make. He shouldn't take more than
four hours. The only tricky bit is sewing the corners of his yellow felt beak
into his face, which is another case of creative pinning and hand sewing.
Apart from this, the hand sewing is really cobbling because the
stitches all get lost in the fur fabric.
When you finish, free all the fur caught in seams; it makes
an enormous difference to his finished appearance.

YOU WILL NEED

- ☐ 50 cm red fur fabric
- ☐ 25 cm yellow fur fabric
- ☐ 25 cm pink fur fabric
- ☐ 20 cm square yellow felt for beak and soles of feet
- ☐ 20 cm square pink felt for tops of feet
- ☐ 20 cm square pale pink (or anything else) felt for eye piece
- ☐ 1 pair 15 mm green safety eyes
- ☐ Sundry sequins to trim face
- ☐ 3 royal blue and 3 turquoise feathers – optional
- ☐ 1.2 metre strong green garden wire for feet
- ☐ About 200 gm stuffing
- ☐ Red, pink and blue cotton for sewing
- ☐ For perch: invisible thread, 1.5 metres of string or cord, 2 tassels, 32.5 cm length of dowelling, metal ring and cup hook

PREPARATION

Trace the pattern pieces (pages 64–68), adding
7 mm to 1 cm seam allowance on all edges
except folds and cheek pieces (see page 10).
If you want to follow this colour scheme, cut up
the fabrics as follows:

- ☐ 2 red fur side body pieces, 2 red fur wings, 1 red fur long tail-piece, 1 red fur short tail-piece
- ☐ Pink fur front gusset, pink fur short tail-piece
- ☐ 2 yellow fur wings, 1 yellow fur long tail-piece
- ☐ 2 yellow felt beak pieces, 2 yellow felt feet pieces
- ☐ 2 pink felt feet pieces
- ☐ 2 pale pink (or anything else) felt eye pieces

Remember to reverse the paper pattern for the
second piece of each pair.

Make the underneath pieces for the wings and
tail a smidgeon bigger all round than the top pieces,
say 2 mm, so that the contrast colour shows
round the outside when the wing or tail piece is
turned through to the right side; pin, tack and
sew the pieces together edge to edge to achieve this.

Cut out pattern pieces, making sure that fur lies
downwards on all pieces. Floyd's front fur lies the
wrong way but he is so eccentric, it doesn't really
matter.

MAKING UP

Sew all pieces of fur fabric with right sides
together. Pin and tack pieces before stitching by
machine or hand.

Join the side body pieces from A to Z along centre back.

Join the underbody gusset from B to Y, snipping seams where necessary. Leave Y to Z, across his tail, open on both sides.

Join his beak section from A to C along curved edge. Trim edges so that there is a minimum of seam allowance left down the centre beak.

Join his beak to his face, matching As, Bs and Ds. I stitched all of his beak in by hand because I found it easier, but there is no reason not to machine it if you wish. Start pinning in the centre top and stitch along this top seam first. Then work your way down each side and under his chin. You will have to snip the corners a fraction as you go.

Trim and clip curved seams and into corners. Turn right side out.

Glue his eye pieces in position, matching Ds and Bs, and fix in his safety eyes, making a hole for the stalks with a pair of sharp scissors. Fix the washers in securely. Sew round the outside by hand. Decorate with sequins now or later (see page 113 for guidance).

Make his two tail pieces by sewing each pair together, leaving straight edge open. Snip into all the corners and curves. Turn right side out and then stitch down dotted lines. Machine the two tail pieces together across the tops of each.

Stuff the parrot firmly, starting with a tiny bit of stuffing in the curved bit of his beak, which is difficult to reach.

Insert the tail pieces 1.5 cm into the end of his body; his breast and the underside of his tail should match and the top of his tail should match his wings and back. You could change this colour scheme, of course, but I tried several variations and this looked the best. Sew tail in place by hand through all thicknesses.

Make his wings up, turn through and hand stitch on to his back – if you are canny, you can stitch the hole up and attach the wing to his back at the same time. I ran two lines of stitching down his wings to secure them firmly to his back because I thought he might be flailed around the room by a wing and the sewing had better be tough enough to withstand the onslaught.

Make his feet up in pairs of contrasting felt – I used pink and yellow, top-stitching round three sides, but not the straight top edge. Taking two 65 cm lengths of strong green garden wire, bend each into the shape shown on the pattern pieces. Twist the edges round so they will not stick out, and twist the doubled loops so that they are firm, as shown on the pattern. Push through the gap at the top of each foot, well down into his toes. Sew up the gap by hand with back stitch, or machine. Sew firmly on to his front with a rectangle of stitching as indicated on the pattern piece. I found the wire did not need to go into the rectangles sewn on to his tummy.

Use the sequins or beads to trim his eye piece and round his beak. You could embroider this instead if you prefer.

I had seen beautiful coloured feathers in John Lewis and longed to use them, so Floyd became a psychedelic cockatoo-type of parrot with a royal blue and a turquoise feather stitched to his topknot and the same stitched on to each wing.

Make his perch with the piece of dowelling and equal lengths of cord or string, attached to a ring. You can pretty up the perch by attaching a couple of tassels to the cord ends where they hit the dowelling. Sew a piece of invisible thread from the ring to the top of his head, make a small stitch and run back to the ring; try the whole thing out for size before you cut and tie the thread. Hang the ring on a cup hook fixed into a beam or joist.

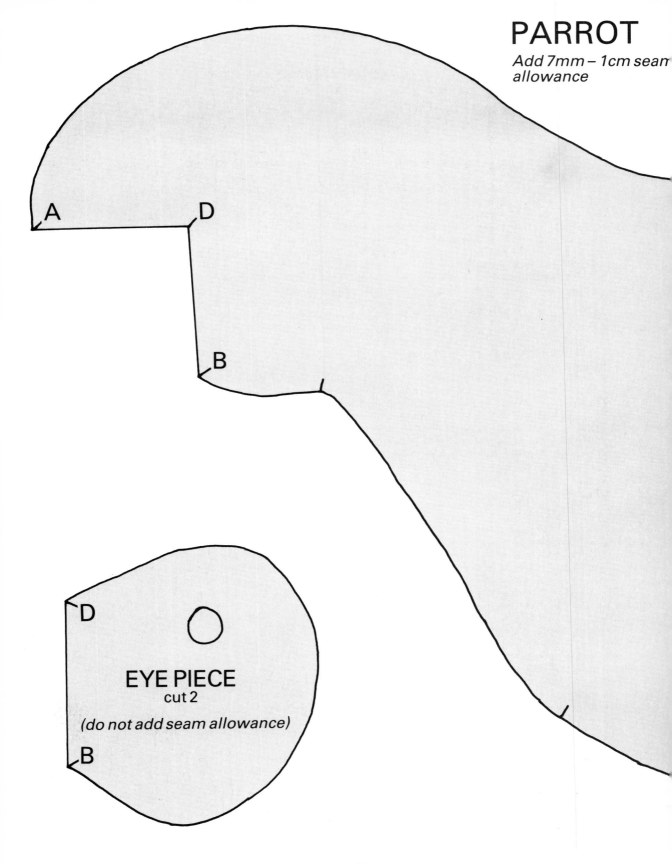

PARROT

Add 7mm – 1cm seam allowance

A

D

B

D

EYE PIECE
cut 2

(do not add seam allowance)

B

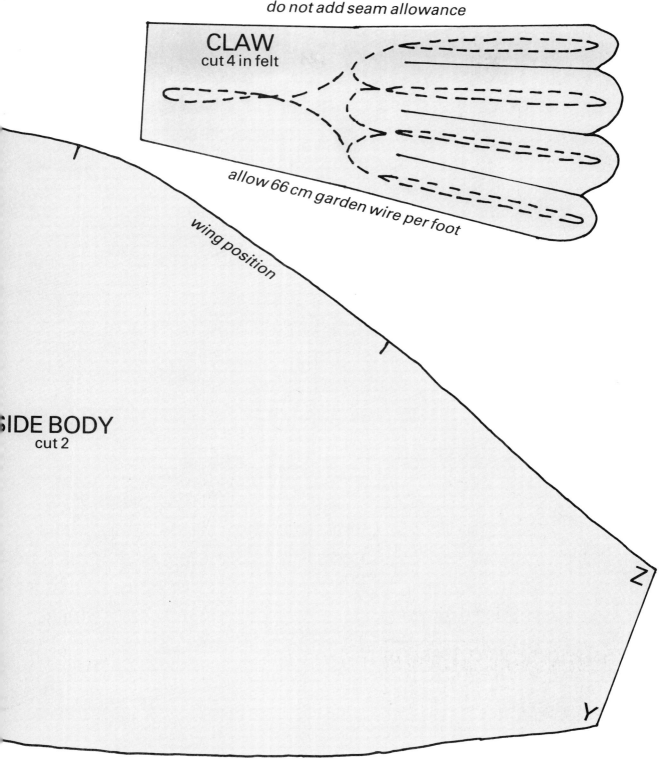

do not add seam allowance

CLAW
cut 4 in felt

allow 66 cm garden wire per foot

wing position

SIDE BODY
cut 2

Z

Y

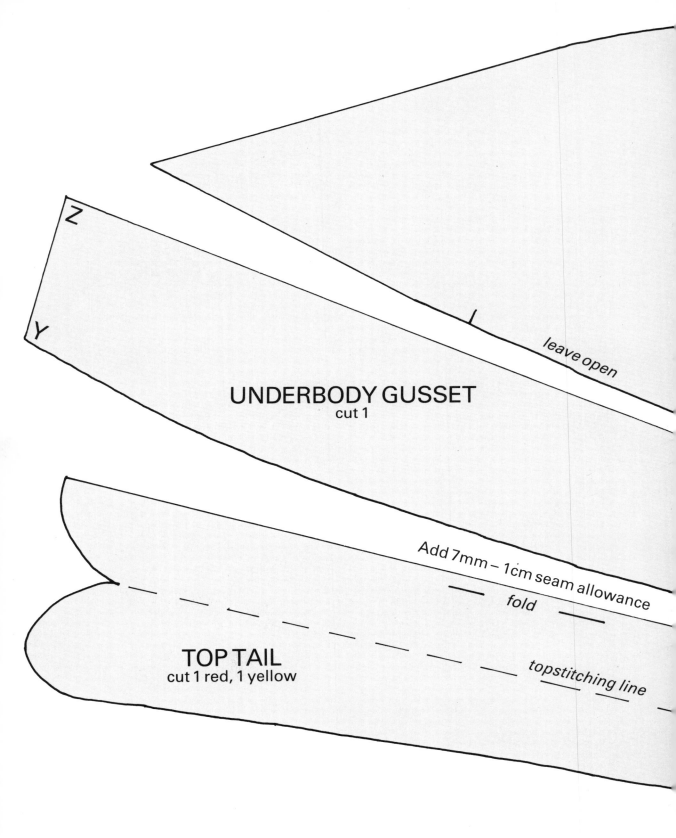

Z

Y

UNDERBODY GUSSET
cut 1

leave open

Add 7mm – 1cm seam allowance

fold

TOP TAIL
cut 1 red, 1 yellow

topstitching line

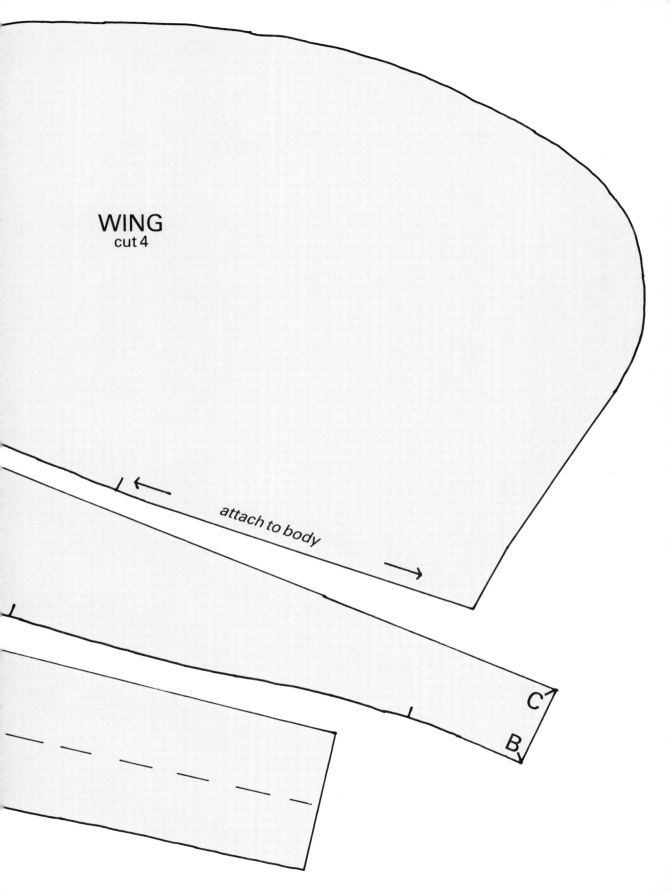

WING
cut 4

attach to body

C

B

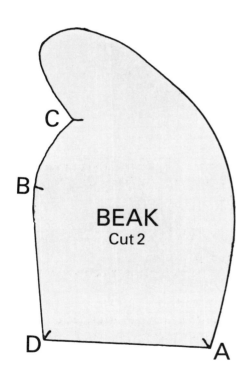

BEAK
Cut 2

C

B

D   A

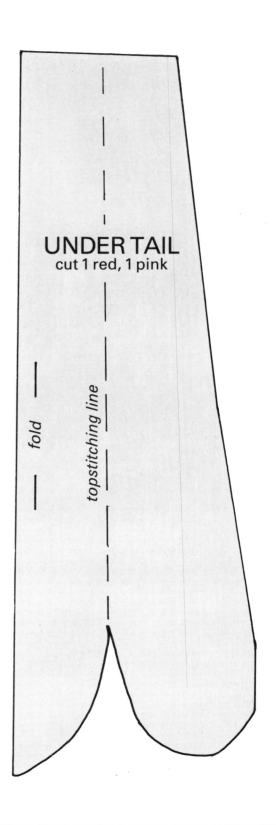

UNDER TAIL
cut 1 red, 1 pink

fold

topstitching line

LEOPARD CAT

*For years I had two cats, one black
and one tabby, who spent their time composedly standing in
front of the fire, paws tucked in and tail tucked round. Now this
one stands by the fender, so much like a real one that visitors are sometimes
very confused and take a few moments to understand that I do not have a baby
leopard in the house. Kate Webster, who is 3, has the prototype of this cat
which started life looking rather butch. She called it Miranda – which
was surprising – and takes it everywhere with her.*

NOTE

The cat is very simple to make. It is made
directly from the stencil which includes a 7 mm
seam allowance.

You can either use bought safety cats' eyes or
make them yourself out of felt, which can be
very effective – the instructions are below. The
ready-made cats' eyes are quicker to fix and
should be available in most stores with
toy-making accessories. You can either buy the
sort with narrowed pupils which are cat-like
but faintly sinister, or this wide-eyed and
dreamy sort.

If you have small children, please be careful
with the whiskers – they seem to be just the sort
of thing toddlers will chew or pull off and poke
in their eyes. It would be safer to sew on wool
whiskers for their sake. If your children are
older then whiskers can be made with fish gut,
or pipe cleaners if fish gut is difficult to find.
The Acton Angling Company very kindly gave
me metres of fish gut to experiment with and
seemed not a whit surprised when I confessed
that my interest in gut was nothing to do with

fishing but soft toy making – they keep various
sorts of gut purely for the BBC props
department.

YOU WILL NEED

- ☐ 50 cm fur fabric
- ☐ Pair of 15 mm safety eyes, or blue and black felt
  and glue
- ☐ About 150 gm stuffing
- ☐ Sewing cotton to match the cat and the eyes;
  contrasting tacking cotton
- ☐ Black wool for nose and mouth
- ☐ Optional: Scraps of red and pink felt for tongue
  and glue to fix
- ☐ 1 metre blue or green ribbon, 1.5 cm wide, and
  bell to trim
- ☐ Black wool or pipe cleaners or fish gut for
  whiskers

PREPARATION

Trace the whole outline of the cat (pages
72–73) and lay it on the material with the fur
pile lying downwards. Cut out the fabric. Use
the same pattern reversed to cut out just the

cat's body but remember to add on 7 mm above the neck for the seam allowance.

Trace off extra pieces, one ear, one cheek, one upper face and one gusset. Lay on fabric, making certain the pile is going the right way in all cases, and cut out. Reverse the ear and cheek patterns to make a pair for each.

Mark the important points on the fabric e.g. where ears begin and end, etc.

From the leftovers, cut out a strip about 10 to 12.5 cm wide and about 30 cm long for the tail. Round the edges of the tail and machine, then turn right side out. Before you start stuffing the tail, push a pipe cleaner to the end so that you can curl the tip when it is finished. Push the stuffing in around the pipe cleaner. A large knitting needle or chopstick is helpful here, both to help turn the band from the wrong to the right side and to push the stuffing in.

MAKING UP

With firm back stitch or machining, sew the cat's face together starting with the two cheeks. Join these down the centre from A to B.

Then sew upper face to lower from C to C, through B, making sure that the centre seam lies flat.

Next sew the ears on.

It is easiest to sew the cat's nose and mouth on now, and add the eyes but not the tongue.

The nose is long stitches of black wool sewn in a fan shape. Put the needle in just below the point B and take it about 2 cm up each side seam to give you the outline to fill in.

The mouth is a triangle of black stitches, just below the nose.

Sew the shape two or three times to make a definite outline. Be careful not to go down too far to the bottom of the face or the mouth gets lost.

Sew the face to the front body from F to F through A.

Sew the front to the back, inside out, in stages. First sew K to F and finish off. Then sew from F round to F and finish off. Then sew from F to G and finish off.

Then stitch the bottom centimetre of back seam from H to J. This makes it easier to put the gusset in.

I found it quicker to back stitch the gusset in by hand. It is up to you whether to pin, tack and machine or pin and back stitch it in.

Clip all the corners. Turn right side out and finish the face.

Carefully push out the corners of the ears and then stitch the line across the base of the ears by hand or machine.

Look at the face and position the eyes in the best place. If you are using safety eyes, take the Quik Unpik and cut a stitch where you choose to insert the eyes. Push the back of the eyes in firmly.

If you are using felt eyes, make up the eyes first. They are two small circles of blue felt, about 17 mm in diameter. Shave the fur behind the eyes and stick on with glue. Sew to secure if this is for a small child.

Cut pupils of black felt, 17 mm high and about 8 mm wide at the widest point and stick these on. Shade the eyes with black felt-tipped pen to give the heavy-lidded look. You can also embroider the pupils in satin stitch with black embroidery silk and blanket stitch round the outside to add an extra dimension to the eyes.

Stuff the cat firmly. Tack opening with the tail in place (seam of tail down), stand the cat up to make certain that the tail is in the right place and then sew up by hand.

Make the tongue up from scraps of red and/or pink felt. Glue on.

Sew securely if the cat is for a toddler. If you are using whiskers of fish gut, sew them in. The only way I found to do this was to sew them on one at a time. Each whisker is about 9 cm long. Put the needle in on the outside, take it through to the inside leaving enough gut for a whisker. Bring it out again and oversew a couple of times. Finish off and repeat for the rest of the whiskers. Trim them all to the right length.

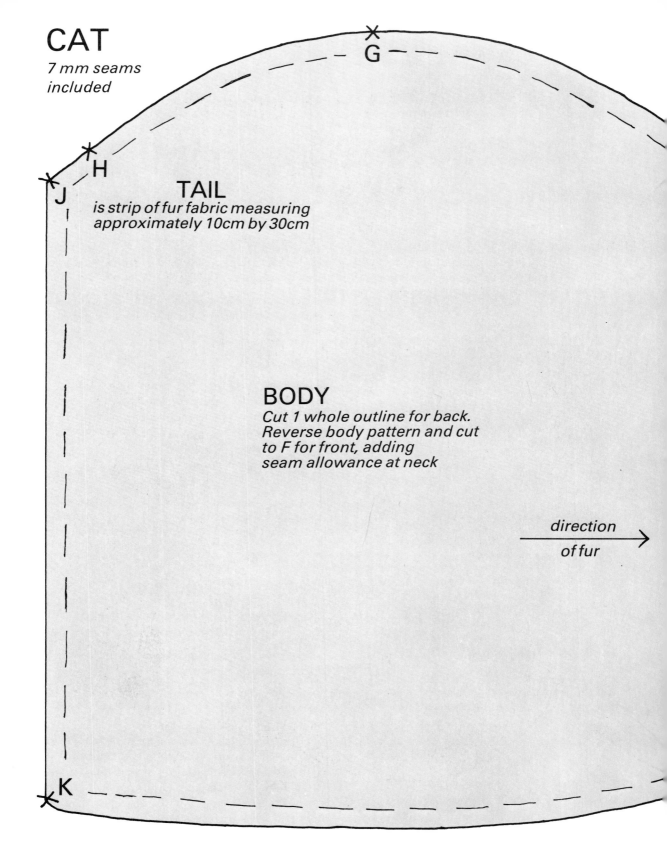

CAT

7 mm seams
included

G

H

J

TAIL

is strip of fur fabric measuring
approximately 10cm by 30cm

BODY

Cut 1 whole outline for back.
Reverse body pattern and cut
to F for front, adding
seam allowance at neck

direction
of fur →

K

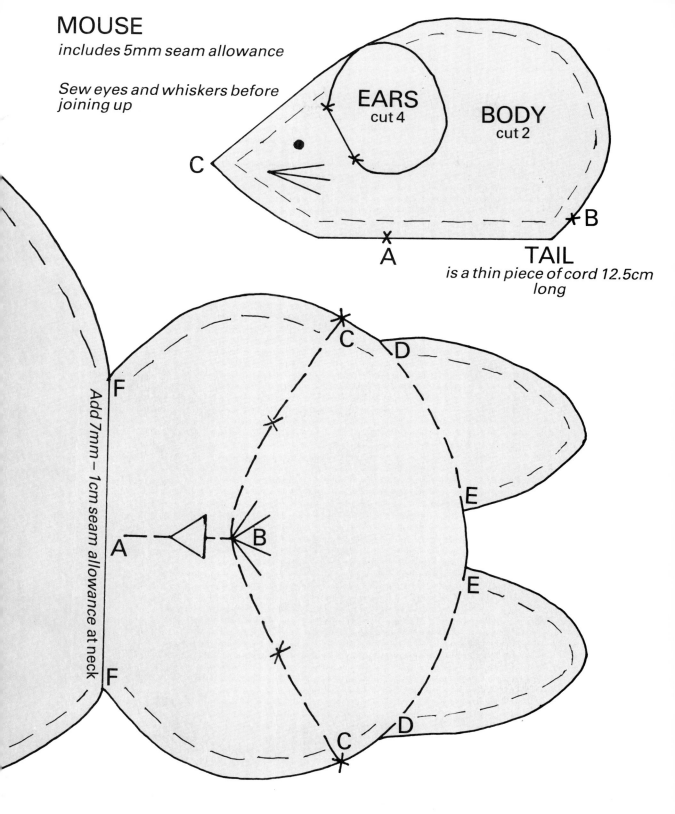

MOUSE
includes 5mm seam allowance

Sew eyes and whiskers before joining up

EARS
cut 4

BODY
cut 2

C

A

B

TAIL
is a thin piece of cord 12.5cm long

Add 7mm – 1cm seam allowance at neck

F

A

B

F

C

D

E

E

D

C

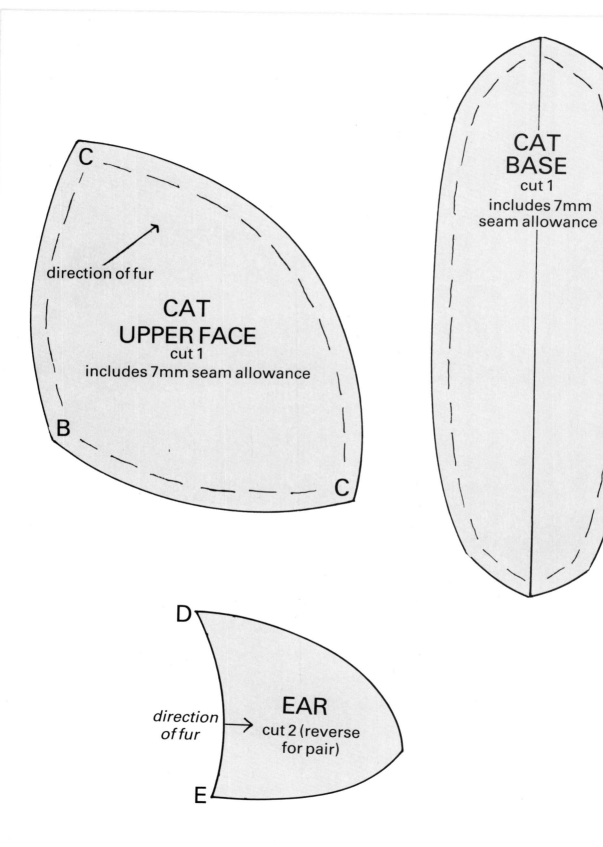

CAT
UPPER FACE
cut 1
includes 7mm seam allowance

direction of fur

C

B

C

CAT
BASE
cut 1
includes 7mm
seam allowance

D

EAR
cut 2 (reverse
for pair)

*direction
of fur*

E

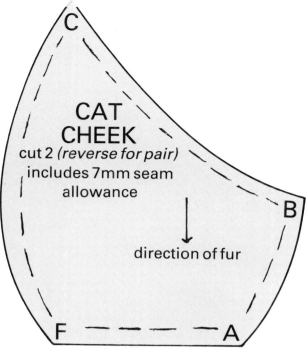

CAT CHEEK
cut 2 (reverse for pair) includes 7mm seam allowance

direction of fur

C

B

F

A

Four whiskers each side seemed adequate to me but you may want to give the cat more.

If you are using pipe cleaners, oversew each one in the middle very *very* firmly. Bend the pipe cleaner at a sharp angle.

Free all the fur round the seams and brush it out in the right directions.

If you want to narrow the space between the eyes and create a slight indication of a bridge to his nose, ladder stitch above the nose for about 2 cm.

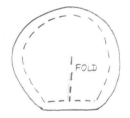

Tie a bow round his neck or put on a small collar and sit in front of the fire, watched by a white mouse.

MOUSE

My brother used to have a white mouse called Gertie when we were little – she was very family minded and produced lots of others and it would be simple to make a whole mouse clan, either all white or different colours.

YOU WILL NEED

- ☐ Small square white felt
- ☐ Scraps of pink felt
- ☐ White, red or pink, and dark brown sewing cotton
- ☐ Tacking cotton
- ☐ 9 cm thick white piping cord
- ☐ Stuffing

MAKING UP

From one 22 cm square of white felt you could make at least four of these white mice. You can hand sew or machine the pieces together.

Trace the paper pattern and cut two bodies and two ears from the white felt and two ears from the pink felt.

Machine or hand sew the body pieces together neatly from A round top to B.

Clip curves and corners, making sure not to cut through to the seam, and turn right side out.

Using dark brown cotton, embroider eyes with a few satin stitches and whiskers with three straight stitches (see page 11).

With red or pink cotton, oversew C to make a bobbly nose.

Sew the ears together with white cotton using one pink and one white piece for each. Make a tiny tuck in the middle.

Sew ears on with a few back stitches along the bottom row of stitching.

With white cotton, sew the cord into the seam for the tail. Knot the cord at the end.

Stuff firmly and then sew up, oversew or ladder stitch.

Squash the mouse down a bit so that he will sit up properly.

SEAL

Add 7mm – 1cm seam
allowances on all edges except
folds

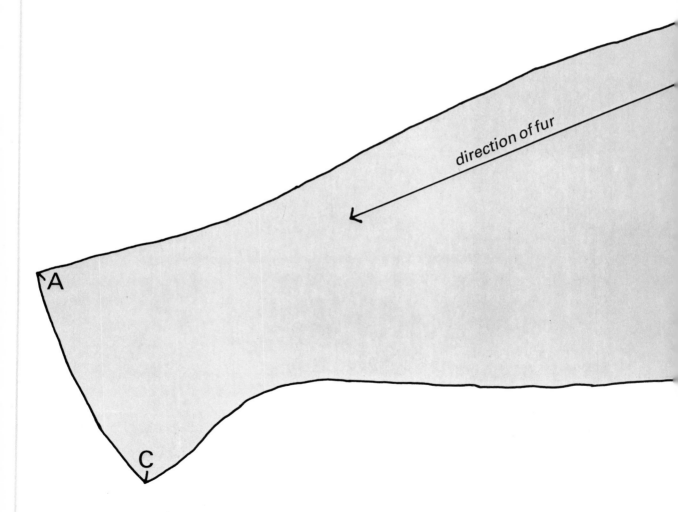

direction of fur

A

C

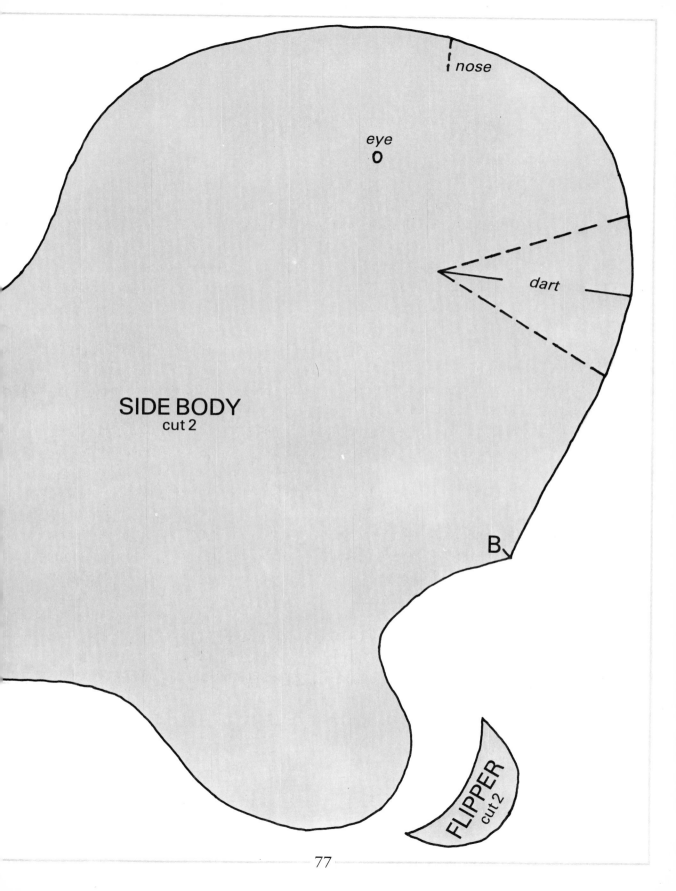

nose

eye
O

dart

SIDE BODY
cut 2

B

FLIPPER
cut 2

SEAL

*My grandmother gave me that lovely book Seal Morning
when I was little and I read it time and again. These nice chaps
are straight out of there. The seals are very, very easy to make, and should
not take more than two hours at the most. One baby seal is made from creamy
fur fabric and his soft, doey eyes are trimmed with brown suede. His nose and
flippers are made from scraps of the same. The other is made from some
scraps in my rag-bag. They are close-pile furry stuff and I have
no memory of buying them. Fleece is the nearest fabric. His
eyes are outlined in black felt pen — to see how it
worked — and his flippers are pink felt.*

YOU WILL NEED (FOR EACH SEAL)

- ☐ 50 cm cream fur fabric
- ☐ 5 small pieces dark brown suede or pink felt
- ☐ 100 gm stuffing
- ☐ A pair of 15 mm safety eyes
- ☐ Brown and cream cotton
- ☐ Tacking cotton

PREPARATION

Trace pattern pieces, adding 7 mm–1 cm seam allowance, see page 10. Note all sewing/cutting instructions and letters. Cut one underbody and two side body pieces, remembering to reverse the pattern for the second side body piece.

MAKING UP

Join all fur fabric pieces wrong sides together; pin and tack before sewing. Join side body pieces together from A to B. Clip and trim seams.

Make the dart by folding on centre line and stitching along dotted line from point to point. Don't make the dart too wide.

Put eyes in as the drawing; you can leave this until just before stuffing if you prefer but you have to wiggle one hand up his body which is fiddly.

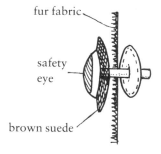

fur fabric

safety eye

brown suede

Join underbody to main body by stitching from C to B across each side.

Trim seams and clip curves.

Turn through to right side and stuff lightly but firmly.

Hand stitch from C to C through A, across tail, to close, see page 11.

Glue and stitch nose in place. Sew brown flipper to each paw.

SEAL

*Add 7mm – 1cm seam
allowance on all edges except
folds*

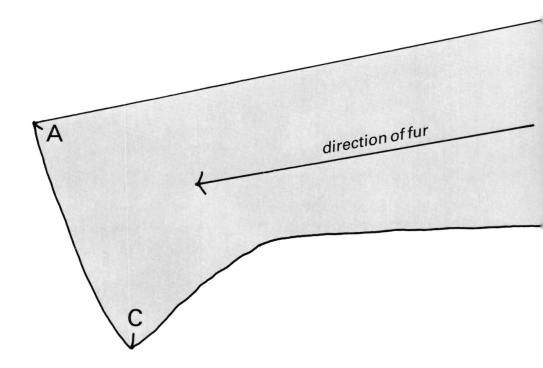

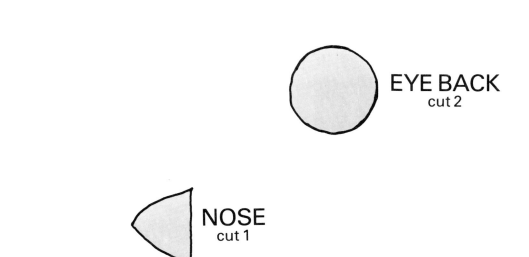

EYE BACK
cut 2

NOSE
cut 1

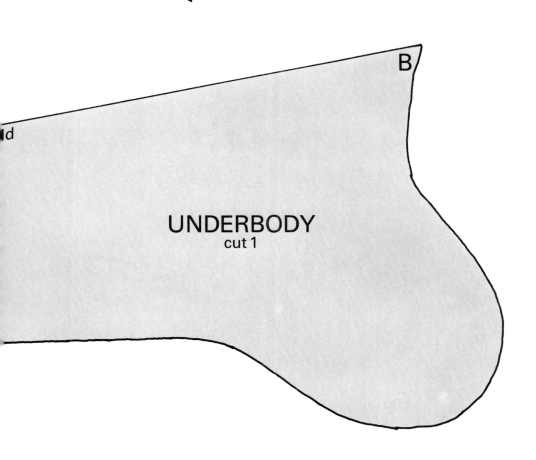

B

d

UNDERBODY
cut 1

81

BENJAMIN RABBIT

*This rabbit started off life in towelling, a
fabric which did not bring out the best in him. Short white
fur is infinitely more flattering; pink or blue towelling is ideal,
however, for ears and paws. This soft and washable toy is perfect
for a baby; it also fits in with many designs for nursery wallpaper. I
made it for Jack Little, who was born on 14 April 1987, and who has a rabbit
frieze in his attic nursery. Like most of my toys, he turned out slightly lopsided,
but this seems appropriate for a loopy white rabbit – it was his nose that
never quite made the middle of his face. He is simple to make; the only
tricky bit is sewing on the base – which
needs a little patience rather than great skill.*

YOU WILL NEED

- ☐ 25 cm white fur fabric – not too shaggy
- ☐ Remnants of pink/blue towelling for inside ears and paws
- ☐ Circle of pink/blue fur, 9 cm in diameter, for tail (or more towelling or white fur)
- ☐ White cotton for sewing; contrasting cotton for tacking
- ☐ 1 pair 15 mm safety eyes – I used blue
- ☐ About 125 gm washable stuffing
- ☐ Darning wool for nose and mouth
- ☐ Ribbon to trim

PREPARATION

Trace the pattern pieces, making sure to transfer the sewing instructions; in particular you will need to mark the letters. Cut out in the appropriate fabric. Remember that you will need two towelling ear shapes and two fur ones. Be careful to allow a seam allowance on each pink towelling paw and each white fur wrist. Add 7 mm to 1 cm on all edges except where fold line is marked (see page 10).

MAKING UP

Start by making his face. Join A to B to form his nose.

Now join his face gusset to his front gusset by sewing from C to C through B.

Stitch the front of the rabbit to each side body piece, by sewing from D to E on both sides.

Clip curves and snip into corners (see page 12).

Join the rabbit down the back from his head E towards his tail F, leaving a good 7 cm (including the space for his tail) to stuff him.

Stitch the base to the body, matching points D, F and G. Pin and tack this carefully first – it is the only bit that can be bothersome.

Trim and clip seams.

Turn through to right side, and position safety eyes – make a hole in the fabric with your

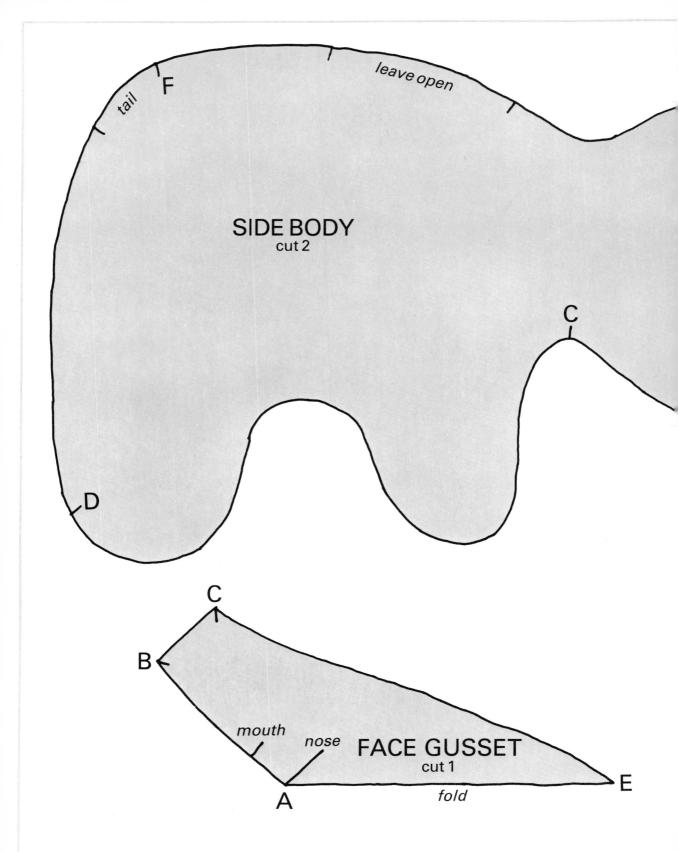

SIDE BODY
cut 2

tail

F

leave open

C

D

FACE GUSSET
cut 1

C

B

mouth

nose

A

fold

E

RABBIT

Add 7mm – 1cm seam allowance on all edges except folds

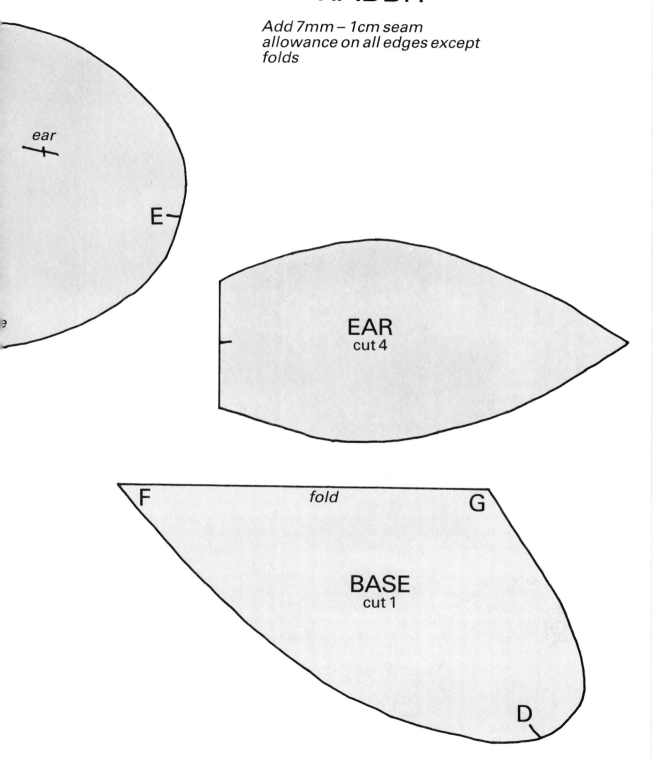

ear

E—

EAR
cut 4

F   *fold*   G

BASE
cut 1

D

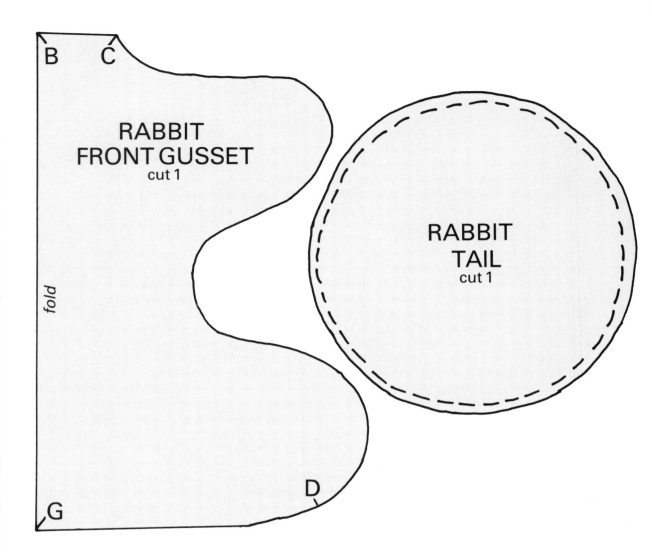

Quik Unpik and push the stalk of the eye through, fixing the washer securely at the back.

Then stuff the rabbit, moulding him carefully into shape.

Sew up the back neatly.

Now make his ears: with right sides together, join a towelling ear shape to a fur one to make the pair of ears. Stitch the two curved sides but don't sew up the base. Trim and clip seams and turn right side out.

Turn in the raw edges, pushing the towelling

slightly further up than the fur so that the fur overlaps the towelling. Slip stitch fur to towelling and then run a couple of long stitches along the base of the ears so that they fold round at the bottom like real rabbits' ears.

Sew the ears to the head, positioning them as you like best.

To make his powderpuff tail, run a gathering thread round the outside of the circle of fur fabric, push a small handful of stuffing in the middle and then draw up the thread. Sew firmly in position.

ELEPHANT

*The little boy in the picture
is David Hearn, who is 2. He adores elephants and
cornflakes so there was no problem about persuading him to
take part in this photograph, although he sometimes got a bit anxious
about how fast the cornflakes were disappearing, usually into his tummy.
He calls all elephants Nellie and says that Nellie is a he – so we all got very confused
and 'it' doesn't have a name at the moment, except that a grown-up suggested it was
really a new species called the Hog-A-Lump.
Whoever it is, this cuddly toy is very easy to make and quite quick, between
three and four hours. If you have small children and want to make it entirely
washable, substitute pink towelling for the felt. Because towelling
frays, you will need to allow 7 mm to 1 cm seam allowance
and turn in the edges of the tongue before you glue and
sew it in place.*

YOU WILL NEED

- ☐ 50 cm fur fabric or other fabric
- ☐ 1 small square each of pink, blue and black (or grey) felt
- ☐ About 150 gm stuffing
- ☐ Glue
- ☐ Grey, pink and black sewing cotton, blue and black embroidery silk
- ☐ Tacking cotton

PREPARATION

Trace the pattern pieces. There is no seam allowance on the pieces so remember to add at least 7 mm (see page 10). You will need to make a separate pattern for the underbody. Place each pattern piece, except the ears and feet, on the fabric. If you are using fur fabric (or patterned fabric), make certain that the fur (or pattern) is lying the right way.

When you have cut out each piece, mark points A and B on the main body and the 'leave open' gap on the underbody with a chalk mark or a stitched cross. *Reverse* the pattern pieces and lay on the material to cut out the pair for each piece. Take the ear pattern and cut out two pairs (four pieces) with the fur all lying in the same direction; the ear pattern is symmetrical so you need not reverse the paper pattern. From the scraps of pink felt, cut out four feet and mark with chalk or a stitch where shown. Cut out one piece for his mouth and put it somewhere safe – it is easy to lose being so small.

Tail From the black or grey felt, cut a rectangle

9 cm long and 5 cm wide. Spread glue on the top 5 cm of the long side and roll up tightly. Sew neatly down the edge to secure. With a small pair of scissors, cut the furled felt at the end in narrow strips about 0.5 cm wide.

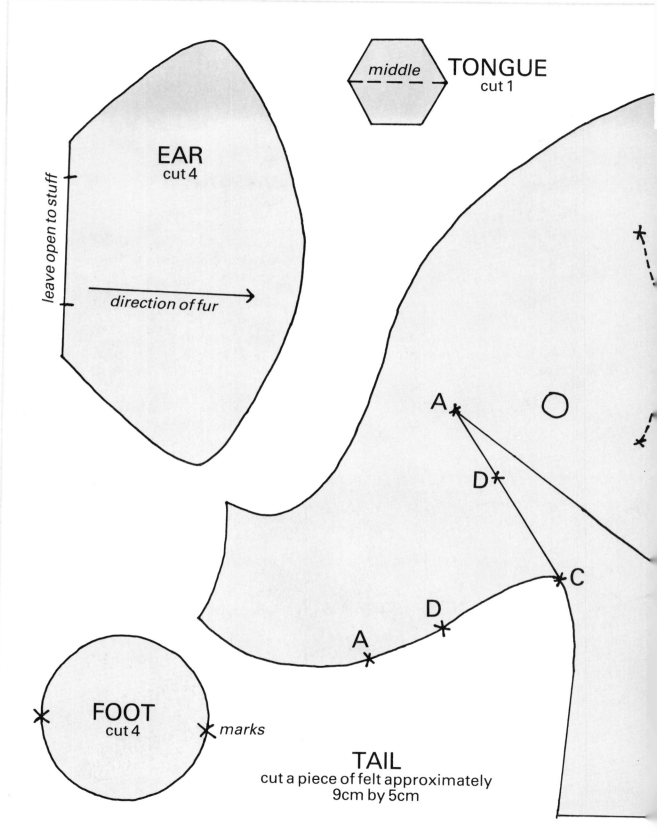

EAR
cut 4

leave open to stuff

direction of fur

TONGUE
cut 1

middle

A

D

C

D

A

FOOT
cut 4

marks

TAIL
cut a piece of felt approximately
9cm by 5cm

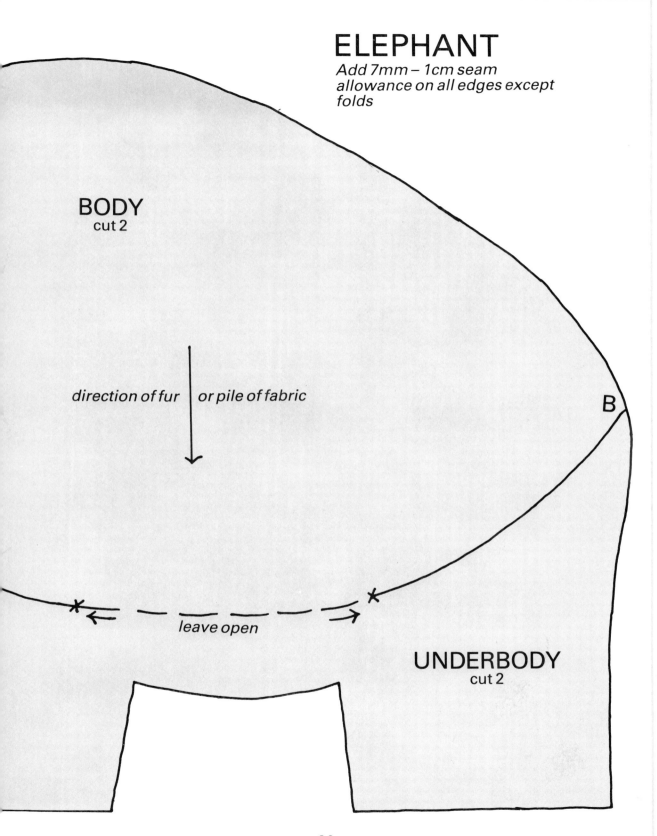

ELEPHANT
Add 7mm – 1cm seam allowance on all edges except folds

BODY
cut 2

direction of fur | or pile of fabric

leave open

UNDERBODY
cut 2

B

Eyes From the blue felt, cut out two small triangles. Put safely with mouth.

MAKING UP

Now start to sew up your elephant:

Join the elephant body pieces together from A to B over the top half of the shape.

Join his underbody from A to B on the curved seam, leaving an opening for stuffing where shown.

Reinforce the two curved seam lines on the main body from A to C with a row of machining.

Pin and tack underbody to main body starting at D, about 2 cm after A – this will be his mouth. When you have tacked, clip the seam allowance from A to C where you have reinforced it, you will then easily be able to machine the body to the underbody. Sew separately round each leg and up to point B. Stop when you come to each front foot, finish off and start again across his tummy, remembering to machine this on a curve. Finish off again at each back foot, and then machine up the back of his back legs. Stop just short of point B, finish off and sew in his tail with firm hand stitching through all the thicknesses of material. You should now have a whole elephant which just needs feet, mouth, eyes and stuffing.

Tack a foot pad to each leg, matching the two marks to the two side seams and sew by hand in back stitch with pink cotton, in a complete

circle overlapping stitching at beginning and end – this is fiddly but not difficult.

Clip into the corners and on the curved seams, being very careful not to clip through to the stitching. Then turn through to right side.

Stuff firmly, moulding into shape and stitch across the opening.

Join ears together along the curved edges, leaving them open along most of straight edge as shown on pattern.

Clip on the curves and corners, turn through to the right side and stuff lightly. Turn in the raw edges and sew together using a running stitch. Pull this up slightly when you finish off, just enough to gather the ear into a slight curve. Sew firmly in position.

Don't worry too much about how you sew it: when the fur is teased out, the stitches don't really show.

Work out where you think his eyes look best and if you have used fur fabric for the elephant, snip the fur in that spot. You need two baldish spots to glue his eyes on. Oversew with blue thread. Embroider the triangle in satin stitch with blue embroidery silk.

Look at his mouth. Pull out the pointed bit which is the end of the two underbody pieces. You should have about 2 cm. This is his lower lip. Fold half of this back on itself – upwards and into his mouth to form the lip – and oversew all round with grey thread.

Take the six-sided mouth piece, and glue the back. Push it into his mouth as shown in the photo. Back stitch across the centre and then sew round the edges with pink thread. This all sounds complicated in writing but it is simple when you are looking at the real thing.

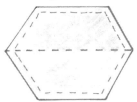

Free the fur round the seams and feed cornflakes.

KOALA

*Sean Edgerton aged 4 has just returned
to England; he spent all four years in Australia running round
barefoot in the sun and cannot understand the cold and convention of
an English upbringing. I made him this curious koala to cheer him up. I am
none too certain what the real thing looks like so this is a personal view of a
koala. All I know about koalas is how slow they are; they sit and blink in trees
and even the blinking is an effort. Sewing
the koala is relatively simple but does call for some creative pinning.
If it is the first toy you make, take your time and read the
instructions very carefully.*

YOU WILL NEED

- ☐ 50 cm grey fur fabric
- ☐ Small piece (about 15 cm by 20 cm) of pink fur fabric for face
- ☐ 2 small pieces of white fur fabric, about 12.5 cm square, for ears
- ☐ Small square or scraps of black felt for nose and paws
- ☐ About 150 gm stuffing
- ☐ Pair of 15 mm safety eyes
- ☐ Grey, white and pink sewing cottons; tacking thread

PREPARATION

Trace the pattern pieces and add 7 mm to 1 cm seam allowances (see page 10). Note all instructions and letters carefully.

Cut out pattern pieces and mark as necessary.

MAKING UP

Sew all pieces of fur fabric with wrong sides together, pinning and tacking before stitching.

Start by sewing the ears on to the front face, from A to B on both sides. Then join the back of the head to the front from C to C through B,A,A,B.

Sew on his black felt nose using blanket stitch or back stitch, inserting a little stuffing just before you finish sewing up.

Put in his safety eyes: unpick a stitch in the fabric on either side of his nose, insert the stalks of the eyes and fasten the washers firmly on the back.

Now his head is finished, move on to his body.

Join the two back side pieces down the straight sides from D to E, but leave a space of at least 7 cm for stuffing the koala.

Take the base piece and match E to E; sew the base to the back all round the curved side, from F to F through E.

Now take the front gusset, match the centre mark on the bottom to the centre of the base and stitch along that line until the base is sewn along the front from F to F.

Cut four rectangles of black felt, 2.5 cm by 2 cm, and pin the longer side into each paw seam. Most of the felt should be on the inside of the koala, so that when you turn it right side

KOALA

For back of head: place on double fabric, centre on fold line. Cut 1, including ears

For face: cut pattern into ear and face. Place ear on single fabric; cut 2 (reverse for pair). Place face on double fabric, centre on fold line and cut 1

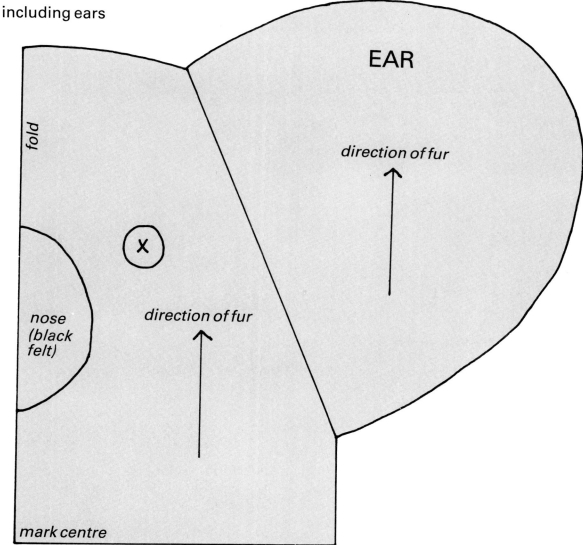

fold

EAR

direction of fur

X

nose
(black
felt)

direction of fur

mark centre

out, the black felt ends up appearing out of his paws.

Now sew up either side of the bear from F to G on both sides: that is, from the corners of the base on either side, round his legs, tummy and arms to his shoulders. You will find that the

seams join quite happily when you pin them if you have joined the base to the back and front first – though it was difficult to make it work when I tried it another way round. You should now have a bear body, with a rounded back and two sticking out arms and legs, sitting on a base.

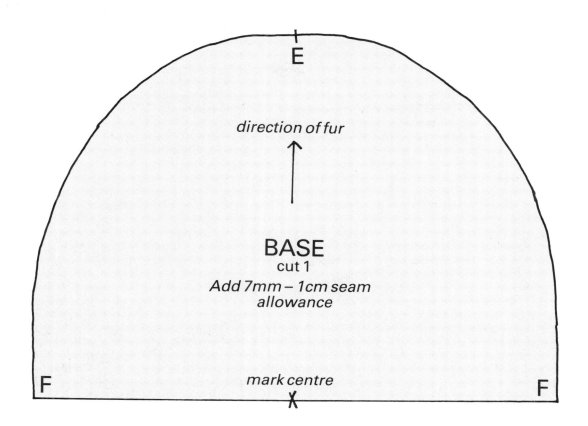

direction of fur

↑

BASE
cut 1
*Add 7mm – 1cm seam
allowance*

F   *mark centre*   F

X

The next thing is to join the body to the head.

Don't try and match up the side seams of head and body; the bear's rounded back depends on having a narrower front than back, so the side seams of the body will not match the head side seams – they will be further round towards his chest.

I found it difficult to sew all round the head/body seam in one go; it was simpler to sew from G to G via D, that is shoulder to shoulder via the back, and then sew the front face to the front body. Where the layers of fabric at seam junctions were too thick for the machine to take comfortably, I finished the seams by hand.

Clip and cut all curved seams and into corners and turn the koala right side out.

Now you can stuff your koala. Start by stuffing the ears lightly and then sew across the AB line on either side. Stuff his paws next and then his head and body. Sew up the back by hand.

Use a small pair of scissors to trim the rectangles of black felt on his paws into fingers. Curious the Koala had four fingers per hand, which may be wrong but looks fine.

Brush out the fur round the seams with a wire brush or needle.

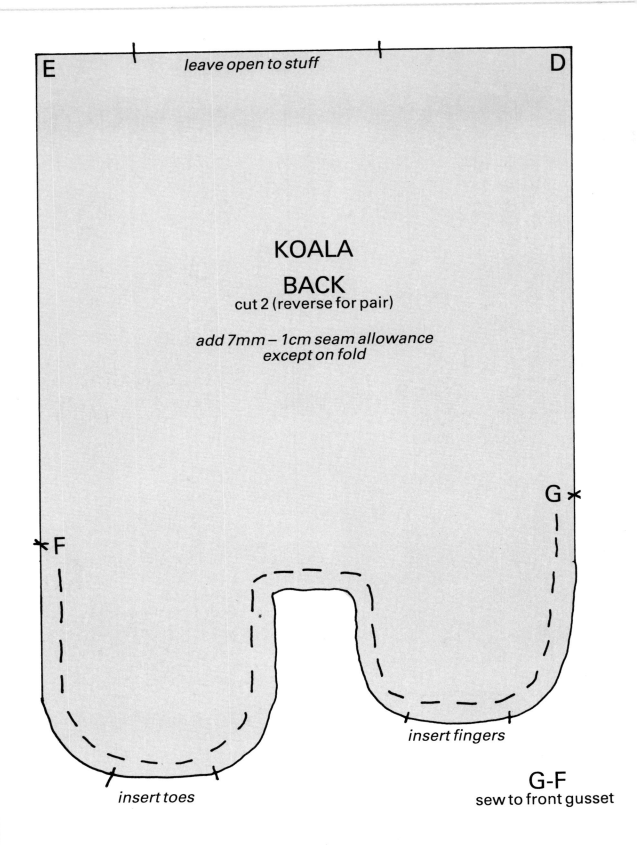

E

D

leave open to stuff

KOALA

BACK
cut 2 (reverse for pair)

add 7mm – 1cm seam allowance
except on fold

G

F

insert fingers

insert toes

G-F
sew to front gusset

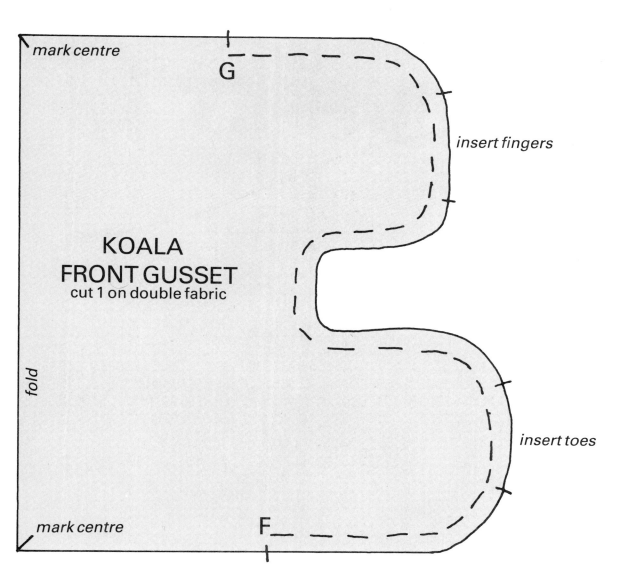

mark centre

G

insert fingers

KOALA
FRONT GUSSET
cut 1 on double fabric

fold

insert toes

mark centre

F

CROCODILE OVEN GLOVE PUPPET

*Rory and Sean's mother
left a frantic message on the answerphone
one day, saying she had urgent news. The news
was that Rory's most successful birthday present was an
animal oven glove, which appeared round doors and leapt out
and frightened grown-ups and ate them up. The only minor problem
was the size, it was a bit big for small hands. What about making up a
pattern for a smaller version and putting it in this book? This one fits the three-
to-five-year-olds who tried it and you can just alter the top stitching to make it
bigger for older children. It is stunningly easy to make and you can use scraps of
old dressing-gowns or anything similar if you don't want to go out shopping.
All the amounts are variable – just use whatever you prefer or have
available for any bit of the puppet. If you buy the quilting, you will
probably have to settle for a third of a metre of each sort
since shops don't readily deal in less.
You can make lots of different animal oven gloves
from this basic idea.*

YOU WILL NEED

- ☐ 20 cm length dingy green quilting
- ☐ 20 cm length pink quilting
- ☐ 1 pair of approx 2.5 cm rolling safety eyes
- ☐ Small (20 cm) square white felt
- ☐ Small (20 cm) square red felt
- ☐ Scraps black and yellow felt
- ☐ Glue
- ☐ Matching cotton for sewing; contrasting cotton for tacking

PREPARATION

Trace the pattern pieces and cut out the pieces of fabric; add seam allowance of 5 to 7 mm to quilting only, not to felt pieces. You should have one top head, one underside, and two feet in green; inside mouth and two feet in pink; inside mouth in red felt; band of teeth in white felt; one black felt diamond and one smaller yellow felt diamond.

CROCODILE OVEN GLOVE PUPPET

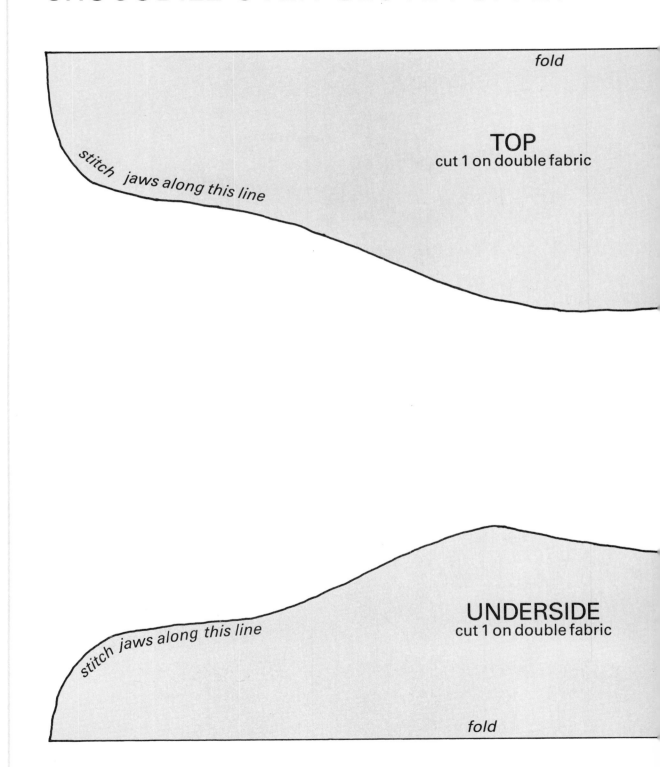

fold

TOP
cut 1 on double fabric

stitch jaws along this line

UNDERSIDE
cut 1 on double fabric

stitch jaws along this line

fold

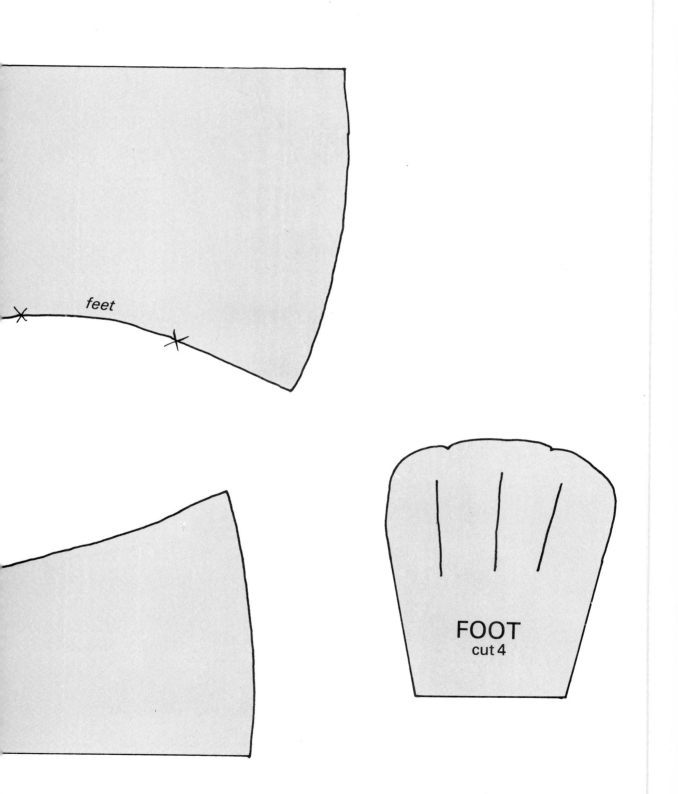

feet

FOOT
cut 4

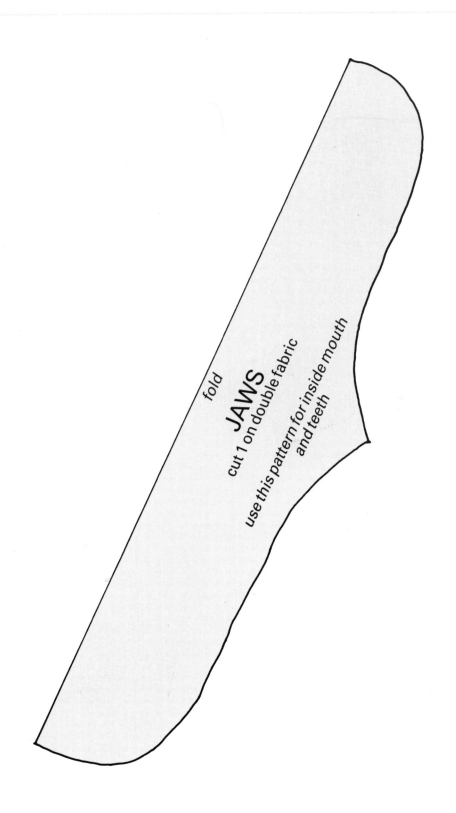

fold

JAWS

cut 1 on double fabric

use this pattern for inside mouth and teeth

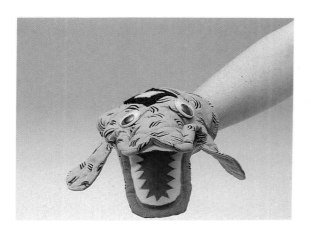

MAKING UP

Make the feet first. Right sides together, stitch green and pink feet in pairs. Stitch where shown on the pattern.

Right sides together, pin and tack the jaws into the top and under pieces.

Pin and tack the top and under pieces together, inserting the feet where indicated on the pattern and then stitch. Cut and clip the curved seams and turn right side out. Turn the raw wrist edge in and stitch – I zigzagged it on the machine.

Oversew a ridge about 4 cm long up the croc's face from his nose towards his eyes.

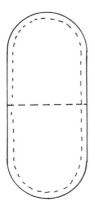

Open his mouth and topstitch round the inside of the mouth piece, about 1 cm in from the edge, but try it on your child for size before sewing down – you can adjust it at this stage.

Cut down the red felt inside mouth by 1 cm so that it fits on to this line, and glue.

Glue the ziggyzaggy oval shape which makes up the crocodilic dentures on to the outside rim of the red felt. Slip stitch these down if the toy is for young children.

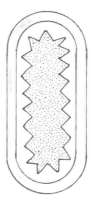

Insert the eyes: make small holes in the fabric first to put the stalks in, then fix on the washers securely.

Glue and stitch the black and yellow diamonds on his forehead. That's it.

LITTLE HORSE

*This is a traditional nursery toy, made out
of felt. I don't know exactly why it has such charm but everyone
loves it. The pattern came from the octogenarian mother of an old
friend. She made toys all her life, immaculately sewn with the tiniest of stitches.
Sadly I never met her before she died, so I only know her through the toys which
have been lent to me for inspiration. You can machine this toy, in which case
add 5 mm seam allowance to the basic pattern, but I prefer to hand sew it
in blanket stitch – it is soothing and simple.
Don't overstuff the horse or the seam junctions may weaken.*

YOU WILL NEED

- ☐ 2 small (22 cm) felt squares
- ☐ Contrasting cotton
- ☐ Ric-rac or felt in contrasting colour for mane and tail
- ☐ Stuffing

PREPARATION

Trace the paper pattern pieces: one whole horse, one gusset.

Cut out two whole horse patterns and two gussets.

MAKING UP

Sew the gusset pieces together from A to B.

Sew the two horse pieces to the gussets – back, front and all four legs. Do not sew over the hooves. Finish off very securely at A and B, oversewing them with a few small stitches.

Cut out four circles of felt 2.5 cm in diameter and stitch into the feet.

Stuff the feet and legs now before you finish sewing up the horse. If you leave it until later, you will find it much more difficult.

Now finish sewing up the horse, leaving a gap from the forelock to the base of the mane and a gap of 1 cm for the tail.

Stuff the rest of the horse lightly but firmly, pushing the stuffing down into his nose. Don't be tempted to overstuff the horse or the legs will stick out at extraordinary angles. Mould the body as you go along.

Cut a 1 cm square piece of felt for the forelock and sew it in to the horse with tiny stitches. Take a small piece of ric-rac, just over double the width of the forelock, and fold it in half. Put it round the forelock, inserting the raw edges into the ears. By hand, stitch round the base of the ric-rac and stitch the bit which is in the horse's ear.

LITTLE HORSE

end mane

tail

HORSE
cut 2

A GUSSET B
cut 2

The next stage will close up the felt horse, so if you want to push in any more stuffing at the last minute, do so now.

Cut two long fans of felt about 2 cms deep – the base should be the same length as the mane from ear to shoulder, and it should fan out slightly at the sides. Sew these two pieces into the neck, thus closing up the horse.

Cut a length of ric-rac just over double the length of the mane. Fold it in half and put the fold at the top of the mane just behind the ears. Using matching thread, slip stitch the ric-rac to the felt neck down each side. Finish off by turning the ric-rac in at the end and oversewing together.

Fringe the mane and forelock.

Make the tail with a square of blue felt, about 5 cm across. Roll it round tightly and sew up for about 1 cm. Insert the tail, using back stitch (instead of blanket stitch) to sew it in. Fringe the tail using small scissors.

Sew round the ears with blanket stitch. Strengthen the seam junctions at back and front with a few overstitches, which will also stop the legs splaying.

Sew his eyes with satin stitch or put on a sequin either side. Trim the little horse with a bridle and rosette if you wish.

THE SWIMMING POOL GAME

---

*This is a fishy game,
played like draughts. The board is chipboard painted like a
blue swimming pool. The counters are red goldfish and yellow
dolphins. Their tails are wired with pipe-cleaners so that the dolphins
can leap and the goldfish curl their tails over their backs. These are simple
enough to be made by children. When a fish
reaches the other side, his important new status is shown by safety- pinning
a tiny fish to his body. I bought little metal minnows at the Hobby
Horse, but you could make flat felt fish or coloured cardboard
cut-outs. The best safety pins are those tiny gold ones which
usually come from the laundry.*

DOLPHINS AND GOLDFISH

You should be able to cut out four sets of three pieces from one 20 cm square of felt. You will need twelve of each fish, so you need three squares each of yellow and red felt. You will also need thread, stuffing and trimmings. Tack and then sew the fish together, leaving a 4 cm gap along his spine. I blanket stitched the fishes in metallic thread, available from craft shops. You could back stitch the seams if you prefer and/or use ordinary coloured cotton; I found machining was too time-consuming to be worthwhile on these fiddly-sized objects but you may be more deft. Don't try and glue the edges – the seams split when you put in the stuffing. Insert the pipe cleaners, as shown in the patterns opposite.

Stuff lightly but firmly and continue sewing up.

Then decorate as you wish with sequins, buttons, etc. It is well worth sewing these in place rather than using glue, which discolours the metallic finish and is less secure.

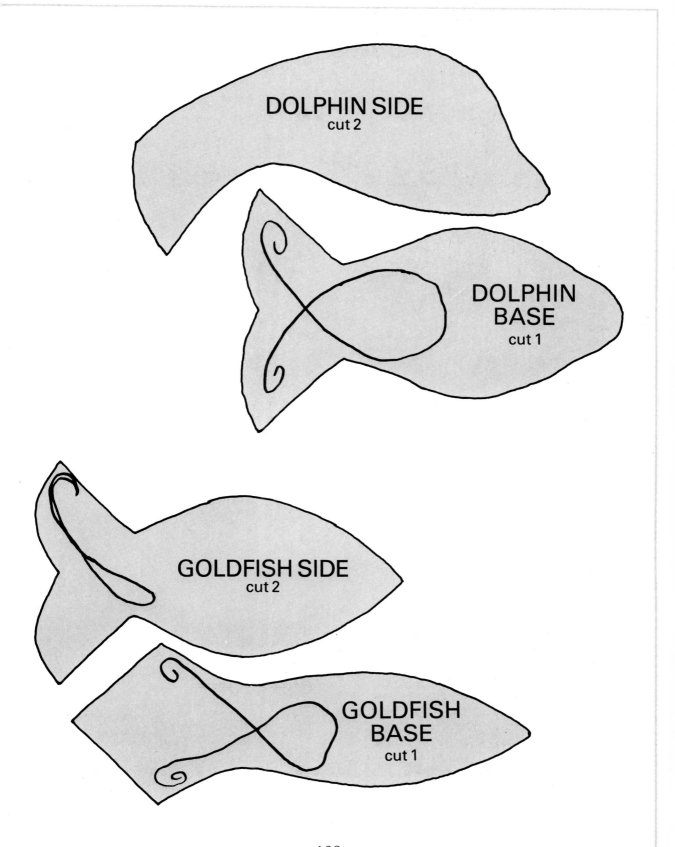

DOLPHIN SIDE
cut 2

DOLPHIN BASE
cut 1

GOLDFISH SIDE
cut 2

GOLDFISH BASE
cut 1

THE BOARD

YOU WILL NEED

- ☐ 70 cm square of 1 cm chipboard (from your local timber merchant)
- ☐ Small pots of gloss paint in two blues, light and dark
- ☐ Small pot black lacquer or black gloss paint
- ☐ 3 paint brushes

NOTE

Prime the chipboard with wood primer before you start painting or you will find, as I did, that the paint sinks relentlessly into the board and you have to do two coats of everything.

Using a ruler, make a border of 3.75 cm round the board. Divide the remaining centre square into 64 7.5 cm squares. Leave the vertical lines straight but make the horizontals wavy.

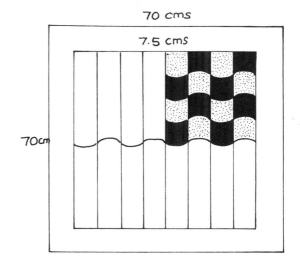

Paint the board in alternate squares of light blue and dark blue gloss paint. Wait until the first colour is dry before you start the second.

Paint the border with the black lacquer when the centre is dry.

CHRISTMAS TREE DECORATIONS

*You can make ravishing decorations very simply
with felt and sparkly trimmings like sequins. I should warn
you that the more I became carried away with beautifying the basic
shape, the longer it took, but the decorations can be packed away to last
from year to year so you can justify the hours of stitching as long term planning.
Children can use the patterns to make their own decorations and the same patterns can
be used to make cards, invitations, party presents, mobiles etc.
How much and exactly what kind of trimming you use is really a matter of
what is easily available and how much time you have. The patterns are
intended as guides only; you could let your imagination run riot.
You could also use other basic shapes and treat them in the same way.
Valerie Mangold gave me unstinting help with ideas for these
decorations and Annie Lickett produced the basic
pattern for the adorable clown.*

The total effect can be seen at the front of the book

FELT TOYS

YOU WILL NEED

☐ Felt, stuffing (cotton wool is fine), coloured cottons, metallic thread, sequins, feathers, beads

NOTE

The birds, butterfly and Christmas trees are pairs of shapes, cut out, stitched up and lightly stuffed. Don't try and glue the felt pieces together if you want to stuff them – it doesn't work.

Felt is available in the most gorgeous bright colours. I found that the dark colours were invariably disappointing for decorations because they look dull. Yellows, pinks, reds, whites, greens and the brighter blues were the most rewarding.

I preferred to sew up most of the toys by hand in blanket stitch using metallic thread. A spool of this is an expensive outlay, but it gives a wonderful finish to the toys and is also useful for making loops to hang them on the tree.

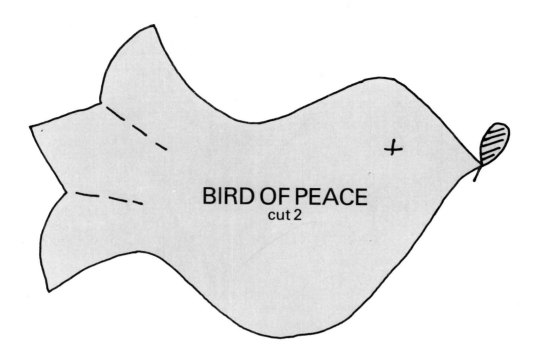

BIRD OF PEACE
cut 2

Sequins, which are available in lots of different shapes and sizes, are instant pzazz, easily available and well worth the trouble of fixing them on. If you want to sew sequins round the edge of a toy, machine or back stitch the edges and then apply the sequins on top. It looks better if you use invisible thread.

It took me ages to work out what seems the most efficient way to sew on sequins so the details are below, in the hope of saving you time.

Lay the first sequin in place; bring your single-threaded needle up from the underside of the fabric through the centre hole, push the needle down to the middle right of the sequin (if you are sewing from left to right). The sequins overlap so bring your needle up middle left of the first sequin and through the centre of the next one; push the needle through the centre of the preceding sequin, take the thread underneath to the left centre of the current sequin, then through the centre of the next and so on.

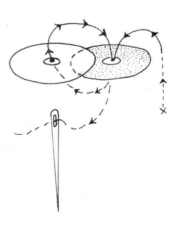

This keeps the sequins securely anchored and you develop a rhythm to work to. Sewing on sequins is slow but tranquil work. The alternative way of fixing them if you are in a rush is to glue them on. This works well in the short term, but they may fall off and the glue tends to discolour the sequins.

BIRDS OF PEACE

Cut out the pattern and lay it on a double thickness of felt. You can make two birds out of a small (20 cm) square, folded in half, four birds from two squares laid one on top of the other.

Handstitch or machine the edges together, leaving a 4 cm gap in the bird's tummy so that you can push a little stuffing in. Stuff lightly and sew up. Then start decorating as you wish. The leaves in their mouths and the feathers on the white bird came from a very ancient bunch of flowers which had adorned my standard going-to-weddings hat.

BABY TEDDY BEAR

For the prototype bear I used contrasting yellow and red felt for back and front, blanket-stitched in gold thread. Sew up his body first, stuff lightly and then sew up his head – you can put a tiny bit of stuffing in his head just before you finish. Remember to sew in the loop.

His eyes are cross-stitched in pale blue cotton, his nose is three tiny satin stitches and his mouth is a feather stitch, both in dark blue cotton (see page 11 for these stitches).

He is trimmed with 15 cm of very narrow blue ribbon, a yellow rosebud and three sequins on his tummy.

MINIATURE CHRISTMAS TREES

Each side takes up a quarter of one of those small squares of felt. You will also need one small square or some scraps of red felt for the pot. I made both white and green trees in red pots, trimmed with anything I had to hand: bows, buttons, sequins, beads, felt presents etc.

Make the red flowerpot first and stuff it lightly, then insert it between the folds of the tree and sew across the base through the four thicknesses of felt. Sew up both sides, either by hand or machine to the top pair of branches, then stuff the tree lightly. Finish sewing up the sides of the tree. Decorate as you wish.

BUTTERFLY

This is made in exactly the same way as the bird and the bear. Cut out the shape twice; sew up all but 4 cm across the top, stuff lightly and then finish sewing, remember to sew in a loop before finishing. Sew along the two body lines; you can draw these partly together in ladder stitch (see page 11) if you want to give the butterfly a more interesting shape – but it is not absolutely necessary. The eyes and antennae are indicated by a little silver bow which seemed a rather cunning idea; make certain the bow is securely stitched on.

Decorate with masses of sequins and beads.

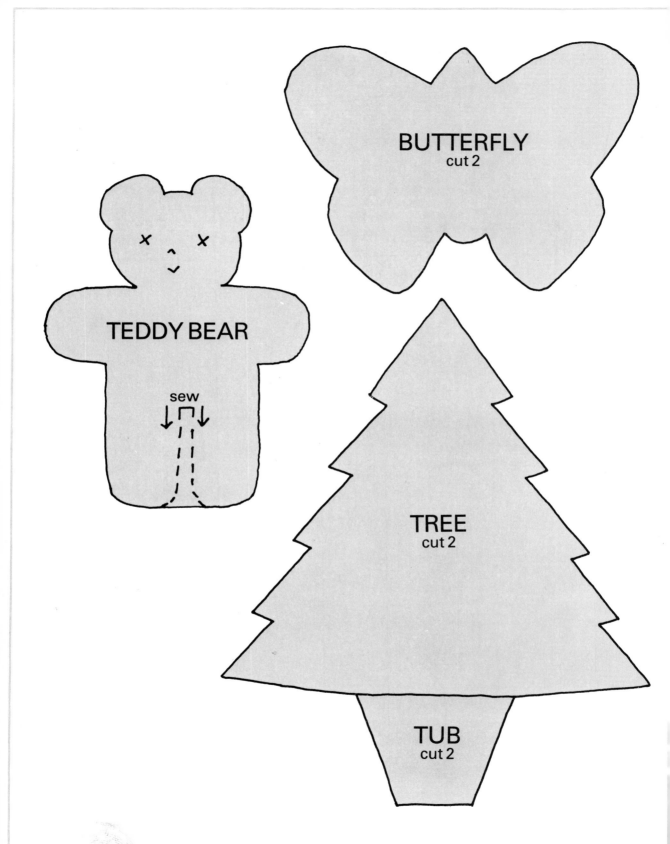

BUTTERFLY
cut 2

TEDDY BEAR

sew

TREE
cut 2

TUB
cut 2

CLOWN COSTUME

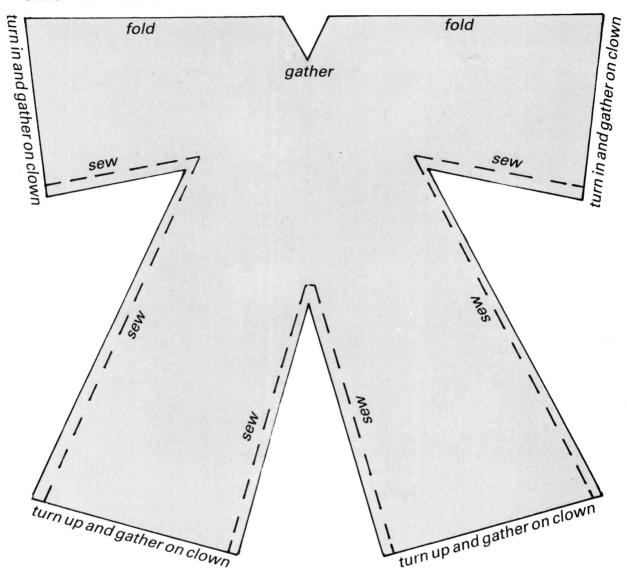

turn in and gather on clown

fold

gather

fold

turn in and gather on clown

sew

sew

turn in and gather on clown

sew

sew

sew

sew

turn up and gather on clown

turn up and gather on clown

sew before fitting on clown; turn
in and gather after fitting

HAT

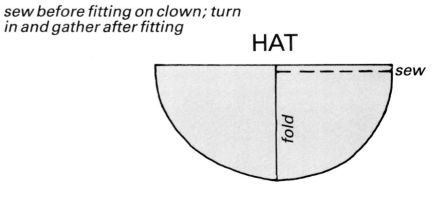

sew

fold

CLOWN

YOU WILL NEED

- 30 cm square of bright cotton material
- Matching cotton
- Scrap of felt 6 cm by 4 cm for hat
- 3 cm diameter polystyrene ball with hole at base (available from Dryad)
- 3 pipe cleaners
- 18 cm of 2.5 cm wide ribbon or lace for ruff
- 15 cm of fairly narrow (about 1 cm) wide ribbon for waist
- Narrow ribbon or metallic thread for loop

MAKING UP

Make the clown's figure by inserting two of the pipe cleaners into the hole in the base of the polystyrene ball.

Twist the two pipe cleaners together a couple of times and then separate to form the legs. Make a little foot at the end of each leg by twisting the pipe cleaner in a circle, flat to the ground. Make the arms with the single pipe cleaner. Bend it in half; twist the 'arms' round the neck twice and then stretch out either side; turn the ends over to make hands.

Fold the material in half to make two 15 cm squares; lay the pattern on the fabric with the shoulders on the fold as indicated. Cut out the costume. With wrong sides together, sew along seam lines by machine or back stitch by hand.

Turn right side out.

Slip clown's body into costume from top. It will look enormous but don't worry — it needs to be baggy.

Turn over wrists and ankles, about 1 cm, and sew with running stitch. Gather tightly and secure with two or three small stitches. Sew with running stitch round neck, gather and finish off.

Sew the ends of the ribbon or lace ruff together with the edges on the wrong side. Run a gathering thread round one edge, slip the ruff over the clown's head with the stitching closest to his neck and pull up the thread. Finish off with two or three small stitches.

Cut the hat pattern out of felt or other stiff material. Fold into cone and sew along dotted line, with small back stitches. Insert thread or ribbon for loop and stitch securely in place. Spread glue round clown's head and stick hat on, with loop out.

Tie bow at waist and stitch once or twice through the knot so that it stays secure.

With fine black felt-tip pen, draw on features as shown in the drawing.

FATHER CHRISTMAS

YOU WILL NEED

- [ ] 6 cm square scrap of red felt
- [ ] Red cotton
- [ ] 10 cm narrow ribbon *or* metallic thread for loop
- [ ] Cotton wool *or* stuffing
- [ ] Glue
- [ ] Walnut or fircone
- [ ] Gold poster paint and small brush

MAKING UP

This simple Father Christmas gives enormous pleasure to children partly because they can make him so quickly. The base is a walnut or fircone painted with gold poster paint (this is non-toxic, in case you are worried). When this has dried, glue on a red felt cone stitched in the same way as the clown hat with a loop popping out of the top. Spread a line of glue round the junction of the walnut (or fircone) and red hat. Roll a little cotton wool or stuffing into a sausage and stick it on to the toy. That's that.

HOBBY HORSE PENCIL

This costs very little to make but looks wonderfully extravagant. It is an ideal Christmas tree or party present.

YOU WILL NEED

- [ ] Scraps of shiny material big enough to make two horsehead outlines
- [ ] Stuffing – could be cotton wool
- [ ] 30 cm of narrow ribbon (4 mm width) to make bridle
- [ ] About 12.5 cm of curtain braid for mane
- [ ] Sequins
- [ ] About 30 cm of brightly coloured ribbon for trim, 1 cm wide
- [ ] White and blue cotton
- [ ] Tacking cotton
- [ ] Glue
- [ ] Pencil

MAKING UP

Cut out two head patterns and two ear patterns.

Machine the head pieces together with a 5 mm seam allowance and turn up the bottom.

Stuff the head, pushing the pencil up the middle.

Using doubled-up cotton, run a gathering thread round the bottom and secure it tightly.

Make a bridle from the narrow ribbon by gluing it on the back and then securing at the noseband with a couple of small stitches.

Sew a sequin on either side for eyes.

Glue the two pieces of shiny material to the ear patterns.

Glue and then sew the ears on.

Sew the mane on down back seam, turning the ends in and neatening off with a few stitches.

Trim with sequins, sewn or glued on to the mane.

Twist wider ribbon round and round the pencil under the hobby horse and then tie in a bow.

Stitch an extra 12.5 cm in a loop and secure behind the ears so that you can hang it up.

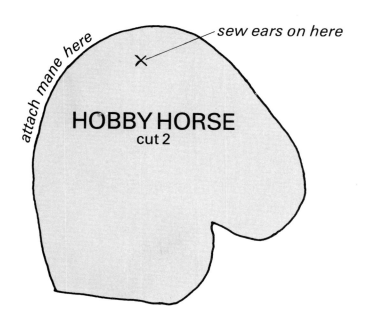

attach mane here — sew ears on here

HOBBY HORSE
cut 2

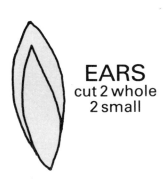

EARS
cut 2 whole
2 small

USEFUL ADDRESSES

John Lewis Partnership, Oxford St, London W1 and branches

The Hobby Horse, 15/17 Langton St, London SW10 and mail order

Dryad Craft Centre, P.O. Box 38, Northgate, Leicester: branches and mail order

B*right*On
Bakes

Jessica Haggerty

Book Guild Publishing
Sussex, England

First published in Great Britain in 2013 by
The Book Guild Ltd
Pavilion View
19 New Road
Brighton, BN1 1UF

Photography and design Stuart Ovenden
Food styling Rosie Reynolds
Typesetting in New Clarendon

Printed and bound in China under the supervision
of MRM Graphics Ltd, Winslow, Bucks.

A catalogue record for this book is available from
The British Library.

ISBN 978 1 84624 716 3

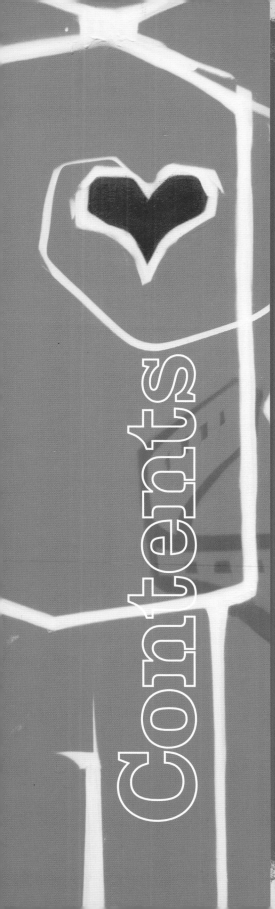

Contents

Brighton Bakes

Rose: 'People change.'

Ida: 'I've never changed. It's like those sticks of rock. Bite one all the way down, you'll still read Brighton. That's human nature.'

Graham Greene, *Brighton Rock*

Why Brighton?

Why Brighton? I remember reading that the Dean of its University described Brighton as 'Like a tart's face: not immediately appealing, but you'll keep going back.'

And the quote itself, whether or not you agree with its frankness, has always rung true with me over the last 15 years of living here, and especially during those few years I exiled myself (and missed the place badly). I set up my catering company in Edinburgh, but it was Brighton that provided the inspiration for experimentation, for the food to really spring to life and become something personal to me. The salty air seasoned my resolve and the town (for it was a town then) provided a haven for yet another wandering soul.

Brighton has always welcomed the weird and wonderful, the unusual and the unexpected. It is home to the second biggest arts festival in the world, an annual naked bike ride and a vintage car rally. Ever since the Prince Regent had his exotic pleasure palace built slap-bang in the middle of town, Brighton has had a reputation for licentiousness and liberality. Whoever you are, whatever you look like, she'll have you – she opens her wide accepting arms and swallows you up into her salty self with the seagulls and the lobster pots.

Maybe that acceptance comes from a lack of perfection in the town itself, those pebbles on the beach making her in some ways a poor cousin of the golden sands of Bournemouth. I always loved the pebbles – each one different, each with its own story. Then there's 'The Lanes', a confusing network of tiny streets that branch off from one another like capillaries and veins, tangled as mermaid's hair. Packed full of the unusual, the colourful and the bizarre: antique jewellery, knick-knacks and collectables, unsightly ornaments and useless bric-à-brac, lovingly polished guns from the Great War....

Bordered by the rolling chalk hills of the South Downs, the Sussex Weald and the sea, Brighton is well placed to take advantage of a profusion of nearby foodie specialities and a generous local larder – the bounty of the waves and the fertile soils combined. Cheeses, sparkling wines, fresh seafood and fruit orchards have resulted in a palette of culinary colours that the best cooks would be proud of. I have greedily stolen bags of roots and edible flowers from my friends' allotments, eagerly plundered farmers' markets for a taste of this and a spoonful of that (getting chased by a live crab in the process!), and unashamedly pillaged every nearby food business and producer I could find.

Seasonal and local foods

And so we move from the compass to the barometer: we're rooted geographically now, but a sense of place only speaks to the home-dwelling, hearth-loving parts of ourselves. The settled, the indoor, the gatherer parts...and, after all, that's where the fire is, the kitchen, the oven, the heat. I'm a home cook – happy in my own kitchen rather than an industrial stainless steel version. But all of us, even the most houseproud, need to venture outside sometimes, even if just to replenish our pantries. And that's where the hunter kicks in.

What could be more natural than structuring a cookery book round the seasons, using ingredients that are local and growing at the time of cooking? The weather outside affects not only the ingredients available to us, but also how we feel, how we function, what we feel like cooking. I know that the 'local and seasonal' mantra can get rather repetitive, and I'd venture that many of us long to revolt, and of course there are exceptions to every rule...but no matter how tempting that peach looks in December, it's going to taste like cotton wool – surely reason enough to fill our plates with food that is naturally primed to be at its absolute best.

But our times of celebrating and feasting are sometimes seasonally unrelated, and bring something more personal to the passing months. Sitting down with those we love, at important times in our lives, to break bread and share much more than the food on our plates transcends much of our everyday existence, and becomes something richer – something that defines who we are. Sometimes those events dictate the menus, and the thought of knowing exactly what to cook can be soothing and reassuring. Sometimes it is liberating to rebel, find your own way: this is your book – chop and change the menus, add your own footnotes, borrow and pluck, magpie-like, from other culinary traditions, familial, inherited, inspired, ancient, contemporary. I always distrust a clean cookbook, a cookbook free of even a smear or a drop of oil. No crumbs squashed between the pages? The book hasn't been used for what it's intended for, that much is plain.

It's the spirit of the town then, rather than faithful recreations of local specialities that I've tried to capture in my food. A local flavour, colour, spice – brash, bright and Brighton. A freedom of approach and a creativity that many Brightonians recognise as their own. And whether you're from Brighton, Budapest, Barbados or Bristol, I hope that the recipes will appeal.

My beginnings

Maybe it sounds ironic, looking to the past for inspiration, for something new, but bear with me...I have a variety of geranium named after me: 'Sweet Jess'. The aptness of the name is questionable, but perhaps my grandmother named those pink flowers with hope, rather than accuracy. As a child I remember her greenhouse as somewhere beguiling, where she was most herself. The musty geranium smell was one that I associated with her always, on her hands and clothes. She developed plants for each of her grandchildren. 'Sweet Jess' can't be used for cooking, but when I started researching this book, the sheer number of geranium varieties that can be astonished me: apple, coconut, rose, lemon, nutmeg, peppermint, ginger, lime, orange...flavours and perfumes that waft through the kitchen, lending their characters and distinct aromas to recipes. Experiment: infuse the leaves in milk and add to muffins, blitz with sugar and sprinkle on biscuits, bake in the oven atop a cake, then soak with sweet wine or citrus syrup. My grandmother, who rarely went near a kitchen, is remembered (despite herself) through my baking.

My baking

My baking encompasses a teaspoon of something unexpected: something once in common use and now forgotten, something locally grown, or something from far away salvaged and used in a new and different way. Familiar names, now reclaimed for our frying pans, our stock pots, our baking trays: geranium, tamarind, rose petals, lovage. Not to tinker, for tinkering's sake, or to deliberately provoke, but because we have a wide, wild palette of flavours, and we can use them to make our cooking our own.

Everything here is baked and fresh from the oven – above all bounteous, overflowing, not necessarily tidy or uniform, but passionate. Let your food reflect you – there aren't any rules here, so experiment away. That might sound dangerous and naive advice to give at the start of a baking book, but as long as you have the proportions of your base (flour, sugar, eggs) right, then you can have as much fun as you like – with added extra ingredients, with the decorations, the moistness of rose water, the brittle snap of salted caramel. If your cake doesn't rise, chalk it up to experience and try something else. What you've created will, in all probability, still taste delicious and be gobbled up by hungry mouths, and some of the best culinary treats were born from culinary disasters.

Baking is the last bastion of culinary apprehension – the worry that an extra spoonful of something will create disaster. It will certainly change the composition, but you will be surprised at how forgiving most recipes are. I have made cakes with bananas and yoghurt instead of eggs (or forgotten them completely), I have dropped cakes on the floor, I have mixed baking powder in far too early and left raw mixes to stand whilst I went on long walks. I make an obstinate habit of adding fresh fruit to plain sponge mixes. Both the taste and satisfaction that you will receive (and of course the praise ringing in your ears) are so disproportionate to the amount of effort involved – I dare you to try just a few of the recipes in this book, lap up the compliments, and feel your confidence growing.

Baking is, after all, just another form of alchemy – and so much greater than the sum of its parts. More than any other style of cooking, a great transformation takes place when the oven door is closed. When you start cooking a stew, you can roughly see your ingredients and the journey they will take to become something rich and sticky and unctuous. Lay out your flour, your eggs, your milk, your sugar...and then start to dream, because more than any other style of cook, a baker needs vision, optimism. Creating fluffy meringues from unpromising egg whites, a crusty loaf from flour and yeast – seeing the potential in the humble, the ability to transform.

Yes there's a science behind it, but there's a magic involved too. And it's a magic that is all the greater for being fleeting, ephemeral. The food is eaten, it's the cause of great happiness in that instance, and it's gone. But those few minutes spent eating, consuming, are remembered. There's no permanent reminder of a meal, hanging on the wall like a painting, just the memories of the diners – and those memories can be some of the most evocative of our lives. Perhaps the reason food affects us so much is that we use all our senses when we're eating – not just taste, but sight, sound, smell, touch. I bake my lemon curd and geranium muffins and I'm back in my grandmother's greenhouse, far more quickly immersed than I would be by looking at a photograph of her.

The joy of these recipes (and the proof that there's more than science involved) is that every person making these recipes, with exactly the same ingredients, in exactly the same environment, will have a slightly different result. Yes, every oven is slightly different, every tin buckled in a different way, but the hands mixing, and the persons creating, are also different. I'm not asking you all to produce baked products that are soggy in the middle, or defective in some way (there are certain rules that need to be adhered to, even in Brighton...), but don't be ashamed if your sponge only rises a couple of centimetres, or your pie filling is a little irregular. There's a beauty in the higgledy piggledy, in the individuality of the slightly wonky, that is very appealing. These scones are 'mine', they're slightly messy like me, they don't conform – but I'm still proud of them, they still taste fantastic. My heart sinks when I see the regularity of rows of baked goods – they speak too much of the machine, of the factory produced.

It's not just sweet treats on offer here. Cakes big and small are arguably the stars of the show, but those that trumpet less loudly are just as delicious: savouries, bread, muffins, pies, bars. From the crowning glory of a baked cheesecake to the intricacy of a cluster of canapés, glistening biscuits that snap when you break them, or dissolve slowly in a mug of hot tea, the glowing, buttery pastry top of a pie, just waiting to reveal its contents, to the sound a freshly baked loaf makes when tapped on the bottom – the joys of baking are manifold.

What we're trying to get at here is the wisdom of the old ways wrapped up with the colour and can-do attitude of the new, the unexpected – the daring that makes Brighton so cutting edge. Local ingredients, organic ingredients, fresh fruit, fresh flowers, herbs and spices – tapping into the zeitgeist with an eye to the past – to the tried and tested, the wisdom of our mothers, our grandmothers. Keeping the connection in families, which can skip a generation, can be transmitted from grandmother to grandson, or ignited when an old recipe book is picked up and well-thumbed pages are opened for the first time in years. My gardening grandmother would do everything she could to stay out of the kitchen – her plants were her passion, she earned the money for the family, and her mother did the cooking. My own mother makes the best scones, the best Scotch pancakes, the best mince pies I have tasted anywhere, ever.

This is a contemporary book then, but one that has not forgotten where my culinary roots lie: in the rich, earthy soils of Sussex. Urban style juxtaposed with an old-fashioned ethos, which I hope will help you find your own way in a sometimes unfamiliar world full of the ghosts of generations gone by. Make it your own, and provide great happiness to those around you – and maybe your own set of memories along the way.

- **When I refer to eggs, they are always free range, and large unless another size is specified.**
- **Butter is always unsalted.**
- **Tablespoons do mean those rather measly looking 15g versions – and it's worth measuring, rather than grabbing the nearest spoon from your kitchen drawers, which can be much too large.**

13

Spring

Spring has sprung afternoon tea

Festival street party

20–30 minute meals

As green, growing things push their way through the soil, be inspired by the shoots, the buds, all the fresh joy in nature, and reflect some of that vibrancy in your springtime menus...

Spring has sprung afternoon tea

I think it's the unnecessary-ness of afternoon tea that appeals to me. The idea of a long, lazy afternoon, the parade of courses: delicate (or not so delicate) cakes and pastries, cup after cup of tea. Afternoon tea is a peculiarly British phenomenon and, by its very nature, it refuses to be constrained by time, by the ability to fit into a working day, by the idea of having to have something savoury before the sweet. Everything about it is obstinate, awkward and fabulously decadent. This is the meal that was created by a duchess to fit in with the aristocratic habit of eating very, very late in the evening – a little something to fill the desolate wasteland between lunch and dinner. The parade of tiny morsels speaks to me of time, of leisure – it can't be rushed, or it is ruined.

Blood orange cake with ginger cream cheese frosting and candied orange slices

The blood orange season is brief, but heralds the start of spring with an evocative fanfare. When you cut into one the deep, ruby-red flesh is always surprising, and its rich citrus tang makes a great flavour base for a light sponge. Contrast the icing with ginger, and candy some slices of orange as an optional (but gorgeous) topping. What I like to think of as the first fruit of the year makes a fitting start to our afternoon tea.

FOR THE CAKE
250g soft butter
250g caster sugar
4 eggs
250g self-raising flour
2 tsp baking powder
juice of 1 blood orange
100ml milk
2 tsp vanilla extract
zest of two blood oranges
FOR THE ICING
500g cream cheese at room
   temperature
200g icing sugar
1 tsp ground ginger
**CANDIED ORANGE
   SLICES**
1 large orange
110g white granulated
   sugar

MAKES
A two-layer 20cm cake
(serves 8)
PREP/COOK
20 minutes preparation
20 minutes cooking
YOU WILL NEED
2 x 20cm springform
cake tins

1 For the candied orange slices: take the orange and slice in half, ideally horizontally so that each slice has an even cross-section of segments.

2 Take the sharpest knife you own, and cut slices about half a centimetre wide through your orange – peel and pith and all. Any thinner and they will break down, any fatter and they won't candy properly.

3 In a large, heavy-bottomed frying pan, bring 375ml water and the sugar to the boil, and then add the orange slices.

4 Let your liquid boil for about 5–10 minutes, turning your slices once or twice. This is perhaps not the time to wash the dishes or feed the cat – boiling sugar most definitely needs all your attention!

5 Reduce the heat to medium and let your orange slices continue cooking for 30 minutes, turning them occasionally. The liquid will soon thicken, and become a viscous syrup. Reduce the heat once more, and simmer the now jewel-like slices for another 10–20 minutes or so, until the syrup has reduced right down and the orange slivers are translucent, but still intact.

6 Remove the pan from the heat, but leave the slices in the pan for 10 minutes until they are cool enough to handle. Please still be wary as you carefully use a plastic spatula or fish slice to take them out of the pan to cool completely on greaseproof paper.

7 For the cake: heat the oven to 180°C/Gas mark 4.

8 Cream the butter and sugar together for a few minutes until light and fluffy, regularly scraping down the sides of the bowl if you are using a mixer. Add the eggs, one at a time, and mix thoroughly until each is incorporated. Your mixture should be pale and cloud-like.

9 In a separate bowl, sift the flour and baking powder together.

10 Add the juice of one blood orange to the milk, with a couple of teaspoons of vanilla extract – the liquid total should be about 150ml. Now add the blood orange zest, and don't worry if the liquid looks slightly curdled at this point.

11 With the mixer on low, add the wet and dry ingredients to the egg mixture in two batches, finishing with a brief whizz to make sure everything is incorporated. Your mixture should now be at the soft-dropping stage, which you can test by spooning some out – it should fall easily from the spoon.

12 Butter and flour the cake tins and divide the cake batter evenly between each. Put the tins on the middle shelf, and bake for 20 minutes, then remove and allow to cool before turning each out and cooling completely on a wire rack.

13 To make the icing: put the cream cheese in a bowl and sift the icing sugar and ginger over the top, then beat well to combine. This amount of frosting will give you enough to fill the centre and frost around the sides and top of the cake.

TIP If blood oranges are out of season, try pink grapefruit or lime. It goes without saying that the more traditional citrus fruits are worthy replacements. If you don't have time to make the candied orange slices, simply finely slice fresh oranges (as thinly as you possibly can) and arrange on top.

Pistachio cupcakes with rose buttercream

There is something about the earthiness of these cakes that sits so perfectly with the perfume of the frosting. Arabian Nights meets English Country Garden. Maybe you're averse to the now ubiquitous cupcake, but let me assure you, the delicate proportions here are utterly correct – bake as a big cake and it loses some of its exotic magic.

210g caster sugar
210g butter, very soft
3 eggs
210g self-raising flour
8 tbsp milk
115g softened butter
500g icing sugar, sifted
60ml milk
2 tsp rosewater
a couple of drops of pink or green food colouring (optional)

TIP To make a buttercream with volume and height, a tabletop mixer is best. You can, of course, mix buttercream with an electric hand whisk, but the minutes required to incorporate the right amount of air does neither the whisk or your wrist much good.

MAKES
12 large cupcakes
PREP/COOK
20 minutes preparation
25 minutes cooking
YOU WILL NEED
A muffin tray

1 Heat the oven to 160°C/Gas mark 3.

2 Whizz the pistachios with the sugar in a food processor until finely chopped into sparkling green flakes.

3 Cream the butter with your jade-coloured sugar until fluffy. It won't achieve the same sort of lighter-than-air consistency as usually expected because the ground nuts add a denseness to the mixture.

4 Add the eggs, one by one, mixing thoroughly until completely incorporated.

5 Place your flour and milk into the bowl, and mix until smooth. You will be left with the palest of green batters, flecked through with small lumps of nut.

6 Divide between cases, then bake for 22–25 minutes until a skewer poked in comes out clean. Cool on a wire rack.

7 To make the icing (see tip also): this sounds like a lot of frosting, and to be honest with you, it is. But we are piping this into great swathes of sugary prettiness atop each cake, so please don't cut back the quantities – cupcakes need dramatic frosting, or they are just lonely muffins. Place the butter into the bowl of a mixer, and add the milk, rosewater and 250g icing sugar. Blitz mercilessly for more minutes than you would think necessary (3 minutes is the bare minimum). Add 125g of sugar and beat for another 3 minutes. Add the last 125g icing sugar, and (you guessed it), at least another 3 minutes of beating. You can now add your colour, if you are using, but remember to start with just a drop or two – you can always add, but you can't take away. Palest of rose petal pinks or pistachio green is what we are aiming for here, not Bollywood bright.

Spelt muffins with gingery peaches

Or, adventures in flour. These rich, chewy mouthfuls work particularly well with alternatives to wheat flour – and indeed spelt gives them a nutty, distinctive chewiness that blends well with the spiced gingerbread doughiness. I've lightened them with fresh peaches – poaching and skinning isn't essential, but makes them tangibly more unctuous, and adds a little luxury to a worthy bake.

PEACH TOPPING
1 large peach, ripe but firm
1 tbsp unsalted butter
1 tbsp honey
1 tsp freshly grated ginger

DRY MIX
100g plain flour
100g wholemeal plain flour
60g spelt flour
200g caster sugar
50g soft brown sugar
1 tsp baking powder
1 tsp bicarbonate of soda
¾ tsp sea salt
1 tsp ginger

WET MIX
85g unsalted butter, melted
180ml milk
120ml sour cream or natural yoghurt
1 large egg
2 tsp freshly grated ginger
3 tsp crystallised ginger, chopped

1 Preheat the oven to 180°C/Gas mark 4.

2 Rub the inside of the baking tins with butter and set aside.

3 Halve the peach, remove the stone and slice thinly. If you wish, simmer the peach in water or fruit juice for a few minutes first, then skin it before slicing.

4 Add the butter, honey and fresh ginger to a frying pan and heat. Stir to combine, and gently add the peach slices. Fry the slices over a low heat for a few minutes.

5 In a large bowl, sift all of the dry mix ingredients together. If you have any larger grains left in your sieve, do add them in anyway as they provide tasty chewiness.

6 Whisk the wet mix ingredients together and add them to the dry mix.

7 Fill muffin tins full (you can mound this mixture higher than you would a sponge cake), and lay a couple of peach slices on top of each, pressing them in slightly.

8 Spoon all that gorgeous golden peachy nectar left in the frying pan over the top of each muffin, and place on a middle shelf in the oven. Bake for about 25 minutes until golden and the peaches have caramelised.

9 Cool on a wire rack.

TIP Remember the muffin mantra of never over-mixing – it's fine to keep small pockets of dry mix uncombined.

MAKES
12 muffins
PREP/COOK
20 minutes preparation and
25 minutes cooking
YOU WILL NEED
A 12-hole muffin tray

Elderflower and rhubarb cheesecake

This cheesecake is a beautiful balancing act of rich decadence and light, springtime flavours, with the perfumed elegance of the elderflower lifting and offsetting the almost cloying sweet milkiness of the cake itself. For all those who declare cheesecake too stodgy, try this, I dare you.

BISCUIT BASE
350g digestive biscuits
120g butter
2 tbsp honey
FILLING
450g forced rhubarb, chopped
3 tbsp caster sugar
5 tbsp elderflower cordial
350g low fat cream or curd cheese
2 eggs
juice and zest of 2 lemons
150g caster sugar
25g arrowroot
1 dsp cold water
FOR DECORATING
fresh elderflower blossoms

1 Preheat the oven to 180°C/Gas mark 4.

2 Crush the biscuits into fine crumbs, either in a food processor or, more stress-relievingly, by placing them in a food bag and bashing merrily with a rolling pin.

3 Melt the butter and honey in a saucepan, and add the biscuit crumbs. Fork through until thoroughly mixed – everything should be clumping together nicely.

4 Grease the base of the tin, and line with greaseproof. Firmly press your biscuit crumbs onto the base (using the back of a spoon for assistance if needed) and set aside to cool for 10 minutes or so.

5 Place the rhubarb, caster sugar and elderflower cordial in a saucepan, and poach gently until the rhubarb pieces are starting to lose their shape. Don't allow them to break up completely though. Check for taste, and sweeten if necessary. Remove the pan from the heat and allow to cool slightly, before spreading half the rhubarb over the biscuit base.

6 Beat together the cheese, egg, lemon juice, zest and caster sugar with an electric mixer or wooden spoon. When it is completely smooth, pour over your berried base, and cook in the oven for 20–30 minutes. Remove and leave to cool.

7 Gently reheat the remaining half of the rhubarb in the pan – these will make a gorgeous pink topping to the cheesecake. Mix the arrowroot with the water, and add that to the pan. Heat for about a minute until the liquid in the pan thickens, and the glaze becomes clear. Allow to cool and spoon over the cooled cheesecake. As a finishing touch, sprinkle with fresh elderflower blossom.

TIP You should be able to find forced rhubarb in shops during spring. It's younger and more tender than rhubarb grown outdoors in summer, and is a distinctive bright pink.

MAKES
One 23cm cheesecake (serves 10–12)
PREP/COOK
20 minutes preparation
30 minutes cooking
YOU WILL NEED
A 23cm springform tin

Brighton biscakes

An old Sussex peculiarity, which I've included here as an intriguing (but delicious) oddity. A hybrid that feels at home in both camps, combining the moistness and body of a cake with the crunch crisp of a biscuit – a talking point for the afternoon tea brigade, most certainly.

1 Preheat the oven to 160°C/Gas mark 3, and grease and line the baking trays.

2 Take the three egg whites and beat them, slowly at first until foaming, then as fast as you can until they are opaque and hold stiff peaks. This will be much easier and quicker in a clean bowl.

3 In a separate bowl, cream the butter, sugar and lemon peel until pale, light, fluffy and fragrant.

4 Beat in the egg yolks, one at a time, until completely incorporated. With a large metal spoon, using as few movements as you can so as not to beat all the air out of the mixture, gently fold in the egg whites along with the ground nuts and orange flower water. Be cautious here, as the amount of air in the mix now will translate to a lovely light biscuit. If everything seems a little stiff, slowly add a small amount of milk.

5 Drop tablespoons of the mixture onto the baking trays, keeping a few centimetres between them as they will spread slightly. Bake for 10–15 minutes until firm and golden.

6 Whilst the biscakes are baking, make your icing. Warm the jam in a saucepan and add the icing sugar and a little lemon juice until you have a firm mixture.

7 Place a teaspoon on each biscake as soon as they come out of the oven, and quickly top with a roasted hazelnut. Pop them back in the oven for a couple of minutes to make sure the topping and nuts are set, then take out and cool on the trays.

TIP Before beating the egg white, run half a lemon round the inside of your bowl to pick up any invisibly lurking fat.

230g self-raising flour
175g caster sugar
115g butter
90g hazelnuts, roasted and ground in a food processor
3 eggs, separated
grated peel of one large lemon
4 tsp orange flower water
FOR THE ICING
2 tbsp apricot jam
175g icing sugar
juice 1 lemon
36 hazelnuts, roasted

MAKES
36 biscakes
PREP/COOK
15 minutes preparation
20 minutes cooking
YOU WILL NEED
2 large greased and lined baking trays

Chilli bread sarnies, three ways

Or, baking as therapy. Yes we can all buy fantastic bread from the bakers and supermarkets now, but there is a feeling of achievement, of proud-as-punch 'I-did-that' about making your own.

BASIC BREAD
500g strong white flour, plus extra for dusting
7g sachet fast-action dried yeast
1 tsp salt
up to 350ml lukewarm water
a little sunflower oil, for greasing
ADDITIONS
5 tbsp olive oil, 1 tsp of sea salt flakes and either:
1 red chilli, chopped (try with mackerel and beetroot)
or a scattering of sundried tomato and olives (try with chicken and tarragon mayonnaise)
or 2 large red onions, sliced, and a handful of rosemary sprigs (try with goat's cheese)

MAKES
One 1kg loaf (or 4 mini loaves or 12 rolls)
PREP/COOK
50 minutes preparation
45 minutes cooking (for one loaf) or 20 minutes cooking (for smaller rolls)
YOU WILL NEED
One 900g loaf tin

1 Tip the flour, yeast and salt into a large bowl and make a well in the middle. Pour in most of the water and use your fingers to mix the flour and water together until combined. You're looking for a slightly wet, pillowy, workable dough – and it is much easier to gauge this with your hands than with a wooden spoon. Get messy! Add a splash more water if necessary, or balance it with flour.

2 Tip the dough out and knead for at least 10 minutes until smooth and elastic. This can also be done in a tabletop mixer with a dough hook, but where's the fun in that? Place the dough in a clean oiled bowl, cover with cling film and leave to rise until doubled in size.

3 Heat oven to 220°C/Gas mark 7. Knock back the dough by tipping it back out onto your flour-sprinkled worktop and pushing the air out (getting your hands dirty again). Mould the dough into a rugby ball shape and place it in the prepared loaf tin.

4 Cover with a clean tea towel and leave to prove for 30 minutes, then dust the top of the loaf with a little more flour and slash the top with a sharp knife if you want.

5 Bake the bread for 15 minutes, then reduce the heat to 190°C/Gas mark 5 and continue to bake for another 30 minutes until the loaf sounds hollow when removed from the tin and tapped on the base. One of the most pleasing sounds in the universe, surely? And, even if you have never made bread before, you will know when it sounds right, trust me.

6 Once you're confident with the basic dough, you can start adding to it. For all three variations, make the dough, but add 2 tbsp olive oil and only a pinch of salt. Whilst the dough is rising, cook the chilli for the chilli loaf, or onions for the onion version in olive oil until soft, then set aside.

When the dough has risen, knock it back, divide and flavour accordingly, and place in a muffin tray, mini loaf tin or swiss roll tin. Prove for 20 minutes, add your extra toppings, then bake until golden.

Violet and sultana scones

In the case of the scone, the less you mess about with it, the better it will rise. And that surely is the goal here – scones that rise like a dream, light as air. This means no flattening, no rolling, and almost no mixing. Keep those eager hands still! I've infused some violets in the milk which adds a gorgeously floral undertone. The purists amongst you are welcome to omit. The addition of seasonal jam or compôte for spreading, before a large spoonful of clotted cream is dolloped on top, is just the thing. An afternoon tea classic, worthily named. I've kept to standard quantities here, and just hope these live up to my mother's light-as-air versions.

300ml milk
20 violet flowers
450g self-raising flour
pinch salt
**100g butter, cold and
  cubed**
50g caster sugar
100g sultanas
**2 medium eggs, made up to
  300ml with violet milk**

TIP If I'm going to give you one order (or at least a strong request): eat them while they are warm!

MAKES
12 small or 8 large scones
PREP/COOK
20 minutes preparation
10 minutes cooking
YOU WILL NEED
**One large greased
baking tray**
Round scone cutter

1 Preheat the oven to 220°C/Gas mark 7, and grease a baking tray.

2 To infuse the milk, pour the milk into a small saucepan and add the violet flowers. Simmer for 3 minutes, then take off the heat and leave for an hour to absorb the flavours. Now sieve and discard the flowers.

3 In a large bowl, sift the flour and salt together. Add the butter and rub in with your fingertips until the mixture forms coarse grains throughout.

4 With a wooden spoon (or your floury, buttery hands), stir in the sugar and fruit until they are incorporated.

5 Mix the egg and milk together with a fork, then add to your bowl, keeping a little back for brushing the tops of the scones and giving them a golden glow.

6 Lightly flour a worktop and flop your scone mix out onto it. Bring it all together with your hands, keeping it loose and light. You aren't kneading it – try to keep as much air in the dough as you can. Either roll out lightly to a 1cm thickness, or simply pat the dough down and outwards with your fingertips until it is about a centimetre thick.

7 Using whatever size cutter you like, cut into rounds. Press together any trimmings and roll them out too.

8 Brush the tops with your reserved egg and milk mixture, and bake for about 10–15 minutes, depending on the size of your scones.

Cinnamon and chocolate stars

Sprinkled prettily over your tablecloth, these make the perfect pick-up-and-munch treat. They're also very useful as Christmas tree decorations, or cookie-break snacks. An all-purpose, buttery, crumbly biscuit then – simple, but all the better for it.

1 Preheat the oven to 160°C/Gas mark 3.

2 Sift the flours and cinnamon together into a large bowl.

3 In a separate bowl, mix the butter and sugar together with a wooden spoon until they are smooth. Add the egg and mix all together well.

4 Combine both the dry and wet ingredients, and mix into a firm dough.

5 Lightly flour the work surface, turn out the dough and knead it lightly until smooth, making sure not to overwork it, or your biscuits will be tough. You're really just making sure everything is fully incorporated and smooth, which you could always do in the food processor, though I would generally advocate the luddite way. Roll to a 5mm thickness.

6 Use a star cutter (or indeed any that take your fancy) to cut into shapes, and place on a greased oven tray. Bake for 10–15 minutes until light golden. Cool on a rack.

7 Melt your milk chocolate in a bowl set over a pan of gently bubbling water. Dip your stars in the chocolate, or drizzle it over them decoratively. Place back on the wire rack to harden.

150g self-raising flour
150g plain flour
2 tsp ground cinnamon
125g butter
100g sugar
1 egg, beaten
100g milk chocolate

MAKES
24 biscuits
PREP/COOK
20 minutes preparation
15 minutes cooking
YOU WILL NEED
A large greased
baking tray
Star-shaped cutter

Festival street party

I toyed with the idea of calling this section 'Bring Out the Bunting'. When we have big occasions to celebrate, we're growing rather fond of a bit of pomp and circumstance, a long holiday from work, and the feeling that we're just that little bit more community-minded these days.

But we shouldn't need excuses to get better acquainted with our neighbours. Every May the traffic outside my house grinds to a halt whilst the local pub holds their annual street party. The smell of the barbeque draws a crowd of seagulls, who perch on chimneypots surveying the scene regally, feigning disinterest until someone drops a scrap.

Probably more than any other section, the recipes that follow are British classics – a pork pie, beef Wellington, coronation chicken, a red, white and blue cake. But the British are a mongrel race, and if you want to play with your flavours and add some spices to your gravy and fruit to your pies, then I'd mischievously concur. I can't guarantee sunshine, especially at this time of year, but dust off your bunting, spread your dishes out on trestle tables and tuck in – they'll all feed a crowd.

FOR THE CAKE
350g plain flour
1 tbsp ras-el-hanout
1 tsp baking powder
1 tsp bicarbonate of soda
½ tsp salt
250ml full fat sour cream
1 tsp red food colouring
1 tsp distilled white wine
  vinegar
1 tsp vanilla extract
330g caster sugar
225g unsalted butter
2 large eggs
FOR THE MACAROONS
170g icing sugar
150g ground almonds
4 egg whites
80g caster sugar
red food colouring
150ml double cream
FOR THE FROSTING
500g cream cheese, room
  temperature
115g unsalted butter, room
  temperature
1 tbsp vanilla extract
400g icing sugar
fresh raspberries and
  blueberries to decorate

MAKES
A two-layer
23cm cake
PREP/COOK
30 minutes (cake),
40 minutes (macaroons)
preparation,
30 minutes (cake),
15 minutes (macaroons) cooking
YOU WILL NEED
Two 23cm loose-based cake
tins; two large baking
sheets; icing bag
and large plain
nozzle

Red, white and blue velvet cake with berries, mascarpone frosting and homemade macaroons

Possibly I got a little carried away here, but if you're going to go down, best it's in a blaze of patriotic cake-based glory: red for the velvet cake (which I couldn't resist spicing up with a little ras-el-hanout), white for the creamy mascarpone frosting, blue for the berries in a glistening heap atop this proud concoction. If you really want to over-egg the pudding, top with freshly baked macaroons.

1 For cake: Preheat the oven to 180°C/Gas mark 4.
2 Butter and flour the two cake tins.
3 Sift all the dry ingredients – the flour, ras-el-hanout, baking powder, bicarbonate of soda and salt – into a bowl.
4 Whisk the sour cream, food colouring, vinegar and vanilla in another bowl. Please don't economise with the food colouring – it really does need to be the good stuff, preferably paste, or your cake will go a dirty, browny pink instead of vibrant red. You need to be shocked by the colour of your liquid – don't forget it will be diluted when we add it to the rest of the ingredients.
5 Using an electric mixer, beat the sugar and butter until light and fluffy, then add the eggs one at a time, beating until well blended after each addition.
6 Now alternate mixing in the dry and wet ingredients in three or four batches – doing this gradually keeps the air in.
7 Divide your ruby batter between the prepared tins and place on the middle shelf of the preheated oven. Bake the cakes for 25-30 minutes until a skewer inserted into the centre comes out clean.
8 Cool your cakes (now slightly less vivid red) in tins on racks for 10 minutes, then turn them out onto racks and cool completely.
9 For macaroons: Preheat the oven to 180°C/Gas mark 4. (These can be made the day before.)

10 Line two large baking sheets with parchment – this is an unmissable step, as you don't want to be scraping your delicate concoctions from the trays with a fish slice (believe me, it has happened...). You can use a little of your macaroon mix to help fix the paper in place.

11 Sift together icing sugar and ground almonds. In a separate (unnaturally clean) bowl, whisk your egg whites until soft peaks form. Sprinkle over the caster sugar, and keep whisking until you get stiff peaks, adding your food colouring near the end. The mixture should be a vivid scarlet, which will fade slightly when the macaroons are baked. Fold the almonds and sugar mixture into your egg whites, beating until the mixture reaches ribbon stage (that is, a ribbon of mixture is distinctly visible, trailing beneath, when you lift your beaters).

12 Take your icing bag, with nozzle inserted, and spoon the macaroon mixture inside. Pipe small circles of mix onto the baking trays, evenly spaced and not touching. You can just use a teaspoon for this, but they will not be as neat. If you have spooned the macaroons, do make sure you leave them time to settle and spread to 4–5cm in diameter. Leave to stand for at least 15 minutes to form a skin, which results in a crispy shell when eating.

13 Bake for 10–12 minutes until they have formed a shiny round dome. There should still be a bit of moist chewiness to them underneath. Remove the trays from the oven and leave the macaroons to cool briefly – it helps not to try and prise them from the paper immediately. They can be delicate, and you might lose a few when you are loosening them, but these delicious mistakes are one of the great joys of being a cook.

14 Cool completely on a wire rack, and then sandwich the macaroons together with the cream, softly whipped.

15 For frosting and decoration: beat the cream cheese and butter in a large bowl until smooth. Beat in the vanilla. Add the sifted icing sugar and beat until smooth.

16 Sandwich the cakes together with frosting and a few berries, then spread the rest of the frosting round the sides and top. Use a palette knife to smooth or make swirls for a more rustic finish. Pile the remaining berries and the macaroons on top.

Goodwood herrings in a box

Goodwood herrings, in the traditional style, are delicious, but fiddly little customers. I've opened out the recipe a little, and roasted the fish with the tomatoes, herbs and breadcrumbs, instead of using them as stuffing. Stop there if you like (just make sure you add a chunk of crusty bread for juice-mopping duties). For a dish fit for a street party, I've boxed it in with shortcrust, and surrounded it with a savoury egg custard. You can roast your filling whilst blind-baking your pastry case to save time (and show off). If you want to quibble, I'll grudgingly admit OK, it's a quiche, but this sounded more British somehow!

375g ready-rolled shortcrust pastry sheet
6 herrings, gutted
6 large tomatoes
4 tbsp breadcrumbs
1 tbsp chopped flatleaf parsley
zest of 1 lemon
knob of butter
1 tsp each dried thyme and dill
salt and pepper
4 eggs (2 yolks, 2 whole)
200ml milk
100g natural yoghurt

SERVES
6
PREP/COOK
1 hour preparation (including 30 minutes resting)
1 hour 15 minutes cooking (including roasting herrings)
YOU WILL NEED
A 12cm x 36cm rectangular tart tin with removable base

1 Blind bake your pastry case: roll out your pastry slightly thinner than it is from the packet – the thickness of a £1 coin is ideal. Lay the sheet over your baking tin (sometimes it's easier to transport your pastry using your rolling pin rather than your warm hands). Gently, very gently, press into the corners of the tin. Using a rolled up ball of excess pastry is much better than fingers, as the object is to keep the pastry as cool as possible to minimise shrinkage. Trim the pastry, leaving an overhang of at least 1cm from your tin edge (shrinkage again), and prick gently all over with a fork. Now put it in the fridge for 30 minutes to settle.

2 Meanwhile preheat oven to 190°C/Gas mark 5.

3 Once you have taken the pastry out, line the pastry case with foil and fill with baking beans (or simply use dried pulses or rice). Bake in the preheated oven for 15 minutes, then take the foil and beans out, and put back in the oven for 5 minutes until the pastry turns a golden biscuit brown. Leave to cool slightly.

4 Meanwhile place your herrings, tomatoes, breadcrumbs, herbs, lemon and butter in a roasting tray, season well, and roast for 20–30 minutes until everything is cooked and fragrant. The fish flesh should come away in your fingers, and you can now remove it easily, being careful to feel for any tiny bones. Rip up the tomatoes roughly, and mix everything in the tray.

5 Place this mixture, neatly or messily, in your waiting tart case. Mix the eggs, milk, and yoghurt in a jug, and season once more. Pour around your fishy islands, making sure that some poke out of the eggy sea.

6 Bake in the oven for 30 minutes, until puffed and golden.

Coronation chicken and mango pies

Travelling round the Indian subcontinent, I fell (juicily) in love with mangoes. Their sheer abundance, the colour of their flesh bright like the marigolds used as religious offerings, juices running stickily no matter the eater's intentions of neat consumption. I've teamed them with an Anglo-Indian gem for our street party fiesta – coronation chicken – and put it all in a pie.

2 x 375g sheets ready-rolled shortcrust pastry
1 tsp turmeric
1 clove garlic, crushed
2cm piece fresh root ginger, grated
1 red chilli, de-seeded and finely chopped
1 additional tsp turmeric
2 tsp cumin
2 tsp coriander
150ml double cream
100ml stock
2 cooked chicken breasts, ripped into bite-size pieces
handful sultanas (golden if you can find them)
1 fresh mango
handful of fresh coriander
1 egg yolk

1 Heat your oven to 190°C/Gas mark 5.

2 Grease the bun trays with butter or oil, for ease of slipping the little pies out later.

3 Sprinkle your pastry with the first teaspoon of turmeric, then roll out to the thickness of a pound coin, making sure the spice permeates the pastry throughout.

4 Use a cup or mug to cut circles of pastry and line the bun trays – you should have plenty to make 24. Keep the leftover trimmings for your pie pastry decoration toppings.

5 Heat a heavy-bottomed, deep sauté pan and add the garlic, ginger and chilli. Fry for a couple of minutes, then add the spices.

6 When you can smell them, add the double cream and stock and bubble until reduced by half.

7 Add your chicken, sultanas, mango and coriander and stir until heated through. Taste for seasoning.

8 Using a large spoon, pile the mixture into the pastry cases, and press down so they are generously filled, without gaps.

9 Cut your leftover pastry into whatever shapes you like, and top your little pies. We aren't looking for full coverage here – seeing glimpses of pie filling peeking out is very attractive. Brush with egg wash and bake for 15 minutes until golden.

TIP If you can't get hold of fresh mango, please don't substitute, willy nilly, any fresh fruit. The mango goes particularly well with Indian spices. It can be substituted for mango chutney in times of storecupboard emergency – a teaspoon in each pie.

MAKES
24 6cm pies
PREP/COOK
35 minutes preparation
15 minutes cooking
YOU WILL NEED
Two shallow 12-hole bun trays,
and pastry cutters (stars
and crowns work well)

Beef Wellington

This is one that needs no introduction. The best British beef encased in a velvety mushroom coating, and crackly, buttery pastry. Street party, Christmas dinner, wedding – the Wellington is king. If you want to feed a crowd, and if you want to be opening your thank-you letters for the next few weeks, take a little time and effort over this great British institution, and triumph.

1kg beef fillet, the best quality you can find

olive oil

250g mixed mushrooms – portobello, shi-itake, chestnut are all fine

3 tbsp butter

2 sprigs fresh rosemary or thyme

100ml stock or wine

Parma ham or prosciutto for wrapping the fillet – you will probably need 10–12 slices, depending on their size

500g block puff pastry

1 egg, beaten, for brushing

1 Preheat the oven to 220°C/Gas mark 7.

2 When the oven is good and hot (this is a large piece of meat you're roasting quickly), place your beef on a roasting tray, brush it with oil and grind some seasoning all over, which you can rub in a little with your fingertips. Roast it for 15 minutes for medium to rare or 20 minutes for medium (which will still have a little pink in the middle). Take it out of the oven and let it cool down; this will take about 15 minutes or so.

3 Whilst your meat is cooling, you can get on with making the mushroom coating that will encase the meat and keep it moist and flavoursome, which is known in cheffy parlance as a duxelles. Chop the mushrooms as finely as you can without them breaking down completely and looking like a brown sludge.

4 Heat a couple of tablespoons of oil and the 3 tablespoons of butter in a pan and let everything melt and bubble. Add your mushrooms and fry with the fresh herbs – your kitchen will smell fantastic at this point! The mushrooms won't take long to cook as they are so small – it should take less than 10 minutes for them all to soften.

5 Pour over the stock or wine, and stir often until all the liquid is absorbed. You will be patting this round the meat, so you don't want everything too runny. The easiest way of telling if it is at the right consistency is if the end of a spoon dragged through the middle leaves a furrow, and the base of the pan stays visible. Remove the pan from the heat, and take the herbs out.

6 Now comes the slightly technical bit: the instructions may sound complicated, but all you are really doing is rolling the beef up in a coating of mushrooms, then encasing it in ham. You need something to roll it all together with, so take two pieces of cling film and lay them side by side. Lay the slices of ham onto the cling film, doubling them from end to end so you have enough surface area to wrap around the meat. Spoon half

SERVES
10–12
PREP/COOK
50 minutes preparation plus
15 minutes frying, 35 minutes
roasting and 15 minutes
standing
YOU WILL NEED
One large greased
baking tray

of your duxelles (it should be thick and pâté-like) evenly onto the ham, then place your fillet on it. Now spread the rest of your duxelles over the top of the fillet, covering all the meat. Draw up the edges of the cling film and roll everything into a cigar shape, twisting as tightly as you can. Refrigerate while you get the pastry sorted.

7 Roll the pastry out on a lightly floured worktop. You want two rectangles here, both the same length (slightly longer than your beef fillet), but different widths. One will sit under the fillet, so needs to be the same width as it, plus borders for sealing. The other needs to be larger, as it will wrap around the fillet. Measure the fillet by placing the palm of your hand over it, and roll out your second rectangle with that much extra width.

8 Unravel your fillet from its cling film wrapper, and place it in the centre of the smaller sheet of pastry. Brush the edges of the pastry with egg, which will act as your sealant when you press the larger sheet of pastry on it. Using a rolling pin, drape or, using your hands if you are feeling very dextrous, place the larger sheet of pastry over the fillet. Make sure you smooth down the sides closely with your hands, to avoid any air pockets.

9 Seal the pastry borders with fork tines, and glaze all over. Decorate with pastry trimmings or as you like. You can chill your Wellington in the fridge for up to 24 hours prior to baking. It's good to give it at least 30 minutes to ensure that the pastry doesn't shrink too much.

10 While your Wellington is chilling, preheat the oven to 200°C/ Gas mark 6. Cook until golden and crisp, and the beef is done to your liking: 20–25 for medium rare, 30 minutes for medium. Stand for about 15 minutes or so before serving, to ensure that the meat is juicy.

25g butter

1 small leek, chopped

3 sticks celery, chopped

1 onion, chopped

2 cloves garlic, chopped

12 'ready to eat' apricots

2 eating apples, peeled, cored and chopped

125ml cider

grated rind of a lemon

2 tbsp chopped fresh sage

salt and pepper to taste

1 tsp ground mace

350g good quality sausage meat

150g tangy hard cheese, e.g. Sussex Charmer

100g fresh breadcrumbs

600g shortcrust pastry

1 egg, beaten, for glazing

MAKES
One 20cm pie (serves 8–10)
PREP/COOK
25 minutes preparation
30 minutes cooking
YOU WILL NEED
One 20cm springform cake pan

Raised Sussex pork and cheese pie

A raised pie simply means one in which you can cram (greedily) twice the filling of a pie of normal (now think diminutive) stature. If you consider pastry and filling in terms of gluttony, rather than worrying about holes and collapse, you will soon be layering with the best of them.

1 Preheat the oven to 200°C/Gas mark 6.

2 Melt the butter in a saucepan, and add the leek, celery and onion, cooking and burnishing them for 2 minutes, before adding the garlic, apricots and apple. Cook the whole fruity, fragrant mixture for another couple of minutes, making sure everything is starting to soften.

3 Pour in the cider, lemon rind, sage, seasoning and mace, and mix everything up, whilst the liquid bubbles. Give it all a good simmer for at least 10 minutes, then set aside to cool.

4 Take a large mixing bowl, then add the sausage meat, cheese, breadcrumbs and all your lovely cooked ingredients. With a large wooden spoon, make sure everything is thoroughly mixed together, as this will ensure even distribution throughout the filling (and, more importantly, everyone getting a mouthful of meat, fruit, spice, cheese and vegetables when it is sliced!).

5 Now, to the pastry. Divide into three equal portions. Grease and flour the cake tin, which will provide much-needed support to the tallish sides of this pie. Roll out one portion of pastry into a circle to line the base of the tin, and another into a wide strip for the sides, which you can secure to the base with beaten egg. You're probably looking at about 10cm high sides.

6 Fill the tin with the pork and cheese mixture, then roll out the third portion of pastry to make a lid, which you can also secure with beaten egg to the sides. Use any trimmings of pastry to make a design of your choosing on the top – get as creative as you like, or leave it plain.

7 Glaze the top of the pie with beaten egg, place in the centre of the oven and cook for 30 minutes. Reduce to 160°C/Gas mark 3 and cook for another 40 minutes until browned and the filling completely cooked through. You can tell by poking the pie with a metal skewer and then touching it carefully – it should be hot to touch.

8 Remove the pie from the oven and allow to cool before easing it out of its tin.

Rosewater cheesecake

This is no ordinary cheesecake – it is encased in buttery shortcrust, as was traditionally the way with British cheesecakes, so is more of a cheesecake tart really. White chocolate, orange flower water and pistachios are all combined to give a light and perfumed centre. This recipe, in all its aromatic, glistening glory, will serve a crowd, and is incredibly easy to prepare in advance. If you'd like to (and I'd like you to), frosted rose petals are an ethereal and worthy accompaniment, and echo the rose-scent in the pastry.

1 Preheat the oven to 200°C/Gas mark 6.

2 Rub the butter into the flour with your fingertips until large sandy breadcrumbs are formed. Mix your egg yolk, sugar and rosewater together, and add to the dry ingredients until you have a paste. With lightly floured hands, on a lightly floured surface, roll out, and use to line a deep flan or springform tin. The pastry will probably be very short, and difficult to work with, as is the wont of sweet shortcrust. Don't worry too much, as any holes can be patched up with extra pastry trimmings.

3 For the filling, whip the cream until thick, and in a separate bowl beat the cream cheese with the sugar. Add the sugary cheese to the cream and beat. In another small bowl, add the orange flower water to the egg yolks, and add the now fragrant yolks to your cream mixture.

4 Finally, beat the egg whites until stiff and holding their shape, and with a large metal spoon fold them into the mixture, together with the chopped white chocolate and pistachios.

5 Fill your waiting pastry case with the mixture, and smooth the top with a spatula. Bake for 10 minutes at 200°C/Gas mark 6, then reduce the oven to 150°C/Gas mark 2 and continue baking until the mixture is risen and set – about 1 hour, but do keep checking. Occasionally the filling will crack, but once out of the oven, baked cheesecakes usually settle down, and with some artful decorating, no one will notice.

6 Once the cheesecake is completely cooled you can sprinkle with ground pistachios and rose petals (if using).

TIP To frost rose petals, simply coat organic petals in egg white (I usually find a pastry brush works rather well here) and then coat in icing sugar. Voilà – a frosty morning dew.

PASTRY
230g plain flour
115g butter, cold and cubed
1 egg yolk
30g caster sugar
1 tsp rosewater

FILLING
300ml double cream
2 x 200g packs cream cheese
120g caster sugar
4 eggs, separated
2 tbsp orange flower water
100g white chocolate
50g pistachios, chopped

FOR DECORATION
Finely chopped pistachios and (optional) frosted rose petals

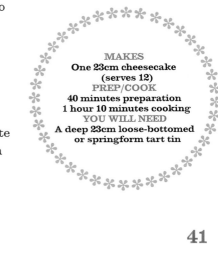

MAKES
One 23cm cheesecake
(serves 12)
PREP/COOK
40 minutes preparation
1 hour 10 minutes cooking
YOU WILL NEED
A deep 23cm loose-bottomed
or springform tart tin

20-30 minute meals
'I don't have time to cook.'

When I look around, I see a blur, I hear a million alarm clocks going off. We're all over-committed, time-poor – a collection of white rabbits, pocket watches ticking, all late, late, for very important dates. Brighton Festival is in full swing in the Spring, the city is alive, bustling, and most of all, busy.

These recipes are the best of both worlds then: delicious, nutritious, and none of them take longer than **30** minutes to get to your plate. Savoury muffins, pies, pasties – vary the fillings as you like.
You're homemaker, you're bounteous creator of plenty, and you're also gaining serious brownie points for 'slaving over a hot stove for hours' (ahem – who needs to know?). Win win.

Tomato, High Weald ricotta and herb tart

If you are lucky enough to be able to find a glorious local ricotta like I did, all the better. With a dish so marvellously short on ingredients, flavour and freshness are paramount.

Using puff pastry as a blank canvas, feel free to experiment with toppings – mushrooms, pancetta and Gruyère perhaps, or cooked leeks, chicken and tarragon – but there is something so vibrant about this combination that it captures all the flavours of the simple, fresh ingredients in a few light-filled minutes. After this picture was taken, the tart was devoured in less than a minute, which should tell you all you need to know.

375g sheet ready-rolled puff pastry
250g High Weald ricotta (or similar)
2 eggs, beaten
50g strong hard cheese, grated
seasoning to taste
a few sprigs of marjoram or oregano – finely shredded (or kept whole for a more rustic look)
5 ripe tomatoes, halved
olive oil for drizzling

1 Preheat the oven to 180°C/Gas mark 4.

2 With the point of a knife draw a border 2.5-cm in from the outer edge of the pastry sheet, being careful not to pierce the pastry all the way through. It should now look like a blank picture frame. And now to your canvas...prick all around the inside of the frame with a fork, which should ensure that this part of the pastry will not rise.

3 Mix together the ricotta, eggs and hard cheese, and season well. Spread generously across your picture canvas, making sure you leave the frame clear.

4 If you want to, shred up the soft fresh herbs as finely as you like. Your whole kitchen will now smell of summer. Scatter the herbs across the cheese layer.

5 Slice or halve your tomatoes, and place on top of the cheese filling. Drizzle with oil and season the tomatoes.

6 Bake for 20 minutes, take out of the oven, stand back to admire your handiwork, and devour at will.

SERVES
6
PREP/COOK
10 minutes preparation
20 minutes cooking time
YOU WILL NEED
One large greased baking sheet

Ham hock and pea pies

Very quick, but oh, so good. I'm rather proud of these little beauties because they scream of long hours in the kitchen, slow simmering on the stove, comfort food that has taken days, nay generations, to be whittled down to its warming, stomach-coating essence; when, in fact, some bought ham hock, peas and crème fraîche are married in a matter of minutes, topped with puff pastry and baked. I won't tell if you don't.

**375g sheet ready-rolled
  puff pastry**
1 tbsp butter
1 big onion, chopped finely
**bunch of sage, leaves
  shredded**
2 cloves garlic, crushed
2 tbsp cider vinegar
**1 Sussex (or any eating)
  apple, chopped roughly**
**350g pack of cooked
  ham hock**
splash of white wine
200ml full fat crème fraîche
1 tsp mustard powder
salt and pepper to taste
handful of frozen peas
milk, for brushing pastry

1 Preheat the oven to 200°C/Gas mark 6.

2 Use your ramekins to cut four equal circles out of the puff pastry sheet, and set aside.

3 Heat the butter in a heavy-based high-sided frying pan and, when it starts to foam, add the onion and cook gently until translucent and shiny. Add the sage and garlic to the pan, and gently fry until it is all soft and aromatic.

4 Turn the heat up and add the cider vinegar – cook briefly until the liquid bubbles and reduces right down.

5 Add all the rest of the ingredients (yes, this really is that easy) and stir until warmed through and simmering. Remove the pan from the heat.

6 Divide your pie filling between four ramekin dishes, making sure that each has roughly equal quantities of ham, vegetables and creamy sauce. Brush the rim of your ramekins with a little milk, and place the circles of pastry over the top, brushing them in their turn with milk. Pierce the middle of the pastry with the tip of a knife, to let the steam out.

7 Bake for 20 minutes until the pastry is golden and risen, and the filling piping hot.

MAKES
4 individual pies
PREP/COOK
10 minutes preparation
20 minutes cooking time
YOU WILL NEED
Four greased individual pie
dishes or ramekins

Red onion and Sussex Slipcote muffins

Having spent a lot of time in New Zealand, I have become rather partial to a muffin. Relatively unknown in the UK, these savoury versions are a super-fast meal in one. You can chuck whatever you like in with the basic muffin mix (and indeed, the Kiwis do, in a sometimes rather cavalier, but generally delicious manner) – just keep your proportions right. I have used a local Sussex goat's cheese, and it provides strong, creamy intensity.

If I can make one caveat: please do eat these warm. Even if just dinged for a few seconds in a microwave, it brings them back to oozing, soft, squishable life, and they lose any firmness they may have acquired since baking.

½ **red onion, chopped**
olive oil
100g log of Sussex Slipcote goat's cheese, or equivalent, chopped or crumbled
small bunch of marjoram, thyme or rosemary, chopped
½ **tsp black pepper**
500g plain flour
2 tbsp baking powder
salt
3 large eggs
450ml milk

1 Preheat the oven to 200°C/Gas mark 6.

2 Meanwhile, fry the onion in olive oil until soft. Once the onions have cooled, mix in the goat's cheese, herbs (saving a small amount for later) and a grinding of black pepper.

3 Sift the flour, baking powder and salt together in a large bowl. Beat two of the eggs into the milk (you will be using the third for brushing over the top of the muffins), and then pour this eggy milk into the flour. Stir two or three times until the mixture is starting to come together, then add the onion mixture. Mix with a large metal spoon with the minimum movements to roughly ripple the filling through – it's really important not to overmix here, or the muffins will be heavy and dense. It's absolutely fine, and indeed desirable, to still be able to see some small pockets of flour.

4 Spoon your muffin mixture into the waiting tins, piling much higher than you would a cake: they do rise nicely, but they stick together in a more dense fashion than a sponge would, so be fearless.

5 Sprinkle a few fresh herbs on top of each muffin, then beat the other egg and brush the muffin tops.

6 Bake for 20 minutes (normal sized) to 30 minutes (Texas) until risen and golden. Try to eat immediately, whilst still warm.

TIP Made tiny, these are wonderful canapés, which can be frozen and reheated when your guests arrive. Simply use two mini muffin trays.

MAKES
12 muffins or 6 Texas-size muffins
PREP/COOK
15 minutes preparation
15 minutes cooking time
YOU WILL NEED
One 12-hole muffin tray, or one 6-hole Texas muffin tray

Local fish pies

I bought my fish for these pies from a fishmonger on the beach, 10 minutes' walk from my house. I honestly believe the pies taste better, not because the fishmonger used to be a pirate and still sports a gold tooth, but because I bought local and sustainably caught fish.

Without waving the worthiness wand, or becoming too strident, I would advise using whatever's available to you nearby. We live on an island – glory in the treasures that surround us, and pop some of them into a golden, crumb-encrusted, creamy pie.

400g skinless white fish fillet

400g skinless smoked fish fillet

500ml full-fat milk

1 small onion, quartered

4 cloves

2 bay leaves

small bunch of parsley, leaves only, chopped

150g crème fraîche

pinch of freshly grated nutmeg

200g breadcrumbs

50g Cheddar, grated

1 Preheat the oven to 200°C/Gas mark 6.

2 Start by poaching the fish: put the fillets in a large saucepan and pour the milk over the top. Stud each onion quarter with a clove, then add to the milk, along with the bay leaves, which will all add delicate flavour to the fish.

3 Turn the heat up and bring the milk just to the boil – you will see a few small bubbles. Now reduce the heat, because you want to gently poach, not fiercely boil, and simmer for 8 minutes. Lift the fish onto a plate, flake into large pieces, and place in four individual pie dishes or ramekins. Now scatter over the chopped parsley, reserving a little for later.

4 Make the sauce: mix the crème fraîche and nutmeg together (shhh – it'll taste just as good as a white sauce, in considerably less time). Season with salt and pepper, then spoon over the fishy pieces in their ramekins.

5 Mix the breadcrumbs with the cheese and the remainder of the chopped parsley, and sprinkle over the pies.

6 Bake for 20 minutes until golden and crisp on top, and warm and melting within.

MAKES
4 pies
PREP/COOK
1 hour (including poaching the fish) preparation
20 minutes cooking
YOU WILL NEED
4 greased ramekins or ovenproof dishes

Raspberry sour cream squares

These moist, tangy squares will do just as well as either pudding, warmly plated, or cooled, hardened lunchtime delight. The recipe is simplicity itself – use whatever fruit you have a glut of, and vary the nuts accordingly – apple and walnut, pear and hazelnut, rhubarb and pecan all work well. Don't be tempted to substitute the sour cream though – the sharpness cuts through the rich, dark sugariness and gives a little palette-cleansing relief. I doubt your trayful will make it into the next day.

200g butter
200g caster sugar
2 tbsp spice (cinnamon works well with apples, ginger with rhubarb)
200g hazelnuts
450g light brown sugar
2 eggs
450g plain flour
2 tsp bicarbonate of soda
pinch of salt
450ml sour cream
300g seasonal fruit – e.g. blackberries, gooseberries, stewed rhubarb, apple

1 Heat the oven to 180°C/Gas mark 4, and line the tin with baking parchment.

2 For the topping: melt 1 tablespoon of the butter, and stir into the sugar with the spice and nuts. This will make your gorgeously crunchy traybake topping later, so don't scrimp. Set aside.

3 With an electric hand whisk, cream together the remainder of the butter and sugar for a couple of minutes until paler in colour and fuller in volume. Add the eggs, and beat thoroughly for another minute or so until wholly incorporated.

4 With a large metal spoon, stir in the flour, bicarbonate of soda, salt and sour cream. Finally, stir in the fruit so it studs the entire mixture with pockets of colour.

5 Pour your batter into the lined tin and sprinkle generously with the topping mixture.

6 Bake for 25 minutes until a skewer inserted in the centre comes out clean.

MAKES
16 squares
PREP/COOK
10 minutes preparation
25 minutes cooking
YOU WILL NEED
A 33 x 23cm tin, greased and lined with baking parchment

Coconut and cardamom macaroons

No, we aren't talking French, fashionable, featherweight pâtisserie – we're talking British, chewy, flaky, smoothg-bottomed clouds of densely textured coconut flakes.

You do not need to be light of touch here – these are easy peasy. The cardamom is just a hint really, a sweet background tone, but it adds an aromatic note that will set your biscuits apart.

1 Preheat the oven to 170°C/Gas mark 3.

2 In a clean bowl, and with an electric beater (unless you're looking for a bicep work-out of course, in which case feel free to do it by hand), beat the egg whites until foaming. Add the cream of tartar and carry on until soft peaks are formed that gently, slowly deflate when you lift the whisk out.

3 Now add the sugar very, very gradually, a tablespoon at a time as if you are making meringue. Feel the mix between two fingertips – you should beat until you can no longer feel the grain between your fingers.

4 Now fold in the almonds, cardamom, salt and coconut, which should make your mixture clumpy and sticky.

5 You can either spoon large rounds of your macaroon mixture onto the baking tray, or use your hands to really clump them together. They look rather lovely with a bit of height, but flattish is fine too.

6 Cook for 20 minutes or so, until they're starting to take on a little colour. You still want off-white and elegant though, so be careful you don't burn the edges.

4 egg whites
½ tsp cream of tartar
150g caster sugar
50g ground almonds
1 tsp crushed cardamom
pinch of salt
400g shredded coconut

MAKES
10 macaroons
PREP/COOK
10 minutes preparation
20 minutes cooking
YOU WILL NEED
A large greased
baking tray

Summer

Sunshine picnic

Glorious garden party

I'm getting married in the morning!

Notoriously temperamental, fluctuating between
glorious, light-filled days, and rain-soaked disappointment.
Make the most of it: take your summertime
food outside, and celebrate.

'On the downs, the beach, at the races, or wherever…'

Sunshine picnic

There is something of the treasure chest about the picnic hamper, even if you have packed it yourself: somehow the food you have prepared takes on a different life, a different constitution when mixed with a sprinkling of pollen, the smell of ozone, and (usually) a generous helping of wasps.

Picnics as a child consisted of sticks of fresh celery dipped into salt, which had a crunch and a crack they always disappointingly lacked at home. Hard-boiled eggs dipped into the same, infinite supply of salt were glistening, velvety prizes. The simplest of treats then, but unimprovable.

I took inspiration from the fields, the hedgerows, the riverbank for these recipes – look around you, at what you're putting your picnic rug on – wild garlic goes a treat with the salmon en croute. Pluck a courgette flower – they look pretty as a picture atop a savoury muffin, or use rosemary to flavour your loaf cake. Go wild in the country!

Beetroot tarts

I know beetroot has become horribly trendy in recent years, but the sweet, earthy flavour and gaudy colour are a winning combination that deserves further investigation. I like to roast the dark roots and slice into a risen, puffed tart case, already lined with cooling sour cream. Stack them between layers of greaseproof paper – they are surprisingly robust and will travel well.

350g small to medium beets
200g ready-rolled puff pastry
zest of 1 orange
garlic clove
a pinch of sea salt
150ml sour cream
2 tbsp olive oil
3 tbsp mayonnaise
2 tbsp chives, snipped

1 Preheat the oven to 200°C/Gas mark 6.

2 Prepare your beets: rub any dirt from the skin and top and tail them (for the faint of heart who don't want to look like Lady Macbeth, rubber gloves are fine here). Roast in 1tbsp oil and sea salt for 20–30 minutes until soft, then slice thickly.

3 Using a small bowl, upturned, cut 15cm circles in your pastry. With the point of a knife draw a border 1cm in from the outer edge, to make a frame, being careful not to pierce the pastry all the way through. Use the tines of a fork to pierce the pastry inside the frame, which should ensure that this part of the pastry will not rise.

4 Bake your empty tart cases in the oven for 10 minutes until puffed and golden. Leave to cool.

5 In a bowl, mix the orange zest, garlic, salt, sour cream and 1 tbsp olive oil until you have a thick, pourable liquid. Add mayonnaise to taste – start with a single tablespoon, and work your way up. Spread the filling thickly inside the cooled tart cases, then top with sliced beetroot and chives.

MAKES
4 tarts
PREP/COOK
15 minutes preparation
40 minutes cooking
YOU WILL NEED
A large greased baking tray

Salmon en croûte with wild garlic cream

This is serious squeal of delight, star-of-the-show stuff. The glorification of the coral fish in its pastry casing, the rich buttery sauce seeping as you slice, the sweet and sour spiciness of the stem ginger and dried fruit. This is probably not paper plate, casual style picnic fare, but the sort when you go all out to impress: wicker hamper, linen tablecloth and glasses would make appropriate accessories.

1kg wild salmon fillet
1 heaped tbsp currants
4 mejdool dates, finely chopped
4 dried apricots, finely chopped
2 knobs stem ginger, finely chopped
70g butter
500g block shortcrust pastry
2 egg yolks
FOR THE SAUCE
300ml single cream
2 egg yolks
2 tsp French mustard
2 tsp plain flour
60g butter
½ lemon
¼ onion, finely chopped
small bunch wild garlic

SERVES
10
PREP/COOK
20 minutes preparation
45 minutes cooking
YOU WILL NEED
A large greased
baking tray

1 Preheat the oven to 200°C/Gas mark 6. Season the fish on both sides and, with a pair of tweezers, remove any small bones that may be lurking. You can lightly stroke the surface of the fish with your fingers to feel for these bones. Tweezer them, pulling with the grain of the fish, not against, then the hole won't be visible. Now cut the fish into two equal pieces.

2 Mix the dried fruits, ginger and butter together, and pour in a little of the liquid from the ginger jar to loosen. This is probably easier with your hands, and you're aiming for a rustic paste-like texture. Use those food-covered hands to smear the mix all over all sides of the fish, thickly. This will melt down into a spiced oil that should permeate throughout the fish, so it is important to get this step right.

3 Roll out your pastry so it is about the thickness of a £1 coin, and cut into two pieces, one slightly larger than the other (say, 15cm x 35cm and 25cm x 35cm).

4 Lay one fillet of fish on the smaller piece of pastry, making sure there is a border of pastry around the edge of the fillet. Brush this border with egg yolk, then lay your second piece of fish on top of the first. Gently drape the larger piece of pastry over all, and press the pastry edges together to seal, making sure there are no gaps in the parcel.

5 Brush all over with egg yolk and bake for 30–40 minutes until golden and crisp on the outside. Cooking times vary depending on the thickness of your fillets – if you have two thick fillets you will need longer. A skewer inserted into the centre should come out feeling warm to the touch.

6 For the sauce: whizz all of the sauce ingredients together in a blender until it is a smooth consistency. Pour into a small saucepan and heat, very gently, for a few minutes until the sauce simmers and thickens. Drizzle over each portion.

Duddleswell and pickle pasties

The classic cheese and pickle sandwich in another form – a cunning solution to the whole soggy bread scenario. Duddleswell is a crumbly Sussex cheese that clumps prettily inside the pasty filling, but Wensleydale or Cheshire will do just as well. Bill's chutney is one that Brightonians know very well, coming as it does from the wonderful greengrocer of that name. Vary your chutney according to your mood: chilli jam and piccalilli also work extremely well.

olive oil
2 large onions, finely chopped
1 tbsp chopped fresh thyme
150g thick slices of ham on the bone, diced (optional – leave out for a veggie version)
100g grated Duddleswell cheese (or similar)
2 tbsp Bill's chutney (or any chutney of your choice)
freshly ground pepper
1 egg
60ml milk
500g block puff pastry

1 Preheat the oven to 200°C/Gas mark 6.
2 Heat a little oil in a heavy-bottomed pan and gently fry the onions and thyme until softened and golden, stirring now and again.
3 Turn off the heat and add the ham, cheese, chutney and a little ground pepper. Stir well and taste for seasoning.
4 Mix together the egg and milk to make an egg wash.
5 Roll out four large rounds of puff pastry, using an upturned sideplate as a guide, brushing the edges with egg wash.
6 Clump some mixture along the centre of each pastry round, slightly higher in the middle, and bring up the pastry. Seal and crimp the edges. Then brush all over with egg wash.
7 Cook in the oven for about 20 minutes until golden.

MAKES
4 pasties
PREP/COOK
25 minutes preparation
20 minutes cooking time
YOU WILL NEED
One large greased
baking tray

Courgette flower frittatas

A frittata made miniature for picnic consumption – simply line your muffin trays with parchment for a portable snack. A courgette blossom is baked atop a savoury eggy mouthful, alive with the flavours of the Med. The courgette flower is woefully under-used on our shores, despite being a favourite in Italian kitchens. Courgettes will grow quite happily in pots or window boxes, or failing that, a local farmers' market should be able to provide you with blossoms during their summer season.

1 Preheat the oven to 180°C/Gas mark 4, and line the muffin tins with parchment or greaseproof paper, scrunched roughly so it will fit. You're aiming for a sort of rustic carrying case.
2 In a large bowl, beat the eggs with lots of pepper. Now crumble the feta in, which should also bring enough saltiness to the frittatas that we don't need to add more. Mix the basil in and make sure everything is thoroughly incorporated – this will be the body of your frittata.
3 Mix in the tomatoes, olives and peppers, and give it a brief stir with a wooden spoon – it doesn't really matter if the filling is uneven or higgledy piggledy when you pour it into your muffin trays – this is part of the charm. Just make sure that they are basically level, and you will then have evenly sized frittatas.
4 Top each frittata with a courgette flower and bake in the oven for about 15 minutes until they are set and golden and puffed. They will shrink back slightly when you take them out of the oven to cool.

TIP Any edible squash blossoms would look lovely here, and indeed you can replace the tomatoes with cooked sausage, or lardons for a non-vegetarian version.

6 eggs
freshly ground black pepper
100g feta cheese, crumbled
small handful of basil leaves, torn up small
100g sunblush tomatoes
100g olives
100g roasted peppers, from a jar
12 courgette flowers

MAKES
12 mini frittatas
PREP/COOK
20 minutes preparation
15 minutes cooking time
YOU WILL NEED
A 12-hole muffin tray

Brighton Rock cake

I knew for a long time I wanted to make a Brighton Rock cake, but it had always been a bit of wordplay that didn't translate to the kitchen. In the end it was one of those ideas that I woke up with, coming to me in the night from who knows what inspiring source…that Jungian collective cooks' unconscious maybe. A cake in the shape of a stick of rock – a roulade if you like, with a sweet billowing meringue batter, fresh cream and berries, and, to continue the theme, tiny broken up pieces of rock inside and sprinkled merrily on top. It's just as ridiculous and wonderful as I wanted it to be.

1 stick of rock

handful of caster sugar –
 this doesn't have to
 be exact

5 egg whites

150g caster sugar

2 tsp cornflour

284ml carton double cream

250g red berries (match
 your fruit colour to your
 rock – blueberries with
 blue, kiwis with
 green, etc.)

SERVES
6–8
PREP/COOK
35 minutes preparation
1 hour cooking time
YOU WILL NEED
A 33cm x 28cm
Swiss roll tin

1 Blitz the rock and the handful of sugar in a food processor until only a few larger pieces remain (so your guests can recognise its origin), then sprinkle thickly all over a sheet of greaseproof paper about the same size as your Swiss roll tin.

2 Heat oven to 150°C/Gas mark 2 and line the Swiss roll tin with baking paper, making sure there is a 5cm overhang on all edges.

3 Whisk the egg whites until stiff (if you are planning on doing this by hand, it will take about 10 minutes), then gradually whisk in 150g caster sugar, until the meringue is stiff and glossy and the grain of the sugar has been absorbed. Whisk in the cornflour and give the whole thing another whizz for a couple of minutes until it's pillowy, shiny and holds stiff peaks.

4 Pour the meringue into the prepared Swiss roll tin and spread using a palette knife or spatula. Cook for 1 hour (turn your oven down if it starts to colour) and cool in the tin.

5 Now comes the fun part: flip the tin upside down onto the rock-sprinkled greaseproof – a quick firm action is required here. The baking paper can now be peeled, gently, from the underside (now the top side) of the meringue.

6 Whip the cream into soft peaks, being careful not to over-whip, and spread thickly over the meringue with the pallet knife, leaving a border on the long side furthest away from you.

7 Scatter the red berries over the cream, then roll up the roulade as neatly or as messily as your meringue allows. Use the border to start you off, and try to roll the meringue reasonably tightly initially. Cracks and unevenness really don't matter here - just patch them up with rock sugar.

Chorizo and spring onion muffins

A visit to a hotel buffet in Yosemite National Park saw me returning to the food table on repeated occasions, determined to try absolutely everything laid out there. It was only when they changed the breakfast table to the lunch spread that I admitted defeat, grudgingly. An elderly gentleman standing nearby saw my expression, took pity on my foodie desire to consume everything in sight, and took me to one side, whispering some sage advice in my ear: 'Muffins'll travel'. Wrapped in a napkin, indeed they did that day, and have on many days since...the perfect picnic food.

More from the muffin stable then, and this is not for the faint hearted, but for those who like their flavours strong and full. The piquancy of the chorizo contrasts with the sharp thrust of the spring onions, which can be pre-fried for a milder version.

300g self-raising flour
200g Manchego cheese, cubed
6 spring onions, chopped
200g chorizo, finely chopped
salt and pepper
2 eggs plus 1 egg for brushing
1 cup buttermilk
80g butter, melted and cooled

1 Preheat the oven to 180°C/Gas mark 4 and lightly grease a muffin tray.

2 Mix the flour, Manchego, spring onions, chorizo and seasoning in a bowl until the whole mix is rippled through with red, white and green – olé!

3 Whisk two eggs and the buttermilk together, and add the melted cooled butter (beware: if it is still hot, you're going to get scrambled eggs).

4 Pour the wet ingredients into the floury mix and very lightly mix until just combined.

5 Spoon the batter into the prepared baking tray, piling quite high to get those enviable muffin tops, and brush all over with the extra egg.

6 Bake for 15–20 minutes until golden, risen and springy to the touch. Turn out onto a wire rack to cool.

TIP *Muffin mantra muffin mantra:* do not overmix or you will have muffins like little lead balloons! Small floury pockets are absolutely fine.

MAKES
6 Texas muffins
PREP/COOK
20 minutes preparation
15-20 minutes cooking
YOU WILL NEED
One Texas muffin tray, or a 12-hole muffin tray

Cocoa Loco gingerbread bars with chilli and crystallised ginger

This really is easy peasy – just melt everything together and give it a good stir. These are rich, midnight-dark and delicious and, if you can find a wonderful local chocolatier (as I did) to provide your chocolate, all the better. You may think that gingerbread is unimprovable, but this recipe keeps that toffee-like, chewy texture, and adds depth – a base note of cocoa. Add in chunks of chocolate and crystallised ginger, plus a chilli hotness, and we have a fiery gingerbread happy to be served alongside the rest of your picnic feast.

1 Preheat the oven to 160°C/Gas mark 3.

2 Line your baking tray with baking parchment, making a little extra height with the parchment, as the gingerbread is about 5–6cm deep.

3 Pour your syrup and treacle into a large heavy-based pan. This can be quite messy. I advise against measuring, though you can weigh the jars to make sure you get pretty much the right amount, but it is also easy to do by sight. Measuring both these substances will result in far more sticking to your spoon or measuring jug than actually going into the gingerbread. Inexactness is fine!

4 Add your spices, butter and sugar to the pan, stir on a low heat, and, as you watch everything dissolve together, inhale one of the most comforting culinary smells in existence.

5 Dissolve the bicarbonate of soda in water recently boiled from a kettle, and watch it start to fizz. Add this to the mixture in the pan, and you should be able to discern some small bubbles appearing. Take the pan off the heat and quickly stir in the eggs and milk, giving everything a good whisking.

6 Stir in the flour and cocoa plus the chopped chocolate and crystallised ginger, and beat vigorously with a wooden spoon. You want a relatively smooth mixture (apart from chocolate and ginger lumps of course).

7 Pour this spiced delightfulness into your waiting baking tray and bake for about 40 minutes until the top has set but there is still a wobble to the centre, which will harden slightly as it cools. Think brownie, not sponge cake – you want squidgy but not completely set.

8 Cool in its tin or a wire rack and slice when cold.

½ jar golden syrup
½ jar black treacle
1 tsp ground cinnamon
1 tsp chilli powder
4 tsp ground ginger
175g unsalted butter
125g dark muscovado sugar
1 tsp bicarbonate of soda
60ml warm water
2 eggs
250ml milk
275g plain flour
40g cocoa, good quality
100g Cocoa Loco or any 70% dark chocolate, chopped
50g crystallised ginger, chopped

MAKES
16 squares
PREP/COOK
20 minutes preparation
40 minutes cooking time
YOU WILL NEED
A large, deep, greased baking tray

Rosemary lemon cake with honeyed muscat grapes and ricotta

Tangy cake, sweet grapes, creamy ricotta – the marriage of these strong flavours is a happy one, and I do urge you to try all the constituent parts together. This cake works particularly well in loaf form, which also makes it easy both to store and slice as picnic fodder. You could take a little pot of the grapes, pre-soaked in honey, and the ricotta, mixed with zest prior to departure.

FOR THE CAKE
75ml milk
10 sprigs rosemary
225g unsalted butter, room
  temperature
200g caster sugar
zest of 2 lemons
3 eggs
225g plain flour
pinch of salt
90g ground almonds
2 tsp baking powder
FOR THE GRAPES
60ml honey
20 muscat grapes
**FOR THE LEMONY
  RICOTTA**
125g ricotta
zest ½ lemon
1 tbsp icing sugar

MAKES
One 1kg loaf – cuts into
8 slices
PREP/COOK
1 hour 30 minutes preparation
(including 45 minutes infusing
the milk)
1 to 1 hour 15 minutes
cooking time
YOU WILL NEED
A 1kg greased and lined
loaf tin

1 For the cake: pour the milk into a small saucepan and add the rosemary sprigs. Heat gently for a few minutes to infuse, then set aside for 45 minutes.

2 Preheat the oven to 170°C/Gas mark 3.

3 Meanwhile, cream the butter and sugar with an electric whisk until light and fluffy, and larger in volume – this should take 3–4 minutes. Add the lemon zest and beat for a couple of minutes. Beat in one egg at a time, make sure each is thoroughly incorporated, and then give the whole mixture a good whisking for a couple of minutes – it should be mousse-like and voluminous.

4 Sift over the flour, salt, almonds and baking powder. Strain the milk and add to the mixture, combining all together until you have a soft mixture that drops easily from a spoon or the whisk.

5 Tip the mixture into the greased loaf tin and bake for 1 hour to 1 hour 15 minutes.

6 Cool in the tin for 10 minutes before turning out onto a wire rack.

7 For the grapes: heat the honey in a small pan, and sprinkle in the grapes. Cook until bubbling and shiny, and just beginning to break down.

8 For the ricotta topping: whip the ricotta with the lemon zest and icing sugar to taste.

9 Serve the cake thickly spread with ricotta, and smeared with the honeyed grapes.

Glorious garden party

I'm just dotty about the idea of using growing things – edible flowers, herbs, leaves, shoots – to add colour and variety to my cooking.

This is what spices are, after all: growing things, bottled and distilled to their essence. Once they were living barks, roots and pods – nature's storecupboard. Vanilla, cinnamon, almond are all favourites of the baker. All from so very far away so why not use what, if we are lucky, we can pick from outside? We may not all have access to the perfect English country garden of course, but most of us can lay our hands on some roses, geraniums, even borage if we try. If we can eat it, and it is delicious and distinctive, then why not reclaim it?

Lamb pies with rosemary pastry

These pies are a Mediterranean creation – I wanted all those sunshine-infused Greek flavours of lamb, feta and sundried tomatoes for my garden party, but in a form that could be prepared in advance, and didn't involve too much messiness or washing up. Yes, you could fry up some lamb patties in advance, and serve with a big bowl of Greek salad if you want something lighter, but here you get the best of both worlds.

500g shortcrust pastry
3 sprigs rosemary,
  chopped
2 medium onions, grated
2 tbsp olive oil
500g lamb mince
2 x 100g bags rocket,
  chopped
200g grated feta
1 egg
handful of breadcrumbs
handful of sundried
  tomatoes
salt and pepper
egg yolk, for brushing

1 Preheat the oven to 180°C/Gas mark 4.

2 Sprinkle your shortcrust pastry with chopped rosemary and roll out so that the fresh herbiness penetrates throughout. Using a small bowl, cut circles out of your herby pastry and use them to line the holes in the muffin tray, pushing the pastry slightly above the rim. With a cup or mug, cut smaller holes from what's left of your pastry – these will be your pastry lids.

3 On a medium heat, in your largest frying pan, fry the onions in the olive oil until soft – this should only take a couple of minutes. Add the lamb mince to the pan and turn the heat up to high. Don't move the meat about too much – you want it to take on some colour. Pour off any excess fat.

4 When the mince is cooked, take the pan off the heat, and add the rocket, feta, egg, breadcrumbs and sundried tomatoes. Taste for seasoning. Pile your mix high in the muffin pastry cups, and press down with the back of a spoon.

5 Brush the egg yolk on the pastry edges, and press your lids down over the top of each pie. Feel free to crimp or fork the edges, for a more traditional look. Poke a small hole in the top of each pie for escaping steam, and brush each with egg yolk.

6 Bake for 15 minutes (your filling is already cooked, and you are really only cooking and crisping the pastry) until the pastry is golden.

MAKES
12 pies in a muffin tray,
6 in a Texas tray
PREP/COOK
35 minutes preparation
15 minutes cooking
YOU WILL NEED
A muffin or Texas
muffin tray

Rose cake with strawberry and rosewater compote, mascarpone frosting and fresh rose petals

This cake has served me well in many guises – as cupcake, wedding cake, in muffin format and as a traybake. It really is one I go back to again and again. As a layer cake it shines though: there is something about the jewel-like berries rippling through the batter that lifts it out of the ordinary. The ground and flaked nuts add a wonderful crumbliness to the texture. Leave it simple if you like, with just a buttercream frosting, and possibly a spreading of jam between layers. But for an outdoor celebration, what could be prettier than layers oozing berry and rosewater compote, a velvety mascarpone frosting, and a topping of fresh rose petals? It always reminds me of a summer sunset.

FOR THE CAKE
375g butter
465g caster sugar
6 eggs
225g plain flour
170g self-raising flour
90g ground almonds
180ml milk
2 tsp vanilla extract
115g flaked almonds
300g fresh raspberries

FOR THE MASCARPONE FROSTING
250g mascarpone
100g sour cream
220g icing sugar
30ml Cointreau

FOR THE STRAWBERRY ROSEWATER COMPOTE
400g fresh strawberries, hulled
50g icing sugar
2 tbsp rosewater
rose petals and fresh berries for decorating

1 Preheat the oven to 180°C/Gas mark 4, and grease and line the cake tin.

2 For the cake: in a bowl beat the butter for a couple of minutes.

3 Gradually add your sugar, a little at a time, and then beat for 3 minutes until the mix is as light and fluffy as a cloud. You want as much air in at this stage as possible, so things don't get too heavy with the addition of the nuts and fruits.

4 Add the eggs, one at a time, and be prepared to see the mixture curdle. Don't panic! This is fine – it's a very eggy mix, and we are going to balance all this moisture out with lots of drying nuts.

5 In another bowl, combine the flours and the ground almonds.

6 Separately add the vanilla extract to the milk.

7 Alternate adding the dry and wet ingredients to the batter in your mixer's bowl, and slowly beat everything together until incorporated. You should have a light, nutty sponge that drops easily from the beaters when they are lifted out.

8 Take the bowl from your mixer and add the flaked almonds and berries, and stir in gently with a large spoon. The mixer would be too harsh at this point – you want raspberry ripple, with dots of vivid colour, not a pale pink batter.

9 Bake the cake for 45–50 minutes, keeping an eye on it. Cover with foil if it begins to darken. The cake is done when a skewer inserted into the centre comes out clean.

10 Leave to cool in the tin for 15 minutes, then turn out onto a

MAKES
A two-layer 25cm cake
PREP/COOK
30 minutes (cake), 10 minutes
(frosting), 15 minutes
(compote) preparation
50 minutes (cake),
5 minutes (compote) cooking
YOU WILL NEED
A 25cm loose-bottomed
cake tin

TIP This does make for a very crumbly, moist cake, and if you are thinking of cutting into more layers than two, simply leave out an egg to firm things up a little.

rack to cool completely. You can now cut horizontally into two (or three if you are feeling brave) layers. Often a bread knife is the easiest thing to use here, or at least something large and serrated.

11 For the frosting: mix all the ingredients together until velvety and smooth. This frosting is far shinier and more unctuously delicious than a buttercream, and far less well behaved. If you want picture perfect, whip up a buttercream (see page 20). If you want a frosting that people will want to scoop out of a bowl with their fingers, I do urge you to try this.

12 For the compote: place the strawberries in a pan with the sugar and cook gently for 8–10 minutes until slightly broken down. Add 2 tbsp rosewater and mix.

13 Assembling: place one of your cake layers on a suitable plate or serving dish, and cover with compôte. Although you are aiming for oozing bounteous plenty here, I have lost count of the amount of times I have been too generous with my between-layer decorations, and I have very quickly realised the error of my ways. Spread compote and frosting (in that order) in what you could consider to be a rather miserly fashion. Rest assured, the weight of the upper layer/s will push the softer frosting and compôte outwards, so you will have that divine dripping effect down the side of the cake, without having to scrape goo from every available surface.

14 Decorate the top with the berries and rose petals.

TIP Please, please spend a little more and buy real vanilla extract – the cheaper stuff is mainly composed of alcohol, and may as well be omitted completely for all the flavour it brings.
I don't like to frost the outside of this cake – I don't think it needs it, and the sponge itself is so pretty, it needs no adornment. Needless to say, berries and rose petals look beautiful on top, but you could be struck by a fit of minimalism as I was when we took the picture on page 77. Sometimes, plain is best.

Lemon geranium muffins
with fresh lemon curd filling

There is a huge variety of scented geraniums out there. These muffins would be perfect with the lemon scented type of course (though watch your variety as some are inedible), but you could also experiment with apple, coconut, rose, orange, etc. The curd filling is optional, but it does provide a sunshine bright burst, and an oozing moistness that pervades the dough. If you are leaving out the curd filling, put a couple of tablespoons of natural yoghurt in the mixture to avoid any dryness.

approx 120ml geranium-infused milk

juice and zest of 1–2 lemons

60g butter

1 egg

200g plain flour

2 tsp baking powder

½ tsp bicarbonate of soda

150g geranium sugar

¼ tsp salt

150g fresh lemon curd

1 Preheat the oven to 160°C/Gas mark 3.

2 Line the muffin tray with papers.

3 To make the geranium-infused milk: chop five scented geranium leaves finely, and add to the milk. Pour into a small pan, and heat until almost boiling. Simmer for 3 minutes, then set aside for 1 hour. Sieve.

4 To make the muffins: zest the lemon(s) and then juice them. When added to the milk your liquid total should be 200ml.

5 Melt the butter, add the geranium-infused milk and lemon, along with the egg. Whisk everything together.

6 In a separate bowl, stir together the flour, baking powder, bicarbonate of soda, geranium (or just caster) sugar, salt and lemon zest.

7 Loosely combine the dry and wet ingredients, always remembering not to overmix (which results in a heavy muffin). Some tiny pockets of unmixed dry powder are absolutely fine.

8 Spoon half your mix into the muffin trays, and then add a heaped teaspoon of lemon curd to each. Top with the rest of your muffin mixture, encasing the little golden blob, which will be molten and delicious once baked.

9 Bake for 20–22 minutes until risen and golden.

TIP You can use the geranium leaves in a number of ways, depending on how strong you want the taste to be: chopped finely and added to the mix is most powerful of all, or you can infuse the milk with leaves, as I have done here. Or, for a less potent taste, put a few geranium leaves in a jar of sugar and leave for a couple of weeks. Use the delicately scented granules here, in place of caster.

MAKES
12 muffins
PREP/COOK
1 hour 20 minutes preparation
(including an hour for
infusing the milk)
20 minutes cooking
YOU WILL NEED
A 12-hole muffin tray

PLATE 7.

Nasturtium cupcakes

How many kinds of sweet flowers grow in an English country garden? It's your flower bed – see what you can find. Really these are just the most basic of vanilla cupcakes, but can be sprinkled with any edible flowers you find for a summery garden party treat. Pansies, violets, apple blossom also work well.

FOR THE CAKES
275g plain flour
1 tsp salt
225g unsalted butter, softened
250g sugar
1 tsp vanilla extract
250ml milk
4 eggs

FOR THE FROSTING
225 unsalted butter, very soft
125ml milk
2 tsp vanilla extract
1kg icing sugar, sifted

FOR DECORATION
nasturtiums or any other edible flowers

TIP Do use a guidebook to make sure the flowers you are picking are edible – not all are.

MAKES
24 cupcakes
PREP/COOK
20 minutes preparation
20 minutes cooking time
YOU WILL NEED
Two 12-hole
muffin trays

1 For the cakes: preheat the oven to 180°C/Gas mark 4.

2 Line the tin with cute cases, if you're using them (and that sort of thing appeals!).

3 Mix the flour and salt and set aside.

4 In a mixer (and it does help if you have one for really light-as-air results), cream the butter and sugar together. It should take about 4 minutes at medium speed and the mixture will be fluffy and pale.

5 Add the eggs one by one, making sure that the sides of the mixer bowl are regularly scraped down, and each egg has been thoroughly incorporated. The batter will now look almost mousse-like.

6 Add the vanilla to the milk. Turn the speed of the mixer right down to minimum, and slowly add the flour and milk, in three separate and alternate batches. Everything should be mixed together, but don't overwork the mix or your cupcakes will be heavy.

7 Bake for 20 minutes, turning the trays after 10 minutes if they aren't browning evenly.

8 For the frosting: place the butter, milk, vanilla and half the icing sugar in the bowl of a mixer. (Again, sorry to repeat myself, but to get really fluffy buttercream the secret is in the mixing.) Beat, slowly at first until everything is incorporated, and you don't get large sweet clouds of icing sugar floating around your kitchen. Speed up to medium and beat, and beat, and beat...for at least 4 minutes. Then add the rest of the icing sugar, about 150g at a time, and beat after each addition for another 3 minutes. (See what I mean about the mixer?)

9 Frost or pipe each cake with frosting however you like it – I rather like a big star nozzle. Then sprinkle happily with any edible flowers. Pretty as a picture!

Pea, spinach and mint pithiviers

Imagine all the flavours of an English summer, in a circular pastry case – the freshest peas, the earthiest spinach, and mint that really zings in your mouth – bound together with lemon and ricotta.

1 Preheat the oven to 190°C/Gas mark 5.
2 Fry the onions in a little oil until softened, then set aside.
3 In a large bowl, mix all the zingy filling ingredients together, simple as that. Season well and taste.
4 Cut the pastry into four larger and four smaller circles, using a saucer and the rim of a mug as a guide.
5 Heap the filling in the middle of the smaller circle, and brush the pastry border with the egg. Then carefully drape the larger pastry circles over the top and seal the edges, brushing the whole case with egg.
6 Bake for 20–25 minutes until nicely puffed and brown.

2 onions, chopped
150g peas, podded
150g spinach, chopped finely
small bunch of mint
125g ricotta
zest and juice of 1 lemon
handful sultanas
seasoning
500g pack puff pastry, rolled to the thickness of a £1 coin
1 egg, beaten

MAKES
4 pithiviers
PREP/COOK
20 minutes preparation
25 minutes cooking
YOU WILL NEED
A greased baking tray

Saffron cake with honey frosting and borage flowers

This is an old-fashioned cake, but none the less appealing for it. I have borrowed from that great Cornish tradition of the saffron bun, which combines a yeast-rich dough with dried fruit, but I have lightened it a little for modern tastes. Baking the cake in a ring mould made sense somehow, and enables ease of slicing. The sweet honeyed frosting should be drizzled somewhat messily, and the borage flowers scattered – the effect being to lighten and prettify a hearty traditional bake.

FOR THE CAKE
1 tsp saffron strands
125ml milk
500g plain flour
**½ tsp fast-action dried
 yeast**
salt
**250g butter, cold and
 cubed**
250g caster sugar
300g blueberries
zest and juice of 1 orange
FOR THE FROSTING
water or lemon juice
300g icing sugar, sifted
FOR DECORATION
**3 tbsp Sussex honey or
 your favourite tasty honey**
borage flowers

1 Preheat the oven to 160°C/Gas mark 3.

2 Firstly, infuse your saffron: add it to the milk, and place in a small saucepan. Heat gently until simmering, and let it bubble (being careful not to let it boil) for a couple of minutes. Set aside to cool.

3 Mix the flour, yeast and salt in a large bowl. Add the butter and caster sugar and rub in with your fingertips until you can feel the mix turn to crumbs throughout.

4 Now, to add the colour and flavour: scatter your berries and orange zest into the bowl. Add the orange juice to the saffron-infused milk and now pour this into the bowl, mixing all together gently.

5 Now for the therapeutic part: turn the dough out onto a lightly floured worktop, and knead – it will be wet, but will come together with patience. A few minutes will be fine, until the dough is elastic, and springs back a little when you press it.

6 Place the dough in a loaf tin or a ring mould, and leave for 40 minutes to 1 hour until it rises.

7 Bake for 40 minutes or until risen and golden.

8 **For the frosting:** this is an old-fashioned drizzled icing. Simply mix enough liquid – either water or lemon juice is fine here – into your icing sugar to make it pourable. You can test with a teaspoon: if it drips off the end without too much coaxing, that's about right. Use the same teaspoon to drizzle icing all over the cake. It doesn't have to be neat, and a little icing pouring down the sides is desirable.

9 If you have some rich local honey, the more the merrier – drizzle some of this over too, and then scatter with borage flowers for that English country meadow look.

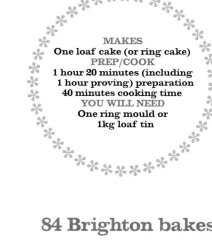

MAKES
One loaf cake (or ring cake)
PREP/COOK
**1 hour 20 minutes (including
1 hour proving) preparation
40 minutes cooking time**
YOU WILL NEED
**One ring mould or
1kg loaf tin**

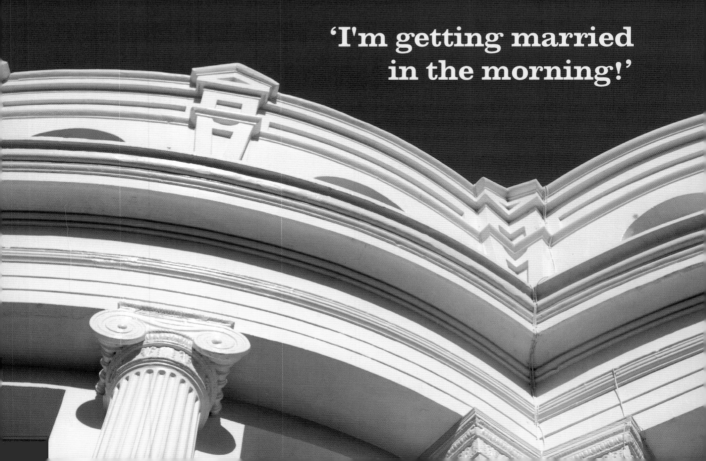

Food as happiness, food as union, food as love

It's probably at a wedding that the above is most true, where the symbolism really hits you in the face. The food is by no means the main event – even with my level of culinary obsession I'd be checking out the bride and groom, not the plate in front of me – but it is true that at a wedding the food is scrutinised more than usual. This doesn't mean your usual cookery style should go out of the window – and if you're cooking for your own celebration, whether barbeque, afternoon tea, buffet or a sit-down meal, the food should be most reflective of you both – vibrant and personal.

Don't be pressurised into adhering to the traditions of the wedding breakfast if the idea of a three-course sit-down meal fills you with horror. I've cooked Mexican, vegetarian, Thai and Moroccan at weddings for over 100 people, and all have been devoured. Do try and get your logistics sorted, and make sure you have lots of willing helpers on the day.

'I'm getting married in the morning!'

FOR THE POTS
2 tbsp roasted garlic

500ml double cream

2 eggs

4 egg yolks

¾ tsp salt

¼ tsp white pepper

⅛ tsp ground nutmeg

FOR THE CRACKERS
220g flour, more as needed

½ tsp salt

3 tbsp Parmigiano
  Reggiano cheese

1 tbsp fresh rosemary,
  finely chopped

2 tbsp black olives, finely
  sliced

2 cloves garlic, finely
  chopped

3 tbsp extra virgin olive oil

60ml single cream

1 tbsp milk, if required

sea salt, coarsely ground
  pepper, sesame seeds or
  poppy seeds

FOR THE SALSA
500g ripe tomatoes,
  skinned and seeded

1 fresh chilli

¼ red onion

small bunch of fresh
  coriander leaves, chopped

about 3 tbsp lime juice

3 tbsp red wine vinegar

150ml extra virgin olive oil

1 dessertspoon Dijon
  mustard

salt and black pepper,
  to taste

Garlicky pots with rosemary olive crackers and tomato salsa

If you are having a hog roast or a barbeque on your big day, sometimes those of a slightly less meaty disposition can feel a little left out in the cold. I have often been asked to cater for weddings that already have the meat feast in place, but are aware they need something extra to make it a fully rounded celebration. These creamy savoury pots are extraordinarily versatile – serve in vintage tea cups as starters or larger ramekins for (veggy) mains as part of a sit-down meal. The crackers and salsa accompaniments aren't optional – they are needed for balance.

1 Preheat the oven to 170°C/Gas mark 3. Set the ramekins in a large deep baking tray.

2 In a bowl, combine the garlic, cream, egg, egg yolks, salt, white pepper and nutmeg – this savoury custard will make the body of the dish. Pour the egg mixture into the prepared ramekins, and place the baking tray containing the custard cups on the middle shelf of the oven.

3 With a small amount of dexterity, carefully pour warm water from a recently boiled kettle into the baking dish, to come about half way up the side of the ramekins. This water will steam the contents of the ramekins, and keep them moist and fluffy inside.

4 Bake for 25 minutes until the tops of the pots are golden brown, and they have puffed up slightly. Take the baking tray out of the oven, but leave the pots in the water to keep them warm for up to 20 minutes, while you make the crackers and salsa.

5 **For the crackers:** grease a baking sheet, and make sure there's a shelf above the custards in the oven.

6 Put the flour, salt, grated cheese, rosemary, olives, garlic and oil into a food processor and pulse until the mixture forms small crumbs. If you'd rather do it by hand, simply whisk all the dry ingredients together first, then add the oil and, using a fork, mix until it looks like coarse crumbs.

7 Add the cream and the mix should come together, either in

MAKES
8 pots, 500ml salsa
and
16 crackers
PREP/COOK
20 minutes each (pots, crackers,
salsa) preparation
25 minutes (pots)
15 minutes (crackers) cooking
YOU WILL NEED
8 ramekins,
one deep baking tray
and one baking
sheet

TIP The crackers can be prepared in advance and frozen.

the bowl of the food processor, or with your hands. You can add a little milk at this point if everything looks a little dry. What you're aiming for is a wettish, firm dough.

8 Roll it out on your baking sheet until slightly less than 1cm thick – you may need to flour your rolling pin and the tray a little.

9 Score the dough with lines as lightly as you can with the point of a sharp knife: this will be useful when you want to break it into cracker shapes later. If you are using salt or any other topping, now's the time to add it.

10 Bake on the top shelf of the oven (above the custards if you are cooking at the same time) until lightly browned and crisp – about 15 minutes. Cool on a rack.

11 Prepare the salsa while the pots and crackers are baking: cut the tomatoes into small dice, and place with their juices into a bowl. Rinse and de-seed the chilli (unless you like things very fiery!), and finely chop. Add to the bowl with the finely chopped onion, coriander and lime juice. Stir and taste – you may need to add more lime, salt, pepper etc – it is very much up to your personal taste.

12 In a small saucepan over a low heat, whisk together red wine vinegar, olive oil, mustard and your salsa base. When it starts to simmer, take off the heat, cover and set aside.

To serve, turn the custards out of their ramekins onto individual serving plates. Spoon warm salsa over each, and place a couple of crackers to one side.

Crab, saffron and leek tart

Or, sophisticated shellfish! A delicate, summery and light dish. It is worth getting your fishmonger to prepare the crab for you – I would advise against using tinned for a special occasion like this. Those of a plucky and tenacious disposition could cook and crack their own crustacean, but please do check and double check for any tiny unwelcome bits of shell.

150g butter
250g plain flour
1 egg yolk
3 leeks, topped, tailed and chopped (about 500g pre-chopping)
2 tbsp butter
1 tbsp white wine
6 eggs
250ml double cream
1 tsp saffron in 1 tbsp milk
1 tsp nutmeg
seasoning
350g white crab meat

1 Rub in the butter and flour with the tips of your fingers until grainy crumbs are formed. I think this pastry is better made by hand, but if you want to blitz it in the food processor, feel free. Add the egg yolk and mix until a soft dough is formed. Be careful not to overmix if you are using a processor, and just pulse briefly until the dough comes together.

2 Roll out the pastry as thin as you dare, not worrying too much if it cracks. Carefully drape over a rolling pin and use to line the tart tin. Patch up any gaps with pastry trimmings. Prick all over with a fork and refrigerate for 30 minutes.

3 Preheat your oven to 180°C/Gas mark 4.

4 Gently fry the leeks in the butter and wine until soft and almost translucent. This will probably take 15–20 minutes – be gentle with them, and don't let them colour too much.

5 Line your chilled case with greaseproof paper and fill with baking beans, or just dried pulses and rice, and bake for 15 minutes. Remove the paper and beans, and put back in the oven for 5 minutes until it has taken on a light biscuit brown colour.

6 Mix your eggs, cream, saffron, nutmeg and seasoning together in a large measuring jug.

7 Line the base of your cooked pastry case with leeks, and then sprinkle the crab meat over the top. Pour the creamy egg mix over all, and then bake in the oven for 25–30 minutes until puffed and golden brown. Leave to settle in the tin for 15 minutes or so if turning out and serving warm.

TIP The pastry for this tart really should be as thin as you can possibly imagine. Not quite see-through, but almost. It is very short, so I wouldn't advise rolling out too much. Simply place into the tin and push gently up against the sides with your fingers or a rolled up ball of pastry. If it cracks (which it probably will), repair it with leftover bits of dough.

MAKES
One 23cm tart (serves 10)
PREP/COOK
45 minutes (including chilling) preparation
45 minutes cooking and settling time
YOU WILL NEED
A loose-bottomed 23cm tart tin

Amity pie

This is really just the famous Homity Pie with a little tweaking, and I couldn't resist playing around with the name either. I've made it a little more wedding-centric: after all you are going to be feeding both your love and your friends, and the name of the dish should reflect that. For those concerned about both budgets and stress on the day, this pie will feed a crowd inexpensively, and can be frozen in advance quite happily.

FOR THE PASTRY
125g butter
100g wholemeal flour
150g plain flour
1 egg yolk
FOR THE FILLING
2 big potatoes (weighing about 350g each) – floury is best
1 onion, sliced
1 red onion, sliced
2 tbsp butter
3 garlic cloves, crushed
150g rocket leaves
150g grated tangy cheese, such as Sussex Charmer
small bunch basil leaves
seasoning
pinch paprika
200ml double cream
seasoning

MAKES
A 21cm pie (serves 8)
PREP/COOK
40 minutes preparation
45 minutes cooking time
YOU WILL NEED
A greased 21cm pie dish or tart tin

1 Rub the butter and flours together with your fingers, or in a food processor, until a crumb texture is achieved. Add the egg and bring everything together until it forms a dough. (If you are doing this in a food processor, the pulse setting is best so you don't overwork the dough.)

2 Roll the pastry out (it might be quite short and crumbly, but don't worry – mistakes can always be rectified with extra pieces of dough) until it is the thickness of a £1 coin, and use to line your pie dish or tart tin. Chill in the fridge for 30 minutes to minimise shrinkage.

3 Preheat the oven to 190°C/Gas mark 5.

4 Meanwhile make a start on the pie filling. Boil the potatoes until tender, then slice into 0.5cm slices. Whilst the potatoes are boiling merrily, gently fry the onions in the butter until they are soft, adding the garlic towards the end of cooking time.

5 Mix the onions, garlic, potatoes, rocket, and most of the cheese together, leaving just a handful of cheese for sprinkling at the end. Season everything well, add the paprika and basil and stir to make sure all the flavours permeate throughout.

6 Place the pastry case on a baking tray, spoon in the filling, and pour the cream over the top, letting it run into all the gaps. It should flow to the top of your case. Carefully sprinkle the remaining cheese on top, and place the tray in the oven. Bake for 45 minutes until the filling is golden, and the pastry is biscuit brown. If you are turning your pie out, be sure to leave it in the tin for 15 minutes to let it settle first.

Hot diggedy dogs

You're rolling sausages and herby tomato relish in a homemade bread dough, and baking them in the oven – what's not to love? They're retro, they're cute, and they're an ideal canapé to send round before your guests are seated. They also work well in a larger size if you'd like something more substantial to nibble on later.

For those feeling somewhat frazzled with the wedding planning, fear not – everything can be baked and frozen, leaving you only a little reheating to do on the day itself.

1 For the rolls: place the warm water, sugar, yeast and olive oil in a jug and leave for about 15 minutes until about 1–2cm of foamy head forms. This means the yeast has come to life and your dough will be light and airy and, if it doesn't happen, your yeast is out of date, and you need to start again.

2 In a large bowl, mix the flour and salt, and slowly add the yeasty water, stirring the whole time. Add the milk, and the whole mixture should start to come together as a dough. Now place on a lightly floured worktop and knead for a few minutes, which will stretch the gluten and give your finished rolls a good consistency.

3 Place your dough in a clean, greased bowl, and cover with a tea towel or greased cling film, and leave for an hour or so until doubled in size.

4 Preheat the oven to 180°C/Gas mark 4.

5 Par-cook your sausages by frying in the olive oil until the outsides take on some colour. This will give the final dogs the mouth-feel of fried sausages, even though they will be baked in bread rolls. When the sausages have cooked slightly, cut each into three equal sized pieces.

6 Fry your tomatoes gently with the garlic and fresh herbs for a few minutes, letting everything reduce down and become the texture of relish.

7 Take a big tablespoon of dough and roll into a 5cm strip. Place a piece of sausage and a spoonful of relish in the centre of each strip, making sure that some of each is visible over the edges, and now roll up the dough over and around them like a blanket.

8 Place your little dogs about 5cm apart on a baking tray and brush with egg. Bake for 20 minutes until the bread and sausages are both cooked and golden brown.

FOR THE ROLLS
1 litre warm water
1 tbsp caster sugar
2 sachets fast-action dried yeast
2 tbsp olive oil
1kg strong bread flour
1 tsp salt
50ml milk
FOR THE FILLING
8 good quality herby sausages
olive oil, for coating
6 plum tomatoes, finely chopped, juice reserved
2 cloves garlic
1 bunch marjoram, oregano or tarragon
1 egg, beaten

MAKES
24 small dogs
PREP/COOK
1 hour 45 minutes (including proving time) preparation
20 minutes cooking
YOU WILL NEED
A large greased baking tray

Fresh Sussex strawberry tart with added passion (fruit)

Why be tied to the idea of a traditional wedding cake? If someone gave me the choice between a dusty fruit cake, and a towering slice of glistening, syrupy, sticky berry tart, oozing a creamy filling, encased in the crispest, lightest, butteriest pastry, I don't think I'd have to ponder my options too hard. It should be all about passion and plenty, not parsimony.

FOR THE PASTRY
225g plain flour
50g icing sugar
100g butter, cold and diced
2 egg yolks
FOR THE FILLING
200ml double cream
25g icing sugar
2 tbsp elderflower cordial
400g strawberries
4 passion-fruits, seeds

TIP I've kept things simple here and given the quantities necessary for a small dinner party, rather than a wedding, but depending on how many guests you have, simply make one per table. It also works very well as individual tarts, piled high on a cake stand.

MAKES
One 23cm tart (serves 10)
PREP/COOK
40 minutes preparation
15 minutes cooking
YOU WILL NEED
A 23cm loose-bottomed
tart tin

1 Preheat the oven to 190°C/Gas mark 5.

2 For the pastry: put the flour in a bowl, add the icing sugar and butter. Then, using fingers, rub the butter in, until it resembles coarse crumbs. Stir in the egg yolk, then squeeze the whole mixture until it comes together into a dough, adding a little water if necessary.

3 Knead lightly until you have a yielding smooth ball of dough, then roll out thinly on a lightly floured worktop. It really doesn't matter if the pastry cracks – sweet shortcrust can be temperamental, and any holes or tears can be patched up.

4 Line your tin with the pastry, pushing it up to the edges with your fingertips. Prick the base with a fork and chill for 15 minutes. Now line the tart with a circle of greaseproof, cling film or foil and some dried lentils or baking beans, and bake blind for 15 minutes. Remove the paper and beans, and cook the tart case for 5 more minutes until pale golden. Leave to cool: if you add your cold cream to the warmed pastry case, you will end up with a runny liquid centre.

5 For the filling: whip the cream with the icing sugar and elderflower cordial until it forms soft swirls. Do taste at this point – you want to be aware of the sweet edge from the sugar, and the perfumed flavour of the elderflower. Spoon gently into the tart case until full, and level the top with a palette knife.

6 Slice your strawberries if they are large, or keep smaller ones whole, and arrange either higgledy piggledy or concentrically on top.

7 If you are using the passion-fruit, sprinkle the seeds on top now, and serve as soon as possible, as this tart won't wait. If you want to get things done in advance (and for a wedding I completely understand why you would), you can bake the tart case a day or so in advance, or even freeze it, waiting to be filled on the day. Fill it as close to the time of eating as possible, to avoid the dreaded soggy bottom syndrome.

Hot chilli cherry meringue pies

Fire and passion – now and in the future – surely the very essence and undercurrent of a wedding day? These are rock 'n' roll rebellion created and plated: the hot-stuff symbolism might be heavy, but the desserts themselves aren't. There's a lip-tingling kick to the cherry compote filling, alongside which the sweet chewy pillows of meringue soothe and cool. Use the tines of a fork to tease your meringue into flame shapes: the heat is on.

FOR THE FILLING
350g frozen/fresh cherries, stoned
200g sugar
zest and juice of 1 lemon
1 tsp fresh chilli, chopped finely
FOR THE PASTRY
250g plain flour
50g icing sugar
125g butter, cubed
1 egg
FOR THE TOPPING
6 eggs, separated
1 pinch of salt
seeds from 1 vanilla pod
300g caster sugar

MAKES
One 25cm pie
or four 10cm pies
PREP/COOK
30 minutes preparation
25 minutes cooking
YOU WILL NEED
One 25cm tart tin or four
10cm tart tins

1 Make your cherry compote filling: cook the cherries, sugar, lemon zest and juice and chilli in a pan on a medium heat for 10–15 minutes until the fruit has broken down and taken on some of those deep, spiced flavours.

2 **To make the pastry:** place the flour, icing sugar and butter in a food processor and pulse until they form crumbs, or rub together with your fingers to the same effect. Add in the egg and pulse again, or simply bring together with your hands until the mixture forms a dough ball. If the mixture is too dry, add a little water until the mixture comes together. Place the pastry in the fridge to rest for 10 minutes.

3 Preheat the oven to 180°C/Gas mark 4.

4 **To make the meringue topping:** place the egg whites in a mixing bowl with a pinch of salt and the vanilla pod seeds. Whisk until light and fluffy, then add in the sugar, one tablespoon at a time, and continue whisking between spoonfuls until all the graininess from the sugar has been absorbed. You want a mixture that is thick and glossy and stays in the bowl when turned upside down (over your head if you dare).

5 Lightly flour a work surface and roll out the pastry large enough to line the big pie dish or four small tart tins. Make sure the pastry fits snugly against the edge of the dish as you don't want it to crack open and the telltale scarlet of the cherries to leak out while cooking.

6 Using a slotted spoon, scoop out the cherries and place in the pastry case. Top the spice-imbued fruits with the meringue until you can't see any red at all, using a fork to whirl your glossy white mountains into flame shapes if you're feeling dramatic and devilish.

7 Bake in the oven for 45–50 minutes (one large tart), or 20 minutes (for individual tarts) until the meringue is golden brown.

Lemony ice cream cone cupcakes with Mr Whippy style frosting

If you're having a seaside-themed wedding, these are the cakes for you. They conjure up connotations of ice creams and beach holidays, and look fantastically inviting lined up in rows. The lemon cakes are baked into their wafer cone holders, then frosted in that unmistakable Mr Whippy style. Add a mini flake for the complete sand-between-the-toes nostalgic feel.

FOR THE CAKES
20 wafer cup cornets (you will need cornets with flat bottoms)
225g unsalted butter, softened
400g sugar
zest of 1 lemon
4 large eggs
60ml freshly squeezed lemon juice (this will probably be about 2 lemons' worth, depending on their juiciness)
180ml whole milk
450g plain flour
2 tsp baking powder
FOR THE FROSTING
225g unsalted butter
1kg icing sugar, sifted
125ml freshly squeezed lemon juice (roughly 4 lemons' worth)
zest of ½ lemon
food colouring (optional)
TO DECORATE
hundreds and thousands
10 flake bars, cut in half

1 Preheat the oven to 170°C/Gas mark 3.

2 Stand the cornets in the muffin tins. In a bowl, beat the butter, sugar and lemon zest together with an electric whisk until light, fluffy and voluminous.

3 Add the eggs one by one, beating after each until fully incorporated in the mixture. Keep beating the mix at a low speed whilst you add the other ingredients.

4 Mix the lemon juice and milk together, and then add alternately with the flour and baking powder, in three batches. Up until you add the flour, it is impossible to mix too much – you are adding air to the sponge, which will get lighter the more you beat it. As soon as you start to add the flour, be very cautious about beating the mixture, as you do not want to overwork the gluten, or your cakes will be heavy and chewy.

5 Spoon or pipe the cake batter into the cornets, leaving a couple of centimetres at the top for them to rise in the oven. Bake for 20–25 minutes until risen and golden, and a skewer inserted in the middle comes out clean. Leave to cool on a wire rack (which may take longer than usual because of their wafer cases).

6 **For the frosting:** Place the butter in the bowl of your mixer, then add half the sugar and the lemon juice and zest. Beat until the frosting is creamy and mousse-like. Add the remaining sugar, 150g at a time, and beat on a high speed for about 3 minutes after each addition. If you want to colour your frosting, now's the time to do it.

7 Spoon your frosting into a piping bag fitted with a large star nozzle, and then pipe swirls on, just as Mr Whippy does. Add sprinkles and a flake.

MAKES
20 cupcakes
PREP/COOK
20 minutes (cakes) 10 minutes (frosting) preparation
20 minutes cooking
YOU WILL NEED
Two 12-hole muffin trays, piping bag and large star nozzle

Margarita cupcakes

Cocktails in cake form – yum! These playful treats work beautifully as wedding favours, or to send round on platters later in the evening to revive flagging spirits.

1 Preheat the oven to 180°C/Gas mark 4.

2 Mix the flour and baking powder together in a bowl, along with the salt. Line your muffin tray with colourful papers – this is a fiesta after all!

3 Add the butter to the bowl of an electric mixer, and whisk for a couple of minutes until fluffy. Gradually add the sugar with the motor running. The mixture will turn very pale, and become light and airy. Keep mixing for longer than you think you should – a good couple of minutes after adding all the sugar.

4 Add the eggs, one at a time, beating thoroughly after each addition, and making sure the batter thoroughly incorporates each one.

5 Tequila Time! Add the lime zest and juice, and the tequila, and mix until everything is combined.

6 Add the dry ingredients to the bowl in three batches, alternating with the sour cream, and beat briefly to make sure everything is blended.

7 Divide the mixture between your paper cases and bake for about 20 minutes until golden and risen, and a skewer inserted in the centre comes out clean.

8 Cool on a wire rack for 20 minutes or so before frosting. If your cupcakes are still warm, the frosting will slide off.

9 For the frosting: beat the butter in the bowl of an electric mixer for 2–3 minutes until fluffy and pale. Now gradually add the icing sugar, beating for a minute or two between additions, being really careful that it doesn't billow out in sweet clouds that coat you and the kitchen. Add the lime juice and tequila and whisk up for a couple of minutes until you have a light buttercream, with a kick in the tail.

10 Frost the cupcakes as desired, and then sprinkle the rims of each with sea salt, and garnish with a lime wedge. Cheers!

FOR THE CAKES
225g plain flour
1 tsp baking powder
1 tsp salt
225g butter
220g sugar
2 large eggs
zest and juice of 1 lime
3 tbsp tequila
150ml sour cream

FOR THE FROSTING
125g butter
500g icing sugar
1 tbsp lime juice
3 tbsp tequila

TO DECORATE
sea salt flakes
fresh lime wedges

TIP Any cocktail will work here – you could make a White Russian cupcake with coffee, for instance. It's up to you to add whatever alcohol you fancy!

MAKES
12 cupcakes
PREP/COOK
20 minutes (cakes), 10 minutes (frosting) preparation
20 minutes cooking
YOU WILL NEED
One 12-hole muffin tray

Autumn

Bonfire party

Harvest banquets

Lunchbox lovelies

Fields are full, and orchards are overflowing.
Jewelled colours, dappled shade and mists surround us.
Harvest your own seasonal bounty,
and turn a meal into a feast in autumn.

'Remember, remember, the 5th of November, with gunpowder, treason and plot...'

Bonfire party

Guy Fawkes may have failed to blow up British Parliament on that fateful evening in 1605, but he did ignite a hot tradition. This after all is the one time of the year that people are allowed to do that most primal of activities – set fire to things. It may be licensed fun, but it's always an incendiary evening – the sky is alight with colour, the pyrotechnics are bone-shakingly loud, excitement crackles in the air along with the smell of gunpowder. Sparklers are fizzy trails of stars, and rockets are man-made comets arcing above. What's not to love?

Food is traditionally classic cold-weather fare, and easily transportable in a gloved hand. Here toffee apples take on a new guise in a hearty crumble, savoury turnovers can be held (but why not fill with rich gamey rabbit instead of beef?), and the sepulchral White Night cake seems to float eerily, and will satisfy those Halloween fans who like their bakes gothic, pale and interesting.

Fig and stilton tarts

If you think of these as cheese scones with chutney, everything sounds much less daunting. All I have done here is add a hint of strong blue cheese to a basic scone dough, which is baked upside down with a base layer of fresh figs and spices. The jammy, figgy reduction is just waiting to be turned out and ooze stickily into the dough. Cheese scones for a grown-up bonfire then.

4 large ripe figs
knob of butter
1 tsp cinnamon
1 star anise
100g grated Stilton
225g self-raising flour
salt
55g butter
150ml milk
extra figs – as many as you
like for presentation

1 Preheat the oven to 180°C/Gas mark 4.

2 Quarter the four figs and fry in butter with the cinnamon and star anise until they break down and you have a juicy, jam-like consistency. This shouldn't take more than a couple of minutes if your figs are ripe, though you may have to persist if they are a little hard.

3 Butter the base and sides of the tart tins and spoon in your figgy compôte.

4 Sprinkle each with a light coating of grated Stilton – don't forget these will be turned out, so you are actually making a cheesy topping for your scone dough here, under the layer of fig chutney.

5 Make the dough: mix the flour and salt together, and rub in the butter with your fingertips. Something would be lost doing this in the food processor – it needs to be a light and airy dough. Stir in the rest of the cheese and milk – the dough will feel wet.

6 Press the dough into a round, and make sure it is no flatter than an inch thick. Use a large biscuit cutter, or an upturned tart case to cut the dough into rounds. Press the dough into the tart tins.

7 Bake for 20 minutes, then take out of the oven and let them stand for a few minutes, so they settle down a little and become easier to handle. Tip them out – if they don't behave you may need to encourage them with the tip of a knife. If any gorgeous spiced juices are left at the bottom of the tart tins, treat as gold dust and spoon them over your scones post haste.

8 Decorate with as many figs as you like.

TIP Handle the dough lightly and as little as possible – you want something that will rise and puff, and it will be a lot more stubborn the more you handle it. These tarts are best eaten warm from the oven as, like any scone, they lose a little something when they are cooled and not completely fresh.

MAKES
Four 15cm tarts
PREP/COOK
25 minutes preparation
15 minutes cooking
YOU WILL NEED
Four 15cm tart tins

Rother rabbit turnovers

These are perfect for a gloved hand on a dark night – rich and gamey. You might meet with an initial rabbit resistance, and indeed might be a reluctant bunny yourself, but rabbits are plentiful and populous on these isles, and eating a diverse choice of meats is important.

1 rabbit, jointed
3 tbsp plain flour
1 tsp English mustard
  powder
50g butter
1 large onion, diced
225g prunes, halved
1 tsp allspice
½ tsp mace
1 tbsp chopped marjoram
seasoning
450ml Dark Star or other
  dark, strong bitter
FOR THE PASTRY
500g plain flour
250g unsalted butter, cold
  and diced
sea salt
1 large egg

MAKES
6 pasties
PREP/COOK
20 minutes (stew), 25 minutes
(pasties) preparation
2 hours (stew),
25 minutes (pasties) cooking
YOU WILL NEED
One large greased
baking tray

1 Toss the rabbit joints in the flour and mustard powder combined. Heat the butter in a large casserole dish and brown the joints on all sides. Remove from the pan.

2 Cook the onion in the buttery rabbit juices until softened and beginning to colour; add the prunes to the pan.

3 Add the rabbit back into the pan and give everything a good mix around. Add the spices, marjoram and seasoning, and cover all with beer.

4 Bring everything up to a boil, then reduce the heat and simmer for 2 hours until the rabbit is tender.

5 Whilst your rabbit filling bubbles away on the stove, you can get started on the pastry.

6 Preheat the oven to 200°C/Gas mark 6.

7 Put the flour into a bowl with the salt, and rub in the butter with your hands. You're aiming for coarse grains throughout. Now add 200ml of cold water and mix it in quickly. Push the dough together with your hands quickly, without overmixing.

8 Separate the dough into six roughly even pieces and roll each of these into a ball. Now, on a lightly floured surface, roll each out into a circle about the size of a sideplate. The pastry should be about 2–3mm thick.

9 Now, with a slotted spoon, grab a large spoonful of juicy rabbit, and place it in the middle of one of your pastry sheets, making sure you leave a border round the edges for sealing. The amount of filling is up to you, and might take a few tries to get it exactly right. Remember the pastry does have to meet its opposite edge, over and above all that filling.

10 Brush the borders with beaten egg and lift and press opposite sides together. You can crimp or twist the pastry edge, or use the tines of a fork if you prefer.

11 Make your other five pasties and put them all on a baking tray. Bake for 20-25 minutes until the pastry is golden.

Garlic plaits

In the dying embers of the fire, wrap these in foil and poke them in, cosily, next to your jacket potatoes. Hot bread for a cold night.

1 Preheat the oven to 200°C/Gas mark 6.

2 In a large bowl, mix the flour, yeast and salt together. Add 300ml of warm water and 3 tablespoons of the olive oil. Mix everything together with your hands until you have a soft, firm dough. You might well need to add a little more water, but you will be able to feel this with your hands. Knead the dough for a few minutes until it springs back and is elastic to the touch. Place it in an oiled bowl, and leave for 1 hour until it has almost doubled in size.

3 Meanwhile, roast the garlic (this makes for a much less harsh version of garlic bread). Simply slice the tops off the heads of garlic and drizzle with the rest of the olive oil. Roast for about 20–30 minutes until the skin has gone light and papery, and slides off easily when you pinch a clove between your fingers. The inside of the clove should now be soft.

4 Place your roasted garlic, the bunch of flatleaf parsley, and a good glug of extra virgin olive oil in the bowl of the food processor, and blitz until you have a vivid green liquid, with no large lumps.

5 Now punch your dough down with your fists, and knock the air out of it. Leave for another 10 minutes in the bowl.

6 Flatten your dough slightly and pour over the garlic and parsley, plus oil and salt. Fold the dough over the filling and then incorporate that as much as you like. A little gentle kneading will result in a dough with green running throughout, whereas simply keeping the parsley and garlic as a large pocket of filling results in a 'hidden treasure' aspect which is fun for a larger loaf.

7 To make plaits, knead the filling into the dough for a few seconds, then separate the dough into four equal pieces. Separate each of these four pieces into three, and roll these into cylinders, about an inch wide and 6 inches long. Plait the cylinders as though you are plaiting hair – over and under in turn.

8 Place your plaits on a greased baking sheet and bake for 25 minutes until golden and risen.

500g strong white flour
1 sachet fast-action dried yeast
1 tbsp salt
300–440ml warm water
5 tbsp olive oil
3 large or 4 small heads garlic
bunch of flatleaf parsley
extra virgin olive oil
salt to taste

TIP It is up to you how you want your final bread to look, but I particularly like the look of plaits here, with the vivid green of the parsley and garlic clinging to the curves and knots of the dough.

MAKES
4 plaits
PREP/COOK
1 hour 30 minutes (including proving) preparation
25 minutes cooking
YOU WILL NEED
A greased baking tray

Sussex toffee apple crumble

All the fun of the fair... Toffee apples, candyfloss – treats of childhood days that memory instils with a magic that doesn't quite transfer to adult reality. This simple, comforting baked crumble combines all the richly remembered caramel and apple flavours with a crumbly roasted topping. A cinnamon or vanilla-spiced custard would be a lovely accompaniment.

**FOR THE
 CRUMBLE TOPPING**
200g plain flour
150g butter, cubed
100g caster sugar
**50g pecan nuts, chopped
 and toasted**
**FOR THE TOFFEE
 APPLE FILLING**
5 large, crisp eating apples
1 Bramley apple
50g brown sugar
1 tsp ground cinnamon
**150g fudge, roughly
 chopped**

1 Preheat the oven to 190°C/Gas mark 5.

2 In a bowl, rub the flour and butter and sugar together with your fingertips until you have a breadcrumb texture. Stir in the pecan nuts and set aside.

3 Cut each apple up finely (discarding the peel and the core), and place in a large, heavy bottomed pan. Add sugar and cinnamon and heat gently (you may need to add a couple of tablespoons of water here to help things along). Cover with a lid and let everything melt and come together. Have a peek and see how the apple mix is doing – it should be breaking down nicely. Cook for another 5 minutes.

4 Butter the serving dish you want to bake your crumble in, and fill it with your apple mix. Dot fudge pieces evenly across the surface, poking them in slightly, but leaving them visible. These will melt down into a beautiful caramel toffee sauce.

5 Sprinkle the crumble evenly over the top, and bake for 20–30 minutes until golden.

**SERVES
4 hungry people
PREP/COOK
30 minutes preparation
25 minutes cooking
YOU WILL NEED
One buttered ovenproof serving
dish about 35cm in length,
20cm in width, and
6cm deep**

Pumpkin bread

A wedge of this bread with any kind of stew or chilli, gathered round the fire, is a joy indeed. It is a quick, moist bread, baked in a loaf tin, sliced and smeared with butter while still warm out of the oven – think banana bread but spicier and denser. It's heavy and cakey and rather wonderful for a few days, even working well toasted, with butter. The recipe is simplicity itself, and a good introduction to baking for the inexperienced.

400g fresh pumpkin, peeled and cut into 2cm chunks
300g plain flour
4 tsp mixed spice
2 tsp baking powder
salt
330g brown sugar
180ml vegetable oil or melted butter (butter will produce a slightly denser bread)
3 eggs
handful of toasted pecan nuts, chopped (optional)
handful of sultanas (optional)

1 Preheat the oven to 200°C/Gas mark 6.
2 Place the pumpkin on a baking tray and roast for 20 minutes until soft. Then whizz in the food processor until you have a purée weighing about 300g.
3 Reduce oven temperature to 160°C/Gas mark 3.
4 Sift together flour, spices, baking powder and salt and set aside.
5 In a large bowl, stir together the sugar, oil and eggs until you have a thick, viscous, opaque liquid. Add the dry ingredients to the wet and mix briefly, then fold in the pumpkin purée.
6 If you want to use nuts and sultanas, add them now, and then spoon your batter into the loaf tin. Bake for an hour or so until puffed and brown, and a skewer inserted in the centre comes out clean, or with just a few crumbs sticking to it.
7 Cool in the tin for 20–30 minutes, then turn out onto a wire rack. Have a sneaky slice, still warm, with butter.

TIP You could use sweet potato or butternut (or indeed any) squash here, in place of the pumpkin. If you are set on a pumpkin, please steer clear of the huge Halloween variety, which are mainly composed of water.

MAKES
One 1kg loaf
(slices into 8)
PREP/COOK
50 minutes (including roasting pumpkin) preparation
1 hour cooking
YOU WILL NEED
One greased 900g loaf tin

Sweet and salty honey peanut cake with honey cream cheese frosting

This is a substantial cake that provides much needed ballast for those cold, hungry explorers in need of sustenance after a long evening outdoors. It expertly balances sugar and salt in a no-nonsense sort of way, and is always a big hit with those who don't like their cakes too tooth-rottingly sweet. The peanut butter replaces butter and the honey replaces sugar, making this a non-traditional take on a traditional formula.

1 Preheat the oven to 180°C/Gas mark 4.

2 Combine the flour, salt and baking powder and set aside.

3 Beat the peanut butter and honey together in a large bowl, until paler in colour and larger in volume. Add the eggs, one by one, beating until fully incorporated. Finally, add the vanilla extract and beat that in turn.

4 Gradually add your flour mixture to the peanut buttery batter, using a spoon now so you don't overwork the cake dough.

5 Pour the dough into the prepared tin, and level with the back of a spoon. Bake for 30–35 minutes until golden and risen.

6 Let the cake cool in the tin for 20 minutes before turning out and cooling completely on a wire rack. The cake will need to be completely cool before frosting.

7 Frosting: this is optional, as the cake serves just as well as a slightly plainer tea-time treat, but the tangy frosting does lift it to another level. Beat the cream cheese and butter together until smooth, which should take 3 or 4 minutes at least with an electric mixer. Add the honey and beat for another minute or so. Then add the icing sugar in three additions, beating for a couple of minutes after each addition.

8 Spread thickly across the top of the cooled cake, using a palette knife to make swirls if you're feeling that way inclined.

FOR THE CAKE
250g plain flour
2 tsp baking powder
1 tsp salt
100g peanut butter
250ml honey
3 eggs
1 tsp vanilla extract
**FOR THE CREAM
 CHEESE FROSTING**
200g full fat cream cheese
60g butter, softened
4 tbsp honey
300g icing sugar, sifted

MAKES
Cuts into 12 small squares
PREP/COOK
20 minutes preparation
35 minutes cooking
YOU WILL NEED
A 23cm greased square
baking tin

White Night cake

White Night is Brighton's annual, free, all-night arts festival. In defiance of the clocks going back and darkness approaching, the people of the city celebrate the light. To reflect the spirit of the evening I wanted to make a cake as light, white and bright as possible. An ethereal, almost ghostly concoction, as befitting this time of year – the palest of pale sponges, four light layers spread with coconut buttercream, as delicate as a lace petticoat, frosted all over, then sprinkled with feathery coconut flakes.

FOR THE CAKE
250g plain flour
¼ tsp salt
2 tsp baking powder
125g unsalted butter, softened
220g caster sugar
2 large eggs, separated
1 tsp vanilla extract
125ml milk
⅛ tsp cream of tartar
FOR THE FROSTING
350g unsalted butter, as soft as possible
500g icing sugar, sifted
125ml milk
2 tsp vanilla extract
300g desiccated coconut
FOR DECORATION
250g coconut flakes

MAKES
One 4-layer 20cm cake
PREP/COOK
25 minutes (cake), 10 minutes (frosting) preparation
25 minutes cooking
YOU WILL NEED
Two 20cm loose-bottomed buttered, floured and lined cake tins

1 Preheat the oven to 180°C/Gas mark 4.

2 Mix flour, salt and baking powder in a bowl and set aside.

3 In a separate bowl, beat the butter with an electric mixer until soft and creamy, which will take about a minute. Add about 150g of the sugar, reserving the rest, and beat until the mixture is light, pale and fluffy – be prepared for this to take another 2–3 minutes. Now add the egg yolks, one at a time, until they are completely incorporated. The mix should take on a yellowness, but look mousse-like and airy.

4 Add the vanilla and beat for another 30 seconds or so.

5 Add the flour mix and milk, alternately, until both are incorporated. This works best with the mixer on slow and continuous, and should take less than a minute as it's important not to overwork the dough here. Once the flour is added you want to be as quick as possible, or the cake will be tough and chewy.

6 In a separate, very clean bowl, whip up the egg whites with an electric whisk. When they start to foam, add the cream of tartar. Then beat a little longer until you have soft peaks, then add the remaining sugar, gradually. After another few minutes of beating you should end up with stiff peaks.

7 Take a large metal spoon or rubber spatula, and fold the egg whites into the cake batter, carefully, so as not to deflate them – use the minimum of movements and try to keep as much air in the mix as you can.

8 Put the batter into the prepared tins, and bake for 20–25 minutes until the palest golden. This is a white cake, and you don't want it to take on too much colour.

9 Set aside to cool in the tins for a few minutes, then turn out onto a rack to cool completely.

10 For the frosting: in a large bowl, beat the butter briefly, and scrape down the sides with a spatula. Add the sifted icing sugar, milk and vanilla, and beat until smooth and light – give it 3 or 4 minutes for a fluffy buttercream.

11 Add the desiccated coconut and beat until combined.

12 To decorate: wait until the cakes are completely cold (or your frosting will slide off), and cut through both horizontally with a serrated knife. It takes a little practice to get your layers level, but don't worry if they aren't: you are frosting this cake completely, so no-one will notice if anything is slightly wonky. Frosting covers a multitude of sins.

13 Place your bottom layer on whatever serving dish you are using, and use a thin layer of frosting to cover the top. Repeat with all three other cake layers. Use the last of your frosting to spread thinly all over the sides and top of the stacked cake layers – a palette knife is useful here. Again, don't worry about neatness, as you are now going to cover the whole thing with coconut flakes. Simply press on with your hands, and enjoy the squeals of delight when you unveil your gothic wonder.

TIP Please don't be tempted to use desiccated coconut for the decoration. It works only in the frosting, as this needs to be smooth. You can find coconut flakes in your nearest health food shop, and only they have the right gossamer-wing quality to coat your cake.

Harvest banquet

We're used to finding whatever we like on the shelves of the supermarket, at any time of year. Whether this is a good thing or not is questionable, but I have to admit to being one of those people who have, rather diva-like, demanded raspberries at Christmas-time in the past, so can hardly point the worthy finger of blame here.

However, even for the lazy cooks amongst us, Nature is going out of her way to make it incredibly easy for us in the autumn. Harvest festivals have taken place since people have been sowing and gathering food. Each country has its own tradition, and its own way of saying thank you to the earth that has borne their crops: Thanksgiving in America, the Harvest Moon Festival in China, Homowo in Ghana. Closer to home, Brighton is positively brimming with foodies at the annual Food and Drink Festival.

Cheesecakes can be eaten two ways – try savoury sheep's cheese and eat with pickled vegetables, or bake up its sweet sister with autumnal pumpkin rippled throughout. Rosehips can be infused in boiling water to make a crystalline sorbet, the colours of the hedgerows beading a delicate glass. Replace hazelnuts with their country cousins cobnuts in accompanying biscotti. Raid your nearby farmers' market for locally foraged mushrooms and fallen quinces, or scrump your own apples.

Shepherd's wheel pie

Mashed potato partitions, like the spokes of a wheel, go some way to explaining this pie's name, which is a sort of grown up version of shepherd's pie. The filling is mutton, but don't let that put you off. The adult sheep is full flavoured and deserving of much more recognition and recipes than it is currently the recipient of. If you have a greedy guts in your family, then simply pre-portion the mashed potato topping accordingly – the wheel spokes don't have to be equidistant!

1 tbsp olive oil

500g shoulder of mutton,
  cut into chunks

1 tbsp butter

1 medium onion, chopped

5 mushrooms, chopped

2 sticks celery, chopped

1 clove garlic, chopped

2 heaped tbsp elderberry
  or fruit chutney

stock to moisten

seasoning

500g cooked mashed
  potato (from 2 large
  potatoes; add milk,
  seasoning and butter if
  desired)

1 carrot, sliced lengthwise
  and blanched

1 Preheat the oven to 190°C/Gas mark 5.

2 In a large, flame proof casserole dish on a high heat, heat the olive oil until rippling. Brown the mutton on all sides, and remove from the pan. Don't worry about cooking it through – this is just to seal the outside and give it some colour. Lay your browned mutton in a pie dish.

3 Add the butter to the pan and reduce the heat. Cook the onion, mushrooms, celery and garlic in the buttery mutton fat until they soften and take on some of the deep, rich flavour.

4 Add the vegatables to the pie dish with a chutney of your choice. Season and add enough stock to moisten the mix and give you a gravy as the filling cooks.

5 Cover completely with mashed potato topping, levelling and spreading right up to the sides of the dish. Make grooves radiating from the centre with the end of a spoon, and lay the carrot slices in them, à la the spokes of a wheel.

6 Bake for 30–35 minutes until the potato topping is golden brown, and the pie filling cooked through and bubbling.

SERVES
6
PREP/COOK
25 minutes preparation
35 minutes cooking
YOU WILL NEED
One greased deep
pie dish

Harvey's hunky loaf

Harvey's ale has been brewed in Sussex for centuries, and it lends a hoppy taste to this loaf. The use of beer makes adding extra yeast unnecessary in this recipe, as it will provide the rise. It also provides a denseness and intensity of flavour. Any hoppy beer will make a good substitute.

This really is better ripped into chunks (or hunks if you're feeling alliterative), and used to mop up whatever meaty juices are left from your Harvest Banquet.

1 Preheat the oven to 180°C/Gas mark 4.

2 Sift your flour. This is an important step for this loaf in particular as it already has quite a compact crumb, as a result of not proving. If you don't sift the flour, the texture becomes very dense indeed.

3 Mix the flour, baking powder, salt and sugar, then pour in the beer. Use a wooden spoon or a whisk to bring everything together so that dry and wet ingredients are incorporated fully.

4 Spoon the dough into the loaf tin, and then pour the melted butter over the dough – this gives a shiny crackly crust to the loaf although, if you prefer a softer crust, you can incorporate the butter instead.

5 Bake for 1 hour until puffed and browned, and it sounds hollow when you tap the underside. Pop back in the tin and cool for at least 15 minutes before turning out.

450g plain flour
3 tsp baking powder
1 tsp salt
60g caster sugar
360ml Harvey's Ale (Best Bitter) or similar hoppy beer
100ml melted butter

MAKES
One 1kg loaf
PREP/COOK
20 minutes preparation
1 hour cooking
YOU WILL NEED
One greased 900g loaf tin

Savoury Slipcote cheesecake

Sussex Slipcote is a wonderful local creamy goat's cheese, and I created this recipe specifically to showcase its depth of flavour. For savoury cheesecakes, the principle is just the same as their sweet sisters, but instead of adding sugar to the cream cheese body, add a stronger cheese such as goat's or Parmesan. Add herbs instead of vanilla, and use wholewheat crackers for the base instead of digestive biscuits. In summer you could try adding basil and sundried tomatoes, in winter cranberries and sage. This makes a beautiful dinner party starter or vegetarian buffet dish, especially accompanied by some home pickled fruit or vegetables by way of contrast.

FOR THE BASE
75g cream crackers
50g hard cheese, grated –
 Cheddar or Parmesan
 are fine
25g melted butter
FOR THE FILLING
2 x 200g packs cream
 cheese
250g Sussex Slipcote,
 or other creamy goat's
 cheese
bunch chives, chopped
2 egg whites
½ lemon, juice and zest
2 tsp gelatine

MAKES
One 20cm cheesecake
PREP/COOK
40 minutes preparation
10 minutes cooking
(for the base)
YOU WILL NEED
One greased and lined
20cm springform pan

1 Preheat the oven to 190°C/Gas mark 5 and grease a 20cm springform cake tin.

2 Make the cheesecake base: grind your crackers in a food processor, or place them in a tea towel and bash them with a rolling pin – either way you want fine crumbs. Add the grated cheese and the melted butter and mix together with a fork until larger crumbs and clumps form.

3 Using the back of a spoon, press down the crumb mix into your greased tin. Place in the oven and bake for 10–15 minutes until crisp and fragrant. Take out of the oven and leave to cool.

4 Make the filling: as this isn't a baked cheesecake, it does take a little gelatine to make it set, but the texture is light as air. In a large bowl, or the food processor, blend the cream cheese and goat's cheese together until smooth. Add the chives, and some seasoning if you like, but do taste it first, as the cheese will probably provide enough saltiness.

5 In a clean bowl, whip up your egg whites until they form soft peaks, then set aside – these will give some much needed air and lightness, and stop the cheesecake being heavy.

6 Squeeze half a lemon and add about 4 tablespoons of water into a small pan, and add the gelatine, stirring to dissolve the powder. Heat until bubbles appear, and pour all into the cheese mixture, stirring in thoroughly.

7 Fold in your egg whites with a large metal spoon. If the cheese mixture looks stiff, stir in a spoonful of whites to loosen it, then fold in the rest, keeping as much air in as possible.

8 Spoon the cheese mix onto the base and level the top with a palette knife. Transfer to the fridge to set, which can take a few hours.

Forager's feast

Our forests and fields yield many riches if you know the right places to look. Sometimes, simplicity is best: foraged mushrooms, fried in butter and herbs, served atop a thickly sliced white farmhouse loaf. Heaven. Not baked exactly, but griddled and grilled, and too good to miss.

2 thick slices of sourdough bread

1 tbsp extra-virgin olive oil

1 small clove of garlic, finely chopped

185g local mushrooms, trimmed

15g butter

handful of parsley, roughly chopped

1 sprig of tarragon, roughly chopped

1 tbsp lemon juice

2–4 slices Parma ham (optional)

50g any melting cheese such as Gruyère or Emmental, grated (optional)

1 Heat the grill to high and line the grill pan with foil.

2 Set a griddle pan over a moderate heat. When hot, toast the bread on the pan for 1½ minutes on each side or until lightly toasted and marked with griddle lines – not cooked through. Place on the prepared grill rack (not under the heat).

3 Now set a small frying pan over a medium heat. Add the olive oil and garlic, and as soon as the garlic begins to sizzle, add the mushrooms and butter and season to taste. Stir-fry briskly for 2 minutes or until the mushrooms are lightly cooked, then add the herbs and lemon juice. Spoon onto the toast, heaping up the mushrooms and dividing the juices equally.

4 Tuck the ripped ham into the mushrooms and top with the grated cheese. Place under the grill and cook for about 5 minutes or until the cheese is bubbling and golden. Serve immediately.

TIP There are a burgeoning amount of foraging courses springing up all over the country (just like mushrooms in fact). Take advantage of an expert in the field and see what you can find.

MAKES
2 slices
PREP/COOK
10 minutes preparation
10 minutes cooking
YOU WILL NEED
A grill and a
griddle pan

Baked pumpkin and pecan cheesecake

This is about as far away from a traditional New York cheesecake as it is possible to get, but I adore it. I was tinkering around with the idea of doing a pumpkin pie recipe, but instead decided to incorporate all the glorious flavours into a baked cheesecake. The base of roasted pecans and gingernut biscuits offsetting the lightly creamy, velvet filling is simply heavenly.

FOR THE CRUST

400g gingernuts

1 tsp ground cinnamon

10 roasted pecans, chopped finely

60g unsalted butter, melted

FOR THE FILLING

400g pumpkin, cut into 2cm chunks

4 x 200g packs cream cheese, at room temperature

330g caster sugar

3 tbsp plain flour

3 tsp ground ginger

4 eggs

3 tbsp whisky

2 tsp vanilla extract

MAKES
One 23cm cheesecake
(serves 10)
PREP/COOK
50 minutes (including roasting pumpkin) preparation
1½ hours cooking time
YOU WILL NEED
A roasting tray and a greased 23cm springform cake tin

1 Preheat the oven to 200°C/Gas mark 6.

2 Firstly roast the pumpkin (this can be done in advance). Cut the flesh into 2cm chunks and place on a greased baking tray. Roast for 20–25 minutes until soft. Now mash with a fork or potato masher, or blitz in a food processor.

3 Put the oven down to 180°C/Gas mark 4 and make your cheesecake crust: bash the gingernuts in a bag or blitz them in a food processor until they are crumbs. Stir in the cinnamon and the chopped toasted pecans, then pour over the butter, mixing it with a fork until all the crumbs are moist and start to clump together.

4 Press the mix onto the bottom of the cake tin, and bake for 10 minutes until crisp. Set aside to cool.

5 When the crust has cooled, wrap the cake tin in foil, and place in a large roasting pan, which will serve as your water bath for baking the cheesecake and keeping the centre moist. This foil jacket is to stop any water leaking into the tin.

6 Make the cheesecake filling: beat the cream cheese and sugar together until they are completely smooth, which may take a minute or two. Beat in turns the flour and ginger, then the eggs, then the previously roasted pumpkin, whisky and vanilla. Pour the whole creamy, fragrant lot onto the biscuit base.

7 Pour recently boiled, but not boiling water into the roasting tray so it reaches 2cm up the cake tin sides. Bake in the oven, in the water bath until the filling is set, but still a little wobbly when you tap the side of the tin. You aren't looking for a great deal of movement here, but just a tremor. It should take about 1½ hours, but keep checking as the water may need topping up in this time.

8 Remove the cake tin from the water bath and let it cool in the tin. When it's cool enough, refrigerate overnight.

9 When you want to serve the cheesecake, release the sides, and run a warm butter knife between the cake and the tin if needed.

Steamed plum and ginger puddings

These are miniature spiced steamed puddings, studded with amethyst plums and flavoured with ginger. The dough puffs up round the fruit, leaving it a hidden treasure to be discovered by spoons and happy diners.

1 In a large bowl, cream the butter and sugars together for a few minutes until light and fluffy. Add the ginger and yoghurt and beat for a few minutes more until the batter has the texture of mousse.

2 Now add the eggs, one by one, making sure each is completely incorporated before you add the next.

3 Sift the flours over the top of the bowl, along with the baking powder, and stir in with a wooden spoon. The mixture should have a soft dropping consistency, and fall easily from your spoon.

4 Take the four serving dishes, and dot them with plum pieces, pouring the maple syrup over the top so that you have little purple islands floating in a lake of syrup. It may seem a little wet and odd, but this liquid will be the very thing that makes the steamed puddings so moist later on as it soaks into your sponge mixture.

5 Blob the sponge mixture over the top of the plums in their syrup, then cover the dishes with cling film. Now place the ramekins in a large saucepan, and pour boiling water from a kettle in the pan until it reaches half way up the sides. Cover the pan and simmer for about 30 minutes, until a skewer inserted in the centre of the pudding comes out clean.

6 Take the puddings out of the pan and cool for about 10–15 minutes before turning them out onto serving plates, and watching all those lovely mapley juices soaking into the sponge.

50g unsalted butter
50g caster sugar
50g vanilla sugar
5cm piece fresh root ginger, finely grated
100g natural yoghurt
2 eggs
40g cornflour
65g plain flour
1 tsp baking powder
8 ripe but firm Victoria plums, stoned and cut into 1cm pieces
150ml maple syrup

TIP To make vanilla sugar, simply add a cut vanilla pod to a jar of sugar, and let it steep and absorb for a week or so – much cheaper and tastier than the supermarket versions.

MAKES
4
PREP/COOK
20 minutes preparation
30 minutes cooking
YOU WILL NEED
4 ramekins or
pudding basins

127

Rosehip sorbet with cobnut biscotti

The elegance hidden away in the hedgerows... crystals of sunset-red sorbet, with a rusty glow imbued from the distilled essence of rosehips. If you have delicate glassware to serve in, all the better, but as you can see from the photograph, this is just as at home in a pewter tankard.

Cobnuts are a native British nut, now found mainly in Kent, but sometimes available at farmers' markets across the south east. They make a delicate biscotti that doesn't overpower the sorbet.

FOR THE SORBET
900ml water
250g granulated sugar
4 tbsp dried or 300g fresh rosehips, crushed
juice of ½ lemon
juice of ½ lime
1 tbsp of finely chopped herbs (lavender, mint, rosemary or scented geranium go well – or experiment with your own)
FOR THE BISCOTTI
225g self-raising flour
100g caster sugar
vanilla pod, split and seeds scraped out
100g cobnuts or hazelnuts, shells removed, chopped
2 eggs
50g butter, melted
25g flour mixed with 25g icing sugar
icing sugar, for dusting the biscotti

TIP If you aren't lucky enough to find cobnuts, hazelnuts make a worthy replacement.

1 For the sorbet: in a large saucepan, bring the water to the boil, and add the sugar, stirring to dissolve, then add the rosehips. Boil for 2–3 minutes until the water has turned a dusky pink, then take off the heat. Add the lemon and lime juice, and the herbs, and let all the flavours diffuse while the liquid cools for 30 minutes. Sieve your mix to ensure a sparkling clear sorbet.

2 Pour into a freezer container and freeze for about 30 minutes. Remove from the freezer, stir gently with a fork, breaking up any large lumps, and return for 30 minutes. Keep repeating this process until the sorbet is frozen and crystallised. If you have an ice cream maker, simply follow the manufacturer's instructions.

3 For the biscotti: preheat the oven to 180°C/Gas mark 4.

4 Mix together the flour, sugar, vanilla seeds and cobnuts in a bowl.

5 With an electric mixer, beat the eggs and butter together until pale and fluffy, which may take a couple of minutes, then slowly add your bowl of flour and beat until a firm dough is formed.

6 Dust a work surface with the flour and icing sugar mix and turn the dough out onto it. Now halve the dough and roll each half into a 24cm long rectangle, 1cm thick. Place the two rectangles of dough onto a baking sheet and bake for 20 minutes, until light golden. This is their first baking, which cooks the dough through, but doesn't give it the crispness necessary for a biscotti.

7 Let the cooked biscuit rectangles cool for 15 minutes, then slice into 12 with a sharp knife. Place each individual biscotti flat on the baking sheet and return to the oven for 15 minutes for their unique second baking. Dust with icing sugar when cool.

MAKES
1kg sorbet and 24
slices biscotti
PREP/COOK
For the sorbet, 5 hours
(including freezing)
preparation and, for
the biscotti, 20 minutes
preparation and 35 minutes
cooking time
YOU WILL NEED
A freezable container
and a greased
baking tray

FOR THE APPLE, MAPLE AND WALNUT CAKE

375g butter
675g dark muscovado sugar
6 eggs, lightly beaten
675g plain flour
4 tsp baking powder
3 tsp ground ginger
3 tbsp maple syrup
3 large Bramley apples, peeled, cored and diced (about 500–600g)
150g walnuts, chopped

FOR THE APPLE AND DAMSON COMPOTE

Makes about 1kg (2 big Kilner jars' worth)
1 kg eating apples, cored, peeled and chopped
500g damsons, stoned
juice of 1 lemon
250g caster sugar
1 cinnamon stick

FOR THE ICING

300g unsalted butter, softened
liquid from a jar of stem ginger
900g golden icing sugar, sifted

FOR THE SALTED CARAMEL SHARDS

500ml granulated sugar
250ml water
1 tsp sea salt

FOR DECORATION

2 eating apples, peeled, cored and sliced
2 tbsp brown sugar
4 tbsp butter

Autumn cake – scrumper's delight

Layers of apple, maple and walnut cake sandwiched together with quince and damson compote, and ginger fudge icing, all topped with shards of salted caramel and an apple rose. Autumn in cake form.

1 For the cake: preheat the oven to 160°C/Gas mark 4.

2 With an electric mixer (it will be easier for this amount of mixture if you have a tabletop mixer), cream the butter for a couple of minutes until light and airy. Add the muscovado sugar and cream the two together. Your butter and sugar mix won't be as fluffy as it would if you used caster sugar, but nevertheless it will still turn paler in colour and the volume will increase as you incorporate more air.

3 Beat in the eggs, one by one, until completely blended in. (With this amount of eggs, the batter may start to look curdled, but keep going.)

4 Add the flour, baking powder and ginger and give the mix a brief beating. Finally add the maple syrup, apple and walnuts and beat for another 30 seconds or so until a uniform texture is achieved.

5 Pour the batter into the two cake tins (use a large metal spoon if you want to make sure they are completely even – spooning in turn into each tin). Bake for 45 minutes to 1 hour until risen and browned. Because the cake is moist, when a skewer is inserted into the centre it should come out with a few crumbs attached. Cool in the tins for 10 minutes, then cool completely on a wire rack.

6 For the compote: combine all the compote ingredients in a large flame-proof casserole and heat gently until the fruit is tender and jammy. This could take up to 30 minutes. It will make a lot more compote than you need, but you could jar some for presents, or try on your cereal, or thickly spread on crumpets. Let the compote cool.

7 For the icing: beat the butter in a large mixing bowl for a few minutes until fluffy. Add the ginger liquid and half the sugar and beat for 3–5 minutes until smooth and creamy. Add the rest of the sugar in three batches, beating for a couple of minutes after each addition.

8 For the caramel shards: place the sugar and water in a medium saucepan and stir to combine. Cook over medium to high heat, without stirring, until the mixture starts to brown, about 14 minutes. Gently swirl the pan until the mixture is an even, deep amber colour, about 1 minute more. Immediately remove from the heat and quickly stir in the salt. Pour onto the prepared baking sheet, spread in an even layer, and let cool. Once cool, break into small pieces, or shards, as you like.

9 For the apple decoration (optional): place a large frying pan on a medium heat, and melt the sugar and butter together. When the brown liquid starts to bubble, throw in your apple slices, and shake the pan around for a few minutes until they soften and become rough round the edges. Using a slotted spoon, take them out of the pan (reserving the juices), and let them cool completely.

And now for the assembly:

10 Take your two cake layers, and make them into four: using a serrated knife (a bread knife is fine), cut horizontally through each layer, trying to keep them even. This comes with practice, and if yours are slightly wonky, it doesn't matter at all as this is a completely frosted cake. You also may be trying to slice through nuts and sultanas, which can make your results a little messier: persevere.

11 Take whatever serving platter you are using, and put one of the cake layers on top. Spread some of the compote thinly over the cake layer, and then spread a layer of frosting thinly over the compote. As with the rose cake, you will need less frosting and compote than you think – the cake layers push everything downwards and out when they are resting on top, and generosity here will be wasted.

12 Repeat for the next three layers, but omit the compôte for the top of the cake, and frost slightly more thickly. Frost the sides of the cake (a palette knife is useful here).

13 You can serve the cake just as it is quite happily but, if you want to be fancy (and sometimes it's nice to be), add the caramel shards to the top edges of the cake. Place the sweetened apple slices in concentric circles on the top, forming a rose shape.

14 Stand back and wait for the gasps of amazement…

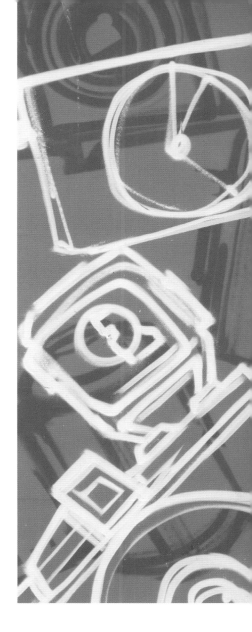

MAKES
One four-layer
20cm cake
PREP/COOK
20 minutes (cake), 45 minutes
(compote), 10 minutes (frosting),
10 minutes (caramel) preparation;
1 hour (cake), 30 minutes
(compote), 10 minutes (frosting),
15 minutes (caramel) cooking
YOU WILL NEED
Two 20cm cake tins and a
large baking tray

Lunchbox lovelies

Step away from the soggy sandwiches! Thinking a little differently about your daily routine can result in a packed lunch that doesn't feel like a punishment. The baking for all these recipes can be done the day before, or even at the weekend, frozen, and simply defrosted in the morning before you go to work.

Just be warned that your workmates will quickly become aware of your newfound culinary prowess: you might need to invest in a padlock for your lunchbox, and prepare yourself for the envious glances...

Coffee cupcakes with mini doughnuts

Doughnuts and coffee – that workplace staple – are combined here in cake form. If you don't want to go to the trouble of making the tiny doughnut hats for the delicately coffee-flavoured cakes, it isn't a necessity.

MAKES
20 cupcakes
PREP/COOK
20 minutes (cakes), 5 minutes (frosting), 2½ hours doughnuts (including proving) preparation;
20 minutes (cakes), 15 minutes (doughnuts) cooking
YOU WILL NEED
Two 12-hole muffin trays lined with paper cases

FOR THE COFFEE CUPCAKES

175g unsalted butter, softened

350g caster sugar

3 eggs

350g plain flour

1 tsp baking powder

½ tsp salt

1 tbsp espresso coffee grounds

125ml strong espresso coffee

90ml milk

FOR THE WHIPPED CREAM ICING

500ml double cream

5 tbsp icing sugar

FOR THE DOUGHNUTS (optional)

500g strong bread flour

7g sachet fast-action dried yeast

100g unsalted butter, softened

45g caster sugar

1 tsp salt

2 eggs

360ml full-fat milk

2 cups vegetable oil

caster sugar for dusting

1 Preheat the oven to 180°C/Gas mark 4.

2 Cream the butter and sugar in an electric mixer until light and fluffy – about 3 minutes should do it. Gradually add the eggs, one at a time, beating until each is incorporated.

3 In another bowl, mix the flour, baking powder, salt and coffee grounds. Now measure out the coffee and milk together.

4 Add your dry and wet ingredients by turn into the butter and sugar, being careful not to add too much in one go, or the mixture will become curdled.

5 Fill your cupcake cases about three quarters full (you can fill a little more if you want domed, rather than flat, cupcakes). Bake for 20–22 minutes until puffed and browned, and a skewer inserted into the middle of one comes out clean. Cool on a wire rack.

6 **For the icing:** whip up the cream until it forms soft peaks, being careful not to overwhip. Add the sugar (it's very much a matter of personal taste here – start with a couple of tablespoons and see how you get on.)

7 **For the doughnuts:** in a small pan on a low heat, warm the milk and set aside.

8 In a large bowl (if you have a tabletop mixer, use this) add the flour and yeast, making sure they are well blended. Rub in the butter until grainy crumbs form. Now rub in the sugar and salt.

9 Add the egg and milk and either mix or knead gently for a couple of minutes in the bowl to make sure they are incorporated. Now either knead vigorously for 10–15 minutes or simply use the dough hook in your mixer to do the hard work for you (it will probably take about 6 minutes on medium speed). You're looking for a dough that is elastic, and springs back when you push it with your finger.

10 Place the dough in a clean, greased bowl, and cover with greased cling film. Set aside for an hour until it rises nicely.

11 Now roll your dough out to a couple of centimetres thick,

trying not to push out all the air. Cut out doughnuts with a pastry cutter, and cut out the centre of each one with a large icing bag nozzle. You should have about 25–30 doughnuts (and their holes!).

12 Place the doughnuts on a baking tray, leaving sufficient space between them, and cover them with greased cling film. Let them rise and double in size for another hour.

13 Heat the oil in a high-sided pan to about 180°C, or use a deep fat fryer. Lower about five doughnuts into the hot oil at a time with a slotted spoon. Fry for a minute or so then turn. When both sides are golden, remove with the slotted spoon and lay on kitchen paper to drain. Repeat until you have fried all your doughnuts, then roll in caster sugar.

14 To make up: the cupcakes look pretty frosted with the whipped cream piped through a large star nozzle, and then topped with a mini doughnut at a jaunty angle.

Triple whammy (fresh, stem and powder) gingerbread

The perfect lunchbox treat: gingerbread is sturdy, transportable, tasty, keeps for days, and needs no adornments whatsoever.

1 Preheat the oven to 170°C/Gas mark 3.

2 Simply chuck the butter, syrup, treacle, sugar, gingers and spices into a large pan and heat gently until you have a bubbling, aromatic lava.

3 Take the pan off the heat and leave for a minute or so to cool down. Dissolve the bicarbonate in 2 tbsp warm water and add it to the pan with your eggs and milk – you should see a faint fizz at this point as the bicarb does its magic.

4 You can either add the liquid ingredients to the flour in its bowl, or sift the flour into the pan – it is up to you and dependent on the size of your pan. It will look runny but that is what you want. Runny = sticky and fudgy and moist later.

5 Pour into your tin and bake for 45 minutes until set on top and firm, but still squidgy underneath. Cool in the tin before turning out and cutting into squares or slices.

MAKES
16 squares
PREP/COOK
20 minutes preparation
45 minutes cooking
YOU WILL NEED
One greased and lined
30cm x 20cm tray

150g butter
200g golden syrup
200g black treacle
125g muscovado sugar
2 tsp finely grated ginger
3 lumps stem ginger,
  chopped finely
1 tsp ground ginger
¼ tsp ground cloves
2 eggs, beaten
250ml full-fat milk
1 tsp bicarbonate of soda
300g plain flour

Lemon poppy seed biscuits

These pale and buttery biscuits are magic: open your lunchbox and I'll guarantee they will disappear. They are the sort of biscuits that would also accompany a mousse or posset admirably, and work very well wrapped in tissue paper as a present too. Tangy citrus and crunchy poppy seeds complement buttery shortbread wonderfully, but do experiment – with rosemary, clementine or cardamom for instance.

250g butter, softened
30ml freshly squeezed
lemon juice
400g plain flour
1 tsp baking powder
½ tsp salt
300g caster sugar
1 egg
2 tsp vanilla
4 tsp lemon zest plus ½ tsp
extra for topping
1 tbsp poppy seeds plus
extra for topping

1 Preheat the oven to 180°C/Gas mark 4.

2 Melt 125g of the butter, and add the lemon juice to the pan. Set aside and let the lemony butter cool.

3 Combine the flour, baking powder and salt and set aside.

4 Now beat the remaining 125g of butter with 250g of the sugar until it is mousse-like and creamy. Beat in your egg followed by the lemon butter and keep beating (this is easier with electric beaters than by hand) for a few minutes until it is light, pale and fluffy.

5 Beat in the vanilla, lemon zest (remember to save some for topping) and poppy seeds until they are fully incorporated, then sift the flour mix over the top and beat gently until smooth.

6 On a flat surface, sprinkle the rest of the sugar, along with the lemon zest. Take a tablespoon of the dough and roll it in your hands to form a ball. Place the biscuit ball on the prepared baking sheet.

7 Take a small glass and moisten the bottom with water. Then dip it into the sugar and lemon zest (which should now be coating the bottom of the glass) and press your biscuit ball down, flattening and adding a sugary coating in one step. Sprinkle with poppy seeds and repeat until you have used up all the dough.

8 Bake for about 12 minutes until slightly golden round the edges – you don't want these delicate shortbreads to take on too much colour. Cool on the trays for a few minutes before transferring to a wire rack to cool completely.

MAKES
36 biscuits
PREP/COOK
15 minutes preparation
12 minutes cooking
YOU WILL NEED
3 greased and lined
baking trays

Blonde Elvis or peanut butter blondies

The king of rock 'n' roll's fondness for peanut butter was legendary and almost matched by my own. Spooned straight from the jar is my preferred way of eating, but sometimes protocol demands sharing. Although I am not generally a fan of the occasionally anaemic blondie (preferring the gooey richness of their darker cousins the brownie), here the nutty butter adds a much needed intensity. These bars were born out of my desire to see a jar of peanut butter go further – though eating an entire trayful is perhaps not the best way of doing so.

200g plain flour
1 tsp baking powder
1 tsp salt
125g unsalted butter,
  melted and cooled to tepid
80g smooth peanut butter
220g soft brown sugar
1 large egg
1 large egg yolk
1 tsp vanilla extract
250g chopped peanut
  butter cups or Snickers
  bars
50g chopped milk
  chocolate

1 Preheat the oven to 170°C/Gas mark 3.

2 Sift together the flour, baking powder and salt and set aside.

3 In a large mixing bowl, stir the melted butter and peanut butter together until you have a loose, runny mixture. Add the brown sugar, egg, egg yolk and vanilla, and stir all these in their turn. Add the chunky peanut butter cup or Snickers pieces. (I defy you not to lick the spoon at this point – if you can resist, you're a stronger person than I am.) Your dough will be thick and chunky, and rather obstinate. Good – this is what you want.

4 Scrape the mix into the baking tin and press it down with your wooden spoon. Bake it for about 30 minutes until the top looks golden and set. You still want a fudgy centre though, so if you insert a skewer it should come out with quite a few moist crumbs attached.

5 Let cool completely in the tin, then turn out. I have a timer on for how long these last…

TIP It's a good idea to have an overhang of lining paper in your tray, as you can then use it as a useful aid for pulling your blondies out of the tin.

MAKES
12 squares
PREP/COOK
20 minutes preparation
25 minutes cooking
YOU WILL NEED
A greased and lined
20cm x 20cm tray

Honey and nut bread

A versatile, easy loaf that doesn't need proving. Because of this the grain is close and dense, and it slices marvellously for sandwiches. There is a sweetness from the honey, and the sprinkling of nuts adds texture. Try it with smoked salmon, hand-cut ham or melting brie.

1 Preheat the oven to 180°C/Gas mark 4.

2 In a large bowl, mix the flour, baking powder, bicarbonate and salt and set aside.

3 Whisk the egg in a separate bowl until paler in colour and fuller in volume (it's fine to use a hand whisk for this). Whisk in the milk, honey and butter.

4 Pour that lovely sweet milk mix over the top of the flour and very gently mix the two together until just combined, no more. Now fold in the chopped walnuts with a large metal spoon, using the minimum of movements.

5 Pour the bread dough into the greased loaf tin and bake for about 45 minutes until it is risen and browned, and a skewer inserted into the middle comes out clean.

6 Cool in the tin for about 20 minutes, then turn out of the tin and cool on a wire rack.

425g plain flour

2 tsp baking powder

½ tsp bicarbonate of soda

1 tbsp salt

1 egg

250ml milk

200ml honey

2 tbsp butter, melted

300g chopped walnuts

MAKES
One 1kg loaf
PREP/COOK
20 minutes preparation
45 minutes cooking
YOU WILL NEED
A greased 900g loaf tin

Lamb and cumin sausage rolls

There is much to be said for the sausage roll, bursting with seasoned pork meat – the sausage made portable in its own pastry case. Much of it has been said already however, and unfortunately buffet tables up and down the land are groaning with the weight of sadly soggy, grey and undercooked specimens. The most important thing to grasp, whether your filling be pork or, as here, gently spiced lamb, is that there should be more meat than pastry. A simple equation, easily followed.

1 onion, finely chopped
1 tbsp butter or olive oil
1 garlic clove
½ red chilli or 1 tsp chilli flakes (optional)
3 tsp ground cumin
1 tbsp ras-el-hanout
400g lamb mince
bunch of finely chopped mint
zest of 1 lemon
500g block puff pastry
1 egg, for brushing
fennel seeds, for sprinkling

1 Preheat the oven to 180°C/Gas mark 4.

2 Gently fry the onions for a couple of minutes in the butter until starting to soften, then add the garlic, chilli, cumin, and ras-el-hanout, and continue to fry for a few minutes until everything is aromatic and soft.

3 Take a large bowl, and add the onion mix, along with the lamb mince, mint and lemon, and mix everything thoroughly together – you are trying to imbue those lovely spicy flavours throughout the meat.

4 Roll the pastry out to a large rectangle, and cut into three columns, about 15cm across. Squidge the meat into three long sausage shapes, and lay down the middle of each of the three columns.

5 Brush each edge of pastry with the egg wash, then pull one side of the pastry up and over the lamb mixture, and bring it down to seal with the other edge.

6 Brush the whole column with egg wash and sprinkle with fennel seeds. Bake for 20 minutes until puffed and golden, then slice into individual sausage rolls, however long you like them.

MAKES
About nine 15cm
sausage rolls
PREP/COOK
35 minutes preparation
20 minutes cooking
YOU WILL NEED
One greased
baking tray

Celeriac and carrot samosas

Or, how Indian street food found its way into British lunchboxes. Here, autumnal vegetables are curried and wrapped in a crunchy filo coating. Although the samosa is traditionally deep fried, a glistening sheen of oil coating its crunchy chickpea flour surface, I wouldn't advocate that preparation method here, unless they were going to be eaten immediately. Anything deep fried loses crispness if it is left hanging around, becoming greasy and limp. Baking is the order of the day here, so the health conscious amongst you can rejoice.

1 Put the diced celeriac, carrot and potato in a large pan and cover with cold water. Bring the water to a boil, and simmer the vegetables until they are tender (the time this will take depends on the size of your dice). Drain and set aside.

2 Heat the olive oil, and fry the onion, garlic, chilli and garam masala together for a few minutes until softened.

3 Stir the onion mix, stock and lots of seasoning into the diced vegetables. If you like, crush some of them slightly, which makes your samosa filling a little creamier. Set everything aside to cool.

4 Preheat the oven to 180°C/Gas mark 4.

5 Making the samosas: this is the slightly fiddly – or the fun – bit, depending what personality type you are. If you have little ones, get them to help you here, as little fingers can be dextrous, and will probably enjoy this no end. Cut your filo rectangles vertically down the centre, making 24 30 x 9cm strips. Brush the first strip all over with oil, and put a heaped spoonful of filling in the bottom right-hand corner. Now take the left-hand corner and bring that up and over the filling, forming that distinctive triangle shape. Fold the pastry up the strip another four times, keeping the triangle as defined as possible. This only sounds complicated on paper – when you have the strips in front of you it makes sense, I promise.

6 Brush your first samosa with olive oil, stand back to admire your handiwork, then make 23 more.

7 Place on a greased baking tray, then bake for 20–25 minutes until crisp.

TIP The quantity I've given you here is so you can freeze some, unbaked, and simply cook from frozen for 10–15 minutes.

½ a celeriac, peeled and diced
2 carrots, peeled and diced
1 potato (300g), peeled and diced
4 tbsp olive oil
1 onion, finely chopped
2 cloves garlic, crushed
1 chilli, finely chopped
3 tbsp garam masala
stock, for loosening (you might need just a few tablespoons)
small bunch of fresh coriander, chopped
12 sheets filo pastry, 30cm x 18cm
oil for brushing

MAKES
24 small samosas
PREP/COOK
1 hour preparation
25 minutes cooking
YOU WILL NEED
Two large greased
baking trays

145

Winter

Christmas brunch

A canapé party to welcome the New Year

Birthday party

Crunchy, crisply, crackly. Food sparkles with the intensity of a frost-filled morning at our wintertime gatherings – markers of warmth and comfort to punctuate the long months of chill.

Christmas brunch

What hasn't been said about Christmas? This is one ancient festival that hasn't shrunk into the shadows, but has continued to grow, a behemoth, ever gaudier each year: more tinsel, more bauble, more...well everything really.

Ever since pagan times people have been having a big old knees-up to mark the turning of the season – the Solstice – a light in the darkness, where the long, cold, bleak blackness slowly, slowly gives way to the springtime, to the sunshine. In Brighton, the Burning of the Clocks is a beautiful and symbolic farewell to the dark days of winter.

I shall leave the turkey/mince pie/Christmas pudding traditions for elsewhere – others have covered them well – they have their own spotlight, and are rarely shy of it. But why not luxuriate in a decadent Christmas brunch, on or around the day itself? Wake up to a delicately puffed lobster soufflé, or the rich oozing velvet of syrupy pecan French toast; let fresh cranberries replace the marzipanned cake of tradition.

Solstice, Saturnalia or Christmas then, gather those you love about you (by force if necessary) and enjoy home, hearth and heavenly eats...

Baked pecan French toast

My all-time favourite brunch dish – and, in my years running a gourmet bed and breakfast, the one dish that was requested over and above any other, time and time again. I've basically crossed French toast with its British sibling, bread and butter pudding. A match made in heaven. This should be enough empirical evidence to persuade you, but if not, let me just say: you can make it in advance, and simply pop into the oven on the day, so ruling out any Christmas morning kitchen stress. It is the best French toast you will ever have. Plain, simple fact.

1 French stick (a day old is best)
6 eggs
750ml full fat milk
1 tsp vanilla extract
250g brown sugar
250g pecans
65g unsalted butter
½ tsp salt
200g seasonal fruit – berries are lovely in the summer, but chopped apple and pears are gorgeous at this time of year
a vat of maple syrup, for serving

1 Cut 20 slices from the French stick about 2cm thick, and put them across the base of the serving dish. You want a single layer of bread here, so they can all have an equal chance of absorbing some of the delicious spiced milk you are about to pour over them.

2 Whisk together the eggs, milk, vanilla and 200g of the sugar and, when the sugar has dissolved, pour this over the bread slices. You might need to do a little bit of jiggling and re-arranging, and you might even need to add the liquid in two batches, depending on how absorbent the bread is. I know it seems a lot of liquid, but be patient, it will take it, and it is what makes your French toast so moist the next day.

3 You can now put the dish in the fridge until tomorrow, and forget about it until you're ready to serve it in the morning.

4 On the day itself, preheat the oven to 180°C/Gas mark 4.

5 Meanwhile, fry the pecans, butter and salt in a pan together for a few minutes until they begin to colour. Sprinkle the salty pecans and the fruit over the top of your soaked bread, pushing them down between the slices too.

6 In a small pan, heat the butter with the remaining 50g of sugar and stir until all the sugar dissolves. Pour this over the bread too, covering the nuts and fruit.

7 Bake for about 20 minutes, until cooked through and bubbling. Serve with as much maple syrup as is humanly possible.

SERVES
6
PREP/COOK
20 minutes preparation
plus 1 day for soaking
25 minutes cooking
YOU WILL NEED
A deep buttered ovenproof
dish, about 30cm in length
and 20cm wide

FOR THE MUFFINS

80g butter, melted

300g plain flour

2 tsp baking powder

250g brown sugar

1 tbsp orange flower water

250ml mandarin juice, freshly squeezed (roughly 5 mandarins)

1 egg, beaten

225g sour cream

zest of 2 mandarins

50g chopped pecans

FOR THE COMPOTE

(makes 500g compote or 1 large Kilner jar)

3 pears, chopped

150g dates, chopped

1 cinnamon stick

1 tsp allspice

375ml apple juice (cloudy is best)

lemon juice and 1 tsp honey to taste

MAKES
12 muffins
PREP/COOK
20 minutes (muffins),
10 minutes (compôte)
preparation
25 minutes (muffins),
15 minutes (compôte) cooking
YOU WILL NEED
One greased 12-hole
muffin tray

Mandarin muffins with spiced pear and date compote

There is something about the flavour of mandarins that screams Christmas to me, though not in a Noddy Holder fashion. They cut through all the richness, the excess and the goose fat – the perfect antidote. Lovely as they are, unadorned, at the bottom of a stocking, they are rarely used as a cooking ingredient, which is a great shame. Although they are often overlooked for their more popular citrus relations the clementines, satsumas and oranges, do give them a try – they imbue these muffins with a taste quite their own.

1 Preheat the oven to 180°C/Gas mark 4.

2 Use a little of the melted butter to grease the muffin tray.

3 In a large bowl, combine the flour, baking powder and sugar.

4 In another bowl, add the orange flower water to the mandarin juice, and then add the egg, sour cream and melted butter.

5 Pour the dry ingredients over the wet and give it a couple of brief stirs (remembering the muffin mantra of never overmixing), and then fold in the mandarin zest and chopped pecans. Some floury pockets are absolutely fine – if you mix it too thoroughly you will have little rocks to eat on Christmas morning, which won't be entirely what you were expecting, I'll warrant.

6 Spoon your muffin batter into the waiting holes of the muffin tray, and bake for 20–25 minutes.

7 For the compote: add all ingredients, except the honey, to a large pan and bring to a boil. Simmer for 10 minutes until everything is starting to break down. Add the honey and simmer for a few minutes more. You can either use as it is, or purée in a blender if you prefer (remembering to take out the cinnamon stick).

TIP If you want to eat these muffins alone, perhaps with some Greek yoghurt and maple syrup, they will be perfectly lovely. However, they are divine with the pear and date compote, which lifts the dish into properly luxurious, aromatic, fully rounded brunch fare.

Jilly and Gabrielle's egg and bacon pie

Another Kiwi institution – the bacon and egg pie – is really a fry-up in pastry. Friends ran a café in Christchurch city centre – The Sauce Kitchen – that sadly bore the brunt of the earthquakes in 2011. Until then, their bacon and egg pie had garnered superlatives from the Prime Minister, amongst many others. This is their recipe, no tweaking – the breakfast, lunch or dinner of champions.

375g ready-rolled puff-pastry sheet
50g grated Cheddar cheese
200g free-range streaky bacon
7 eggs
bunch of chopped flatleaf parsley
seasoning
2 large ripe tomatoes, sliced

1 Preheat the oven to 180°C/Gas mark 4.

2 Roll out your sheet of puff pastry to the thickness of a £1 coin. Cut a 20 x 35cm rectangle from the pastry, and use to line the tart tin with 3–4cm pastry overhang along both the long sides (this will help to join the pie lid on later).

3 Spread the base of the pie all over with the grated cheese, then lie the bacon on top, making a complete meaty layer.

4 Carefully crack in 6 of the eggs, trying to keep the yolks as whole as you can. It helps if you make little indentations in the bacon with the back of a spoon first.

5 Sprinkle the eggs with the parsley and lots of seasoning, then lay the sliced tomatoes over all, very gently so as not to crack the eggs.

6 Cut an 8cm x 35cm rectangle from your pastry trimmings (you may have to re-roll). Place this lid on top of the pie, and use the leftover egg, beaten, to brush over the top of the lid. Now take the overhanging pastry at the sides of the tart tin, and fold them inwards, so they create a seal. You can crimp the edges with the blunt side of a knife or use your fingers if you like.

7 Score the pastry in a criss-cross or lattice pattern, and bake for 35–40 minutes until puffed and golden brown.

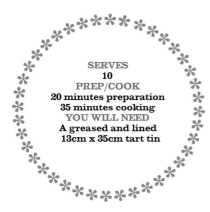

SERVES
10
PREP/COOK
20 minutes preparation
35 minutes cooking
YOU WILL NEED
A greased and lined
13cm x 35cm tart tin

Seafood soufflés

A lobster and crab soufflé seems to epitomise the luxury of the Christmas we would all like to have in our wildest, most Great Gatsby-esque dreams. Soufflés do need a little care and attention, but, as long as you make sure the beaten egg whites stay fluffy and instil the mix with that all-important lightness, your soufflé will rise.

500ml fish stock
100ml white wine
1 onion, quartered
4 cloves
2 bay leaves
500g assorted shellfish and white fish – lobster meat, crab meat, raw scallops, raw sustainable white fish of your choice (gurnard, pollock, hake, etc. are all good here)
seasoning
BÉCHAMEL SAUCE
4 tbsp unsalted butter
4 tbsp plain flour
400ml milk
6 eggs, separated
500g of grated tangy cheese (try your local hard cheese)

1 Preheat the oven to 180°C/Gas mark 4.

2 First add your stock and wine to a large flame-proof casserole dish and heat gently. Add the onion quarters, each studded with a clove, and the bay leaves, and bring up to simmering point.

3 Poach the fish in this liquid very gently, until just cooked through – this should take only 5–8 minutes or so. Gently remove from the pan and flake your fish, mixing with any already cooked shellfish. Season well.

4 Make a béchamel sauce: In a high-sided saucepan, melt the butter gently, and when it starts to bubble, add the flour, a spoonful at a time, stirring for 30 seconds or so after each addition to make sure it is properly incorporated. When you have added all the flour, keep stirring to cook it out completely.

5 Slowly pour in the milk, stirring the whole time as you do, so that the paste is gradually loosened.

6 Take the pan off the heat and beat in the egg yolks, one at a time. Now stir in the grated cheese, which should mean your mixture is now unctuous and golden.

7 Very gently stir in the shellfish and fish, and taste to see if it needs more seasoning. Allow to cool.

8 In an inordinately clean bowl beat your egg whites. Keep beating through the foamy stage until soft peaks are formed.

9 Now is the time for a steady hand – you want to keep as much air in the soufflés as possible for that magical rise. Using a metal spoon, stir one spoonful of egg white into the fish mixture to loosen it slightly. Now very gently fold in the rest of the egg whites, a spoonful at a time, until the batter is mousse-like and airy.

10 Pour or spoon into the greased ramekin dishes and bake for 20 minutes, then increase the oven temperature to 200°C/Gas mark 6 for the last 5–10 minutes until the soufflés are risen and browned on top.

11 I don't have to say: serve immediately!

MAKES
4 soufflés
PREP/COOK
1 hour (including poaching the
fish) preparation
20 minutes cooking
YOU WILL NEED
4 greased ramekins or
ovenproof dishes

Cranberry brunch cake

Yes you can eat Christmas cake for breakfast! I've lightened up the whole stodgy dried fruit idea here, and made something much more similar to what the Americans would call a coffee cake. This may sound confusing but a coffee cake contains nothing of the sort, and is actually a cake that is particularly appropriate to eat with coffee – usually a sweet, buttery cake with fruit and nuts. The result is something that is still very festive, but more accessible (and brunch-appropriate) somehow.

3 eggs
450g sugar
175g butter, softened
1 tsp vanilla
300g plain flour
350g fresh cranberries
100g toasted flaked
  almonds

TIP Sprinkle muscovado sugar over Greek yoghurt and leave overnight for a caramel flavour. Delicious as an accompaniment to the warmed cake.

1 Preheat the oven to 180°C/Gas mark 4.

2 Beat the eggs and sugar until pale and thick and double in volume. When you lift the beaters out of the batter, they should leave a ribbon trail behind them. This will take about 5–7 minutes in a tabletop mixer, so be prepared. The air from beating your eggs will act as a raising agent, so cutting corners here may result in a rather disappointingly heavy cake later.

3 Add the butter and vanilla and mix for a few more minutes. Your mix should look gorgeously light and fluffy at this point. Sift over the flour, and stir in briefly with a wooden spoon. Add the cranberries and almonds, and stir to mix and ripple them throughout.

4 Spoon into the buttered tin, and bake for about 45 minutes until golden (not dark) brown, and a skewer inserted in the centre comes out clean. Cool in the tin for 15 minutes, then either serve warm for best results, or turn out and cool on a wire rack.

MAKES
Cuts into 12 squares
PREP/COOK
20 minutes preparation
45 minutes cooking
YOU WILL NEED
A buttered
23cm x 32cm tray

Mulled chai cakes

Your Christmas morning cuppa, in cake form.

1 Preheat the oven to 180°C/Gas mark 4. Line a muffin tray (if using) with suitably festive papers.

2 Place the teabags in a small bowl, pour over the boiling water and leave them to steep for 10 minutes. When you take the bags out, squeeze them as hard as you can, without breaking them, to extract as much flavour as possible.

3 Sift together the flour, baking powder, spices and salt in a bowl. I've deliberately left the quantities of spices vague, as it is down to your personal taste – anything from a tiny sprinkling to 2 tsp of each is fine.

4 Beat the butter with the sugar until pale and fluffy – this should take a few minutes. Add the eggs, one at a time, and beat thoroughly after each addition until completely incorporated, scraping down the sides of the bowl regularly.

5 Add the tea mixture to the yoghurt, and whisk together. Alternately add this tea mixture with the dry ingredients to the batter in the bowl while the mixer speed is on continuous low. Three or four batches of each should be fine, with a brief beating at the end to ensure everything is incorporated.

6 For small cakes: spoon the cake batter into the papers, filling to about three-quarters up to the top. Bake for 20–22 minutes until puffed and browned.

7 For a big cake: simply spoon into a large tin, level the top, and bake for about 1 hour.

8 For brunch, only a light festive dusting of icing sugar is necessary, but if you were serving this cake later in the day, you could go the whole Christmassy hog, and make some spiced buttercream (simply add 1 tsp of your chosen powdered spice to the vanilla buttercream recipe on p.82), topping with decorations such as whole cloves, cinnamon bark pieces or cardamom pods.

6 chai teabags
125ml boiling water
450g plain flour
1 tsp baking powder
cinnamon, ginger, cardamom, cloves, nutmeg, black pepper
1 tsp salt
120g unsalted butter
220g light brown sugar
3 eggs
250ml natural or vanilla flavoured yoghurt
icing sugar, for dusting

MAKES
15 individual cakes or one 23cm cake
PREP/COOK
25 minutes preparation
22 minutes (individual)/1 hour (large) cooking
YOU WILL NEED
A 12-hole muffin tray or a 23cm loose-bottomed cake tin

A canapé party to welcome the New Year

Or, of topsy-turvy endings and new beginnings...

Our Roman forbears had a god with two faces – Janus – one looking back at the old year, one looking ahead to the new. The finality of the beginning of the evening gives way to the heart-in-mouth excitement as midnight approaches. Surely the only night then, that ends with a beginning.

Much as I love to gluttonously fill myself, fit to bursting, on any social (or solo) occasion I can get away with, it is tonight, maybe more than any other, you will probably have visitors of the transient variety, and therefore nibbles are the order of the evening.

There will be many people, and many parties, and a very high level of expectation, fuelled by fizz, and perhaps too much bubbling goodwill to sit and really concentrate on a traditional meal. Let these distinctive bite-size beauties be your guide and support – serve on boards or platters with whatever leftover festive greenery you can find. Much can be done in advance, so the Christmas-weary host or hostess can also join the fun.

Sesame crusted duck breast on flatbreads with tomato chutney

My most requested canapé. The Asian flavours are light and sophisticated, and just the thing for palates tired of heavy festive offerings. For the duck, you could go down the road of two-day cooking, marinating, hanging from the ceiling and drying with a hair dryer, but a sliced, juicy duck breast works just as well, with far less bother. This is not the time of year that many people have oodles of time to spare in the kitchen.

FOR THE FLATBREADS
300g strong white bread flour
1 tsp sea salt
1 tbsp baking powder
3 tbsp olive oil
FOR THE CANAPÉS
2 duck breasts
2 tbsp olive oil
2 tbsp sesame seeds
24 tsp fresh tomato chutney
small bunch of chives, chopped

TIP Do let the duck breast rest for at least 20 minutes after cooking – it results in a much juicier mouthful.

MAKES
20–25 canapés
PREP/COOK
1 hour (including proving) preparation
20 minutes cooking
YOU WILL NEED
A large, heavy based frying pan

1 For the flatbreads: mix the flour, salt and baking powder in a bowl. Add the olive oil and about 5–6 tablespoons of water from a recently boiled kettle.

2 Use your hands to bring the dough together. If it is too dry, add another tablespoon of water. Lift the dough out of the bowl, and place on a lightly dusted worktop. Roll your sleeves up, and knead, knead, knead. You want the dough to be smooth and springy, and this will take about 10 minutes.

3 Place the dough in a clean bowl and cover it, and set aside for about half an hour. You don't want a big rise – these are flatbreads – by their very nature they aren't going to puff up.

4 Tear small pieces of dough, and in moistened hands, flatten and press them into small bite-size rounds of about 6cm circumference. The dough should make about 25 rounds.

5 Heat a large, heavy-based frying pan on medium, and fry about five flatbreads at a time. Keep checking the undersides, and when they are golden, flip them and fry the other sides. It will probably take about 3 minutes for each side.

6 To assemble the canapés: first, fry your duck breasts. Rub the oil over the skin, and season. Heat a large heavy-based frying pan to medium high, and press the breasts, skin side down, onto the hot pan. Don't move them, just keep frying for about 8 minutes until the skin is crispy and brown.

7 Turn the breasts over and fry the undersides for another 8 minutes (medium rare). Take the breasts out of the pan and rest them for at least 20 minutes. Press sesame seeds all over.

8 Cut with the sharpest knife you have into 1cm slices, and lay one or two slices on each flatbread. Top with a teaspoon of tomato chutney and some chopped chives.

duck

Little charmers

Warm cheese-flavoured choux buns (gougère), served with sweet chilli sauce for dipping. Sussex Charmer is a local hard, tangy cheese that cleverly combines the best aspects of Cheddar and Parmesan, and adds sharp bite to these airy mouthfuls. Charming indeed.

FOR THE CHOUX BUNS
125ml water
50g butter
100g strong bread flour
salt
3 eggs
FOR THE FILLING
300g cream cheese
**150g grated Sussex
  Charmer (or similar)**
3 chopped spring onions
pinch paprika
FOR DIPPING
sweet chilli sauce

1 Preheat the oven to 180°C/Gas mark 4.

2 Make the choux balls: pour the water into a pan, and add the butter. Bring to a boil and then pour in the flour. This will look very unpromising, but take the pan from the heat and stir, as fast as you can, until the mixture comes together, and starts to leave the sides of the saucepan. Leave it to cool slightly.

3 Add the eggs to the pan, one by one. Each time you add an egg, keep the faith, and keep vigorously beating with a wooden spoon, and the dough will come together again. After the third egg has been incorporated you should have a smooth, glossy pastry, which is easily pipeable.

4 Spoon into a piping bag fitted with a 1cm plain nozzle, and pipe into 3cm balls onto the baking tray. Bake the balls until golden and puffed, about 6–8 minutes, then remove and leave to cool. Now poke a little hole in the bottom of each choux bun with the end of a spoon. Don't worry – they won't deflate!

5 Make the filling: whip the cream cheese, grated cheese, spring onions, paprika and plenty of seasoning together until smooth. Spoon this into a piping bag, and use it to fill each of the choux buns with a couple of teaspoons of the cheese mixture.

6 They are now ready to serve, and are quite delicious alone, though a bought sweet chilli sauce makes a suitable dipping partner.

MAKES
24 choux buns
PREP/COOK
40 minutes preparation
10 minutes cooking
YOU WILL NEED
A piping bag fitted with a
1cm round nozzle and a
greased baking tray

Stuffed chillies

This is more of a dare than a dish, to be completely honest. It depends how brave (read foolhardy) your guests are, but definitely warn them in advance that these mouthfuls will be hot stuff; serve them on forks, and do pass round napkins for people to wipe their fingers on.

They would probably make the perfect hen or stag night starter, or you could play a foodie game of Russian Roulette with them – maybe putting a couple in with a wholly calmer platter of stuffed Romano peppers. Anyway, you have been warned!

10 of the largest chillies you can find

200g Sussex Slipcote or other creamy goat's cheese

few sprigs fresh thyme leaves, chopped

small bunch fresh basil leaves, finely chopped

1 egg, beaten

seasoning

TIP It's important to use the largest chillies you can here, as the larger they are, the milder they are as a rule. Definitely do not make this dish with either Scotch Bonnet or the small Thai chillies – you will live to regret it!

1 Preheat the oven to 180°C/Gas mark 4.

2 Using gloves, halve the chillies and carefully deseed them.

3 Place them on the baking tray, and brush with the olive oil. Roast in the oven for 5–10 minutes until they are softened and have lost a little of their heat.

4 Meanwhile, make the stuffing: Simply beat all the cheese, herbs, egg and lots of seasoning together.

5 Take the chillies out of the oven and heap with the stuffing – you want them quite generously filled so the creamy freshness balances out the fiery pepper.

6 Bake for another 5–10 minutes until the stuffing has taken on some colour. Serve warm.

MAKES
20 chilli halves
PREP/COOK
20 minutes preparation
20 minutes cooking
YOU WILL NEED
A greased baking tray

Crab tartlets with avocado

Crisp bread casing crackles against soft melting avocado and light as feather white crabmeat. Sometimes the craving at this time of year is for something light, fresh and clean, and this delivers on all counts.

400g white crabmeat

small bunch tarragon, chopped

200g mayonnaise

juice of 1 lemon

2 avocados, as squishy and ripe as you can find

12 slices white bread, day old

olive oil, for brushing

1 Preheat the oven to 180°C/Gas mark 4.

2 Make the filling for the tartlets: mix the crabmeat, tarragon, mayonnaise and the juice of half a lemon with lots of seasoning in a medium bowl, and set aside.

3 Prepare the avocados: roughly mash the avocado with the juice from the other half of the lemon, season well and set aside.

4 Make the bread casings: grease the muffin trays. Flatten 12 slices of day old white bread with a rolling pin, and then use a 6cm pastry cutter to cut two circles out of each. Brush both sides with more olive oil, and press into the muffin trays.

5 Bake for 5 minutes until starting to go golden, then flip out of the muffin tin and put on a large baking tray upside down. Put back in the oven and bake for another 5 minutes to ensure crispness throughout.

6 Once the cases are cool, put a couple of teaspoons of avocado mash in the bottom, and then top with the crab mixture.

MAKES
24 tartlets
PREP/COOK
40 minutes preparation and 10 minutes cooking time
YOU WILL NEED
Two 12-hole muffin trays and one baking tray

Chocolate bites with salted caramel frosting

This is a rich one-pan chocolate cake, cut small into bite-size beauties. You could get away with a simple dusting of icing sugar at this time of year, piling them happily into a big tumbling mound for people to serve themselves. For smarter canapé parties, I have created a gorgeously grown-up salted caramel frosting. For these rather posher versions, line up in amassed ranks on an attractive serving plate.

1 Preheat the oven to 180°C/Gas mark 4.

2 For the bites: combine the sugar, flour, cocoa powder, baking powder, bicarbonate and salt in a bowl. Then pour in the egg, oil, vanilla extract and the buttermilk. Mix everything together gently. The batter should be runny, which will equal a lovely moist mouthful.

3 Pour into the baking tray and bake for 20 minutes or so until set. A skewer inserted in the middle should come out clean. Let cool in the tin before turning out and cutting into neat squares. If you are topping with frosting, the cake needs to be completely cold first.

4 For the frosting: combine sugar and water in a saucepan. Heat over medium high, and stir with a wooden spoon while the sugar dissolves. Bring the sugar to a boil and stop stirring. Let it boil for a few minutes until amber, but be careful not to let it turn dark brown, as this means the caramel has spoilt.

5 Remove the saucepan from the heat and stir in the first lot of butter and the cream. Be prepared for some spluttering and hissing and stand well back! Add the sea salt, and beat until everything comes together. Cool to room temperature.

6 Now transfer to a bowl, and add the second lot of butter. Beat with an electric mixer until light and fluffy – this should take 3–4 minutes of continual beating. Gradually add the icing sugar, 100g at a time, beating for a minute or two after every addition.

7 You can now use a palette knife to spread frosting over your bites, or pipe on top using an icing bag and nozzle.

FOR THE BITES
250g caster sugar
150g plain flour
100g cocoa powder
1 tsp baking powder
½ tsp bicarbonate of soda
½ tsp salt
1 egg
60ml vegetable oil
1 tsp vanilla extract
250ml buttermilk or sour cream

FOR THE FROSTING
220g caster sugar
1 tbsp water
60g unsalted butter
125ml double cream
1 tsp sea salt
115g unsalted butter, softened
500g icing sugar, sifted

MAKES
20 bites
PREP/COOK
15 minutes (cake), 20 minutes (frosting) preparation
20 minutes (cake) cooking
YOU WILL NEED
A greased and floured 30cm x 20cm baking tin, icing bag and nozzle (if using frosting)

169

Orange flower water pavlovas with Nyetimber mousse topping

Nyetimber is a sparkling wine from Sussex, the geology of the vineyards here mirroring that of the Champagne region of France. The wine is every bit as delicious as its French cousin. These pavlovas are light as air, individual clouds of meringue delicately perfumed with orange flower water. The frothy, bubbly mousse topping injects a note of fun into proceedings...this is New Year's Eve after all.

FOR THE MERINGUES
2 large egg whites, room
   temperature
120g caster sugar
1 tsp cornflour
¼ tsp white wine vinegar
1 tbsp orange flower water
FOR THE MOUSSE
80g sugar
5 egg yolks
300ml double cream
60ml Nyetimber or similar
   sparkling wine
FOR DECORATION
fresh orange zest

TIP If you can, leave your mini meringues in the oven overnight with the door open to cool gradually, which reduces cracking.

MAKES
20 bite-size meringues
PREP/COOK
10 minutes (meringues),
15 minutes (mousse)
preparation
20 minutes (plus overnight in
the oven) cooking
YOU WILL NEED
A large baking tray, lined
with baking paper

1 Preheat the oven to 110°C/Gas mark ½.

2 For meringues: beat the egg whites until soft peaks begin to form – this will probably take a few minutes, and shouldn't be rushed. Beating continuously, add the sugar, a tablespoon at a time, very gradually. Beat between each tablespoon until completely incorporated and not grainy to touch. The meringue should be getting stiffer now.

3 Mix the cornflour, vinegar and orange flower water together so that the cornflour dissolves. Add this to the meringue, and keep beating until you have glossy peaks that stay upright when you lift the beaters out.

4 Take large tablespoons of meringue and place them on the baking paper. You could pipe them, for neatness, but I rather like a little irregularity. Make a slight indentation in each with the back of your spoon, so the mousse has somewhere to sit.

5 Bake the meringues until they are crisp and dry to the touch – about 20 minutes. You want them to take on as little colour as possible, so do keep checking them. Turn the oven off and prop the door open with a tea towel. Cool in the oven for at least an hour, or overnight.

6 For the mousse: combine egg yolks and sugar in a Perspex bowl, or one that will withstand heat without cracking. Set the bowl over a pan of boiling water. Using an electric mixer, beat the eggs and sugar for a few minutes until thick and pale.

7 Take the bowl from the heat and beat in the double cream until the whole lot is foamy and light, and the cream is softly whipped.

8 Now whisk in the wine, gently, trying to keep some of the bubbles visible throughout. Spoon or pipe onto the pavlovas, and top with some grated orange zest.

'Nothing is certain but death and taxes'

Benjamin Franklin

Birthday party

Well I'd disagree with him because birthdays have a habit of appearing, and can be relied on to be a little more regular than the Brighton buses. They're milestones that traditionally involve epic portions and consumption of cake.

However, I'm never one to be satisfied with a one-course meal, so why not create a full-on birthday banquet? This is 'spoil-'em-rotten' territory after all. Yes there may be favourites requested, in which case, I'm not sure you can refuse (today is not really the day for going your own way).

As for that all-important cake, whether it's dark and rich, or individually portioned prettiness, it's up to you how accurate (read cruel) you are with the candles!

Dark Star birthday cake

Dark Star is a boutique brewery in Brighton, and was the inspiration for this grown-up chocolate cake. I wanted to bake a cake that reflected the poetry of their name – deep and dark and rich, with the beer a properly discernible flavour. The stout adds an earthy moistness.

MAKES
One 23cm cake
(serves 10)
PREP/COOK
20 minutes (cake), 5 minutes
(frosting), 15 minutes
(decoration) preparation
45 minutes (cake), 10 minutes
(frosting) cooking
YOU WILL NEED
A greased loose-bottomed
23cm cake tin

FOR THE CAKE

300g butter, cubed

100g dark chocolate, as high a cocoa solid content as you dare, chopped

500g light muscovado sugar

330ml Dark Star beer, or stout

3 eggs

200ml buttermilk

350g plain flour

2 tsp baking powder

FOR THE FROSTING

125g butter, softened

50g cocoa

60ml milk

1 tsp vanilla extract

250g icing sugar, sifted

FOR DECORATION

200g dark chocolate, melted or half dark, half white

TIP Although I have used a chocolate frosting here, if you want to lighten the whole concoction up a little, a cream cheese frosting works well in its place or, if you want to be really grown up, frost with a rich chocolate ganache.

1 Preheat the oven to 160°C/Gas mark 3.

2 In a large heavy-based pan, melt the butter and chocolate together, stirring. Brown, velvety and shiny should be the order of the day here. Then add the muscovado sugar, and stir until incorporated and no grains remain.

3 Pour the beer into the pan, and don't worry if everything seems runny – this is a very moist cake. The hoppy spices should fill the kitchen with a comforting aroma.

4 Whisk the eggs into the buttermilk, and then pour this mixture into the pan.

5 Sift over the flour mixed with the baking powder, and gently mix all together until combined.

6 Pour the batter into the cake tin, and bake for 1 hour to 1¼ hours. You may need to cover with foil if it is going too dark on top during this time – it is a deep cake, and will take a lot of cooking. Start testing after 45 minutes, then every 15 minutes or so. It is done when a skewer inserted into the centre comes out with a few moist crumbs attached.

7 Leave to cool in the tin for an hour or so before turning out and cooling completely on a rack. The cake needs to be completely cold before frosting.

8 For the icing: simply whip up all the ingredients with an electric mixer for 3 or 4 minutes until you get the desired consistency. This is quite a light cocoa frosting, to offset the dark cake.

9 For the decoration: place a sheet of baking parchment on a baking tray. Pour the melted chocolate onto the parchment and spread out with a palette knife or spatula.

10 Refrigerate until just set and then scrape with the edge of a palette knife to make curls, or simply break into shards.

11 Cover the top of the cake with frosting and make a jagged star in the centre with your chocolate shards.

Walnut and blue cheese straws

These are our old friend the cheese straw, fancied up for the birthday brigade. This is an ultra-flexible recipe – you can sprinkle with paprika, or spread with grainy mustard. You could use any nut and cheese combination, and cut into any length. Do make sure to serve them warm though, and do be generous with your flavours.

150g plain flour
180g blue cheese
120g mature Cheddar
150g butter, chilled and diced
1 tsp cayenne pepper
1 tsp salt
2 tbsp milk
1 tsp Worcestershire sauce
60g chopped walnuts

1 Combine the flour, cheeses, butter, spice and salt in a bowl and rub together with your fingertips until a sandy breadcrumb-like texture is achieved. Add the milk and Worcestershire sauce and bring the mixture together in your hands. Now add the nuts and firmly mix them throughout, clumping everything together to form a smooth dough. Wrap in cling film and chill until you want to bake the straws.

2 Preheat the oven to 180°C/Gas mark 4.

3 Dust the worktop with flour, and place the dough onto it. Roll the dough out to a rectangular shape about 30cm in width, and about 0.5cm thick. This isn't an exact science, so don't worry too much if your dough doesn't stretch to that surface area. Using a sharp knife, cut vertically down the length of your pastry rectangle, dividing it into 1cm wide strips. Twist the strips and place them on the greased baking sheet.

4 Bake for 12–14 minutes until golden and crisp. Serve immediately.

MAKES
30 twists
PREP/COOK
25 minutes preparation
14 minutes cooking
YOU WILL NEED
Two greased baking trays

Baked gurnard pots

These work equally well as one large pot for sharing, or the slightly more selfish individual birthday-style portions we have pictured here. The flavours are those of the summer, and it makes a tasty, healthy dinner in the heart of the winter, with the promise of things to come. It's often made in Italy as a classic Christmas Eve dish, and is a doddle to prepare in advance. If you are planning on making one of the cakes that feature in this chapter, this is a hassle-free main course that doesn't take up too much of your time, but is still special enough to fool the birthday recipient into thinking you have spent hours in the kitchen.

2 tbsp butter

2 onions, sliced

3 large floury potatoes, peeled and chopped into 2cm dice

454g can cherry tomatoes

400ml good quality fish stock

150g Kalamata olives, stoned

1kg gurnard fillets (or other white fish), skinned and chopped into 2cm chunks

small bunch fresh herbs, chopped

juice of a lemon

1 Heat a large heavy-based frying pan with a tight fitting lid, and melt the butter. Fry the onion slices for a couple of minutes until softening. Add the potato dice, and cook for a few minutes more, until starting to turn golden.

2 Stir in the can of tomatoes (I do feel that this is your best bet at this time of year, though feel free to buy fresh if you prefer) and the stock, and turn the heat up. Everything should now be bubbling and reducing nicely – allow the liquid levels to reduce by half. This will intensify the stock flavour and the richness of the tomato sauce.

3 Stir in the olives and now cover the pan. Turn the heat down, and let everything simmer, under the lid, for 20–25 minutes until the potatoes are tender.

4 Preheat the oven to 200°C/Gas mark 6.

5 Decant the stew to either a large ovenproof serving dish, or four smaller ones. Nestle the fish in amongst the onions, potatoes and tomatoes, and pop the dish or dishes in the oven for about 10 minutes until the fish is cooked.

6 Sprinkle with fresh herbs and lemon juice as soon as the dish is out of the oven, and serve immediately to take full advantage of the lovely fresh flavours.

TIP If you can't get hold of gurnard, this dish is just as lovely with any sustainably caught white fish such as pollock, hake or coley.

SERVES
4
PREP/COOK
20 minutes preparation
45 minutes cooking
YOU WILL NEED
One large ovenproof dish
or four smaller ones

Upside down onion tart

Or a savoury tarte tatin – the onions caramelised and juicy just like their appley counterparts. Cook them long and cook them slow, for the necessary dark, deep toffee layer. This is the all important step, and it's essential not to rush, as this is the filling for your pie in its entirety. This makes an unusual vegetarian main course, needing only a peppery rocket and goat's cheese salad as accompaniment.

4 tbsp butter
leaves from 3 sprigs thyme
2 tbsp sherry vinegar
1 tbsp redcurrant jelly
3 large onions, peeled and
  cut into 1.5cm slices
1 tbsp honey
375g sheet ready-rolled
  puff pastry

1 Melt the butter in a heavy ovenproof frying pan, add the thyme leaves, sherry vinegar and redcurrant jelly, and let it bubble for a couple of minutes.

2 Add in the onion slices and fry gently for 20–25 minutes, flipping them half way through.

3 Drizzle the honey across the slices, which should be soft and yielding. Make sure you are happy with your slice placement, as this will be the top of the tart when you turn it out. Try to ensure there aren't too many gaps.

4 Roll out the puff pastry to a circle slightly bigger than the pan circumference, and carefully lay over the top of the tart, tucking in the edges with the blunt end of a knife. Chill in the fridge for half an hour to minimise shrinkage.

5 Meanwhile preheat the oven to 200°C/Gas mark 6.

6 Bake the tart in the oven for 30 minutes until the pastry is puffed and golden, and the onions caramelised and cooked through.

7 Using oven gloves, take the frying pan out of the oven, and let it sit for about 10 minutes, right side up, to let everything settle. Have a board to hand, then fearlessly flip it upside down onto the waiting board. You may need to loosen the edges of the tart first, and there may still be onions sticking to the pan when you lift it off, but these can be eased back into their gaps on the tart surface without too much trouble.

8 Serve warm.

MAKES
One 25cm tart (serves 8)
PREP/COOK
15 minutes preparation
1 hour cooking
YOU WILL NEED
A heavy, ovenproof frying
pan 25cm across

Oven baked risotto

I can hear the purists amongst you screaming, and I know that in an ideal culinary universe we would all be stirring our risottos on the hob, ladling our homemade stock in by the slow spoonful, and imbuing them with all the love and undivided attention we can for an hour or so to achieve the right balance of creamy deliciousness.

I don't usually advocate a short cut, but this risotto does keep true to the spirit of the original, with an almost comparable level of unctuous ooze, with far less sweat and arm ache.

1 Preheat the oven to 200°C/Gas mark 6.

2 In a large, flame-proof casserole dish, fry the lardons or pancetta cubes until crisp. Take out of the pan with a slotted spoon, and set aside. Now melt the butter in the pan, and fry the onions and garlic in all those buttery, meaty juices. Cook for a few minutes until softened, then add the leek.

3 Fry the vegetables for another 5 minutes or so, stirring often, then add the mushrooms, and give it all another couple of minutes.

4 Pour in the wine and turn the heat right up, watching as it bubbles and reduces down by half.

5 Add the risotto rice and mix it all well until you can see every grain of rice is coated in shiny juices from the pan. Now add the stock and your reserved lardons, put the lid on, and bake for 20–25 minutes until cooked.

6 Take the pan out of the oven and stir through the lemon juice, 100g of the Parmesan and the mascarpone. Put the lid back on and leave for at least 5 minutes before serving, sprinkled with the tarragon and the rest of the Parmesan.

300g lardons or pancetta cubes
3 tbsp butter
1 onion, chopped
2 cloves garlic, crushed
1 leek, topped and tailed and sliced
150g chestnut mushrooms, quartered
250ml white wine
500g risotto rice
900ml stock – chicken is best
juice of 1 lemon
150g Parmesan, grated
120g mascarpone
small bunch fresh tarragon, chopped

SERVES
4
PREP/COOK
25 minutes preparation
40 minutes cooking
YOU WILL NEED
One ovenproof casserole dish

Montezuma's fiery birthday brownies

Montezuma – Aztec ruler and award-winning chocolatiers based in Brighton. These brownies are a happy marriage of fiery chilli heat and dark intense chocolate. If you use chocolate already pre-blended with chilli, as I have here, there is no need to add further chilli heat to these bars. For a birthday celebration, cut into slabs, add candles and pile higgledy piggledy.

350g Montezuma's chilli chocolate, or other good quality chilli chocolate, finely chopped
120g butter, chopped
80g caster sugar
2 eggs, beaten lightly
150g plain flour
1 tsp chilli powder (only if you like things hotter!)
100g chunks additional good quality chocolate (you could use chilli, plain dark, milk or white for a contrast)
icing sugar, for dusting

TIP Line the base and opposite sides of the tray with greaseproof paper, leaving an overhang which you can use to lift the brownies out with later.

1 Preheat the oven to 180°C/Gas mark 4.

2 Combine the chocolate and butter in a medium saucepan and heat very gently indeed, stirring all the while until melted. Be cautious not to overheat or the chocolate will seize and go grainy.

3 Add the sugar and heat, stirring continuously for another couple of minutes. Your chocolate mixture should be shiny and smooth, with no graininess from the sugar. Remove from the heat and let it cool for a couple of minutes.

4 Add the eggs, flour and chilli powder, if you're using it, and whisk briskly until all combined. With a wooden spoon, stir in the additional chocolate until the chunks ripple the batter.

5 Spoon into the prepared baking tray and level the top. Bake for 25–30 minutes, though check after 20 minutes. You want a set top and the all-important squidgy middle.

6 Cool in the tin for at least 1 hour and use the greaseproof paper to lever the brownies out. Cut into squares, dust with icing sugar and serve.

MAKES
Cuts into 9 squares
PREP/COOK
20 minutes preparation
30 minutes cooking
YOU WILL NEED
A buttered and lined 19cm square baking tray

Suppliers

✽ Delicatessen
Bookham Fine Foods Ltd
Bates Green Farm
Arlington,
Sussex
BN26 6SH
www.bookhams.com

✽ Meats
Brighton Sausage Company
28a Gloucester Rd
Brighton
BN1 4AQ
www.brightonsausageco.com

✽ Cake decorations
Cakes Cookies & Crafts Shop
Unit 2, Francis Business Park
White Lund Ind Estate
Morecambe
Lancashire
LA3 3PT
www.cakescookiesandcraftsshop.co.uk

✽ Chocolate
Cocoa Loco
The Chocolate Barn
Hill House Farm
West Grinstead
West Sussex
RH13 8LG
www.cocoaloco.co.uk

Montezuma's
Montezuma's Mail Order,
Birdham Business Park,
Birdham,
West Sussex
PO20 7BT
www.montezumas.co.uk

✽ Dairy
High Weald Dairy LLP
Tremains Farm
Horsted Keynes
West Sussex
RH17 7EA
www.highwealddairy.co.uk

✽ Alcohol
Nyetimber
Gay Street
West Chiltington
West Sussex
RH20 2HH
www.nyetimber.com

The Dark Star Brewing Co. Ltd
22 Star Road,
Partridge Green
West Sussex
RH13 8RA
www.darkstarbrewing.co.uk

Harveys
The Bridge Wharf Brewery
4-6 Cliffe High Street,
Lewes,
BN7 2AH
www.harveys.org

Edible flowers
1st Leaf Produce Ltd
Blaenafon
Brynberian
Crymych
Pembrokeshire
SA41 3TN www.firstleaf.co.uk

Fresh fruit and veg
Barcombe Nurseries,
Mill Lane,
Barcombe,
Nr. Lewes,
East Sussex
BN8 5TH
www.barcombenurseries.co.uk

Bill's Produce Store
The Depot
100 North Road
Brighton
BN1 1YE
www.bills-website.co.uk

✽ Ceramics
Sweet William Designs
12 Kinlet Road
Shooters Hill
London
SE18 3BY
www.sweetwilliamdesigns.com

✽ Props
Mr Magpie
94a Gloucester Road
North Laines
Brighton
BN1 4AP www.mr-magpie.com

Thankyou...

Thanks to everyone who made this book possible:
Stu for the beautiful pictures and expert guidance, and Rosie for interpreting my food probably better than I ever could (with a cheeky smile on her face).

To Carol for having enough faith in me and this project to make it real, and to all my friends at Book Guild.

To the local suppliers and producers who gave freely of their ingredients, time and advice.

To Sylvi, for a week of her time, baking (and gossiping).

Most of all to my mum, who continues to inspire me, both inside the kitchen and out...

...and to Toby and bump, who have taught me that cooking isn't everything, or even close.

Index

Ingredients included in a recipe but obviously not one of the main ingredients are not indexed. Page numbers followed by *a* indicate use of this ingredient as an alternative in the listed recipe.